GREG HONEY
A HONEY AGENCY NOVEL

By the Author

Blue

Greg Honey

GREG HONEY
A HONEY AGENCY NOVEL

by

Russ Gregory

A Division of Bold Strokes Books

2013

GREG HONEY: A HONEY AGENCY NOVEL

© 2013 By Russ Gregory. All Rights Reserved.

ISBN 13: 978-1-60282-946-6

This Trade Paperback Original Is Published By
Bold Strokes Books, Inc.
P.O. Box 249
Valley Falls, NY 12185

First Edition: September 2013

Credits
Editors: Greg Herren and Stacia Seaman
Production Design: Stacia Seaman
Cover Design by Sheri (graphicartist2020@hotmail.com)

Acknowledgments

Publishing takes teamwork, and Bold Strokes Books has one of the best teams in the business. I'd like to single out Greg Herren for his thoughtful editing that turned my repetitious ramblings into a story.

Writing comedy can be a little daunting. Let's face it—jokes tend to fall flat on or about the sixth reading. I owe much gratitude to Travis Hanes, who lent fresh eyes to parts of the story. I'd be remiss if I didn't thank Vicki McKain for providing inspiration for the character Willa. Willa is not Vicki, but I drew much of her pluck and steadfast views on friendship from the Vic's example.

Lastly, this story could not have been written without the prodding I received from my dear friend Dan Sucher. Danny challenged me to write with humor. In his words, "The sad stuff is okay, I guess, but you really need to write something that's less of a downer." I forced Dan to read through numerous early versions, and he succeeded with almost no whining. Anyone who knows Danny understands the effort that took.

I hope this story makes you laugh, Dan. I hope it makes everyone laugh.

For Kendall

CHAPTER ONE

My head was pounding as I stared at the letter in my hands. It told me that Mother expected me to marry a woman, produce offspring, and find Jesus (preferably in that order). Briefly I considered whether the emotional toll of matricide would be worth the bliss of being rid of her. That's when the cat's tail swished.

He was a gnarly, fat tom with a surly attitude and quite possibly ringworm. He came with the office. I watched him perched on the windowsill, staring intently through the glass. I couldn't figure out what had grabbed his attention, so I wadded the letter into a ball and tossed it at him.

He hissed at me without turning from the window.

The wind-up clock on my desk read 10:14 and my computer screen showed a bank account balance of $253.17.

Twenty-eight years old with a nagging mother, failing business, and $253.17 to my name...and the office rent was due on Monday. Swish went the tail, tick went the clock, and thump went my head.

I was considering which kidney to sell when the phone rang.

It was Willa.

"Whatcha doin'?"

"Busy," I said, not because I was busy but because it was Willa and once she started talking it was like a rolling mudslide, full of debris and impossible to stop.

"I went to see *Brokeback Mountain* at the Arbor last night. The place was full of gay guys. Felt a little like a night at the bars. You know how I love that heady mix of testosterone and hair-care products. Sure, it's a gay movie and all that but I still say it's the best chick flick since *When Harry Met Sally*. You just can't beat a movie with gay cowboys and horses."

Ugh! My head throbbed and the cat's tail twitched again. I pleaded, "Kind of busy here, Wil," trying to stanch the flow down the soggy hillside, but even as I spoke, I knew the onslaught was inevitable.

"Heath Ledger is so hot in that movie, such a loss. I particularly liked the scenes where they're mounting each other in the tent. There's nothing like a couple of hot guys doing the nasty to get my juices flowing. Throw in a bunch of sheep and it's a country girl's fantasy, like watching a pair of stallions humping. All muscle and snort and…" Yammer, yammer, yammer.

I tuned her out, speculating about the taste of cat meat and thinking I was kind of partial to my right kidney when Willa mentioned Matt Kendall and my boy parts started tingling. I tuned back in to Willa's drivel because Matt Kendall was just about perfect in every way.

I don't mean to imply that he walked on water, but for me, he was pretty much perfect in all the ways that mattered. At age twenty-eight, the way that mattered the most involved condoms and anti-friction products. Matt was the man of my dreams, literally. I dreamt about him all the time—sometimes wet dreams. (The fact I still was dealing with wet dreams at age twenty-eight said all there was to say about my sex life.)

Willa was working her way through a detailed description of her third movie when I broke in to ask, "Wait, what did you say about Matt?"

"What?"

"Matt Kendall—you said you saw him?"

"Oh yeah. I ran into him in the theater lobby, he asked about you. Boy, that lobby smells bad—a little like jellybeans and poo…with about a gallon of pickle juice mixed in. Some would say they need to clean it but it would be safer just to burn the whole place down and start again because there are just some smells that you can't…"

Again with the yammering as my heart began to flutter and my chest felt like it was going to explode. Then the feeling moved lower and I wasn't sure if I was about to sing for joy or crap my pants.

I interrupted again. "What exactly did he say?" I emphasized "exactly," hoping she would get to the point.

"What did who say?"

"Matt, Willa. What exactly did Matt say?"

"Oh, well…like I said, we were in the lobby. I was buying peanut M&Ms 'cause I like the blue ones…the yellow ones are scary and don't even get me started about the brown ones…it's like eating sheep poop, for God's sake…whoever thought little brown balls of candy-coated chocolate would…"

See what I mean? An absolute mudslide.

"Jesus, Willa! Concentrate, honey. Tell me about Matt."

"I'm getting there. So he like comes up and I said 'hi,' and he said 'hi,' and I said 'I was at the show last night,' and he said 'what'd you think,' and I said 'it was good but I don't like the new Mimi,' and he said 'no one does,' and I said…"

I hung on to the phone like I was about to backhand a service return; at times conversation with Willa can be very infuriating. Finally, she got to the point.

"And then he said 'where's your hot friend Greg, haven't seen him in a while,' and I said 'he's been busy,' and he said 'well, I better get to my seat.'"

I tuned out the rest of her blather because I had just heard that Matt Kendall told Willa Jensen that I was hot. That caused the angels to sing in my head. And not a wimpy Britney song either—we're talking Mahalia Jackson and the Brooklyn Tabernacle Choir!

When I tuned back in, Willa was going on about some lame TV show and I broke through the static to ask, "Are you going to the theater tonight?"

I could tell my question took her by surprise because she was momentarily silent, and Willa is only silent when she is either stunned or unconscious.

After a pause she said, "I guess so, *Rent*'s still on and I love those songs."

"You think you can get me in?"

Willa works in the box office at Zachary Scott Theater, and I figured if the house wasn't sold out, she might let me in for free.

"Sure, come on by, you want to go to dinner first?"

"Got no money, but sure would love to eat." I let my voice trail off in an unspoken request I knew she would pick up on.

"Jesus! Honey, you beg more than a Tibetan pilgrim. Maybe you should shake a little cash out of the family tree or buy a guitar and strum it in the subway."

"Austin doesn't have a subway."

"Sure it does, I like their foot-long Italian meatball."

I laughed, not because it was funny but because I wanted her to think I thought it was funny. She sighed, pretending to be put out, but I knew it was an act because there is absolutely nothing Willa Jensen likes better than company willing to listen to her incessant drivel over dinner.

"I'm broke, Willa. What can I say?"

"I guess I can swing it if you're really broke. But you better appreciate me, mister."

"I appreciate you, Willa, you're a life saver—you're the best."

Then she launched into another twenty minutes of pointless yammering while I sat with the phone wedged between my shoulder and ear, half-listening. I interjected an occasional "uh-huh" and smiled like a Chucky doll. I was happy because dinner on Willa sure beat *arroz con gato*, and the thought of seeing Matt at the theater filled me with… let's call it *optimism*.

When Willa finally finished her mind-numbing verbal onslaught I said good-bye and hung up, still smiling. The cat had disappeared, along with my headache, and the clock on my desk told me it was 11:43; time for lunch.

I taped the Gone Fishing sign on the plate glass door and caught the bus home.

❖

I live with my mother and grandmother—well, not exactly *with* them. My abode is a red brick gatehouse barely on the Lost Wind compound grounds. The Honey women share the palatial limestone edifice four hundred yards farther up the driveway. My grandmother named the place Lost Wind after the gentle Pemberton breezes, but most of the locals just call it Passed Gas because of the odors that occasionally waft over from the water treatment facility.

My family is rich in the *Beverly Hillbillies* sort of way. It's not that Grandmother stuffs her money in a mattress or that we don't know it's a swimming pool and not a cement pond, but the money did arrive unexpectedly from a hole in the ground.

It all started with my great-great-grandfather, Belton Honey. He was a rancher. Well, he was *sort of* a rancher. He owned twelve sections of bone-dry, hardscrabble desert in West Texas. He purchased the spread, paying a penny an acre after the Civil War when everything was cheap and land was plentiful. He was *sort of* a rancher because the entire place was so dry and inhospitable that it could only support about fifteen head of cattle, and with those numbers he needed a Cheyenne tracking party to locate the bovines in the brush.

The family was dirt poor until a pair of local wildcatters persuaded Winston Honey, Belton's grandson and my grandfather, to let them drill in 1939. They struck a gusher and the site reached peak production about the time World War II caused the oil industry to boom. Almost overnight the Honeys were rich. Grandmother Lucille went on a shopping spree that didn't end for sixty years. Her biggest and most renowned purchase was made in 1966. She bought the Tiger's Eye—a gaudy fourteen-carat yellow diamond that even today occasionally graces the gooseflesh skin of her neck, though in recent years Mother is more likely to lug the rock around in order to impress well-heeled guests.

After the oil hit, the entire Honey clan relocated to Austin in search of the good life. Grandfather Winston bought Lost Wind on Niles Road and set about expanding and remodeling. When she wasn't shopping for clothing and jewelry, Lucille wrote obscenely large checks in support of the arts in an attempt to establish status, and it pretty much worked. Up until a decade ago, she was a familiar face in the society pages. My earliest memories of her were flashes of an elegant woman dressed in flowing silks with feathers in her hair. The feathers were her signature fashion statement. Of course, that was before the alopecia. Now if she wanted to wear feathers she'd have to glue them to her head.

Mother married into the family and set up shop at Lost Wind. Over the years, the shift of power from Lucille to Livia has been gradual but unstoppable.

As for me, I am relatively happy in my role as the black sheep of the family, camped out at the end of the driveway and held at bay, as far from the royal jewelry as possible without complete banishment to the real world. I live in a kind of no-man's-land hovering between obscene wealth and abject poverty, teetering on the cliff of family indifference, perched between the gulf of Mother's refusal to recognize my "gay" lifestyle and the chasm of her need to exert control over my destiny.

Thus far the family connection has delivered free housing, free electricity, and the seed money for my failing one-man private detective agency.

❖

The bus dropped me one hot, sticky block from home. The temperature in Austin that fine August morning was roughly two hundred degrees, but you could still hang meat safely in the gatehouse because the electricity for the mansion and the cottage were jointly metered. Mother took care of the bill and I lived in seven hundred square feet of refrigeration all summer long. As I entered the icy cool I considered begging Dolores to stock my pantry. Then I could give up trying to make a living and spend the rest of my life in a coma on the couch. Dolores was Mother's cook, an absolute magician with a frying pan and a can of Crisco. (I have other friends that are good with Crisco too, but that's another story altogether.)

I lunched on a peanut butter and jelly sandwich made with matzo…and if you think that sounds good, try spreading grape jelly on a cracker. I was wiping the last of the jelly from my T-shirt and trying to come up with an intelligent way to ask Mother for financial assistance, knowing that in her view the only acceptable justification involved marriage and children. That's when I heard a knock on my front door. The sound took me totally by surprise because access to the property was strictly controlled. Anyone coming down from the big house would undoubtedly arrive at my back door, and the gate to the street was always locked. The only other way inside the compound involved scaling a fence or parachuting into the yard. There was a buzzer, of course, but it rang in the big house and no one who pressed it ever came to my door.

I peered through the spy hole cautiously. Russ Buttons stood on my porch looking like a grape smoothie in skintight purple slacks, purple shoes, and a sparkly purple pullover. I tugged the door open and said, "How very Prince of you."

"Plum is this year's black, Mr. Honey."

Russ popped his *p*'s and hissed his *s*'s like an deflating tire. I had a momentary flashback to the time I first introduced him to my mother. He actually kissed her hand and said, "That's Russsssss, with six *s*'s."

Russ is quite possibly the gayest man in the state of Texas (that may be a point of contention with anyone who has actually met our governor).

I said, "Come inside, you're clashing with the lawn furniture."

I led the way to my kitchen where half of my PB&J on matzo rested on a paper towel next to the sink.

Russ said, "Swanky lunch, what's for dessert? Cherry sauce on fish sticks?"

"Why are you darkening my life with your horrendous presence?"

"Because I have a job for you. An honest-to-God detective job."

"I'm listening."

"I need you to find my brother."

"You have a brother? I thought you were grown in a garden."

"Are you trying to be insulting?"

"Sorry. Why do you want to find your brother?"

"None of your business. Do you want the job or not?"

"Depends."

"On what?"

"On what's the catch."

"There is no catch, just find him and let me know where he is."

"And if he's dead or someplace dangerous like Yemen or Akron…I don't have to retrieve the body, right?"

"Right, you can leave the body buried in Akron."

"Then yes, I want the job." I said this, smiling at the prospect of avoiding office eviction.

Russ told me his brother had been estranged from the family since 1988. Milton left home after a horrible fight with their father, Hiram Buttons. Hiram passed away in the 1990s, leaving Milton as Russ's only surviving relative. There had been no contact between the two in twenty-three years and now Russ wanted to reconnect.

"This sounds like a challenge, and I can't give you any guarantees, but if you're willing to pay my rate, I'm willing to try to locate your brother."

Russ studied me warily. "I didn't expect you to work for free, but what's this going to cost me?"

I said, "My rate is nine hundred up front to cover my start-up costs, then five hundred if I find him this weekend. If he's not found by Monday I'll show you all the info I've been able to dig up and we can decide where to go from there."

Russ looked at me for a few seconds with squinty eyes, then he extended one heavily jeweled hand and we shook.

He offered to give me a ride back to my office so he could sign the necessary client agreement and fork over the check. I bolted the rest of my PB&J on matzo and followed him out the door. I was turning the key in the deadbolt lock on my porch when I remembered something.

"How'd you get in here anyway? I assume you didn't climb the fence." I waved a hand toward the ivy-covered brick wall, and Russ looked at me in horror. Russ was definitely not the climbing type. He might break a nail or snag his shiny shirt, for heaven's sake.

"I walked through the gate, of course," he said, pointing to the ornate wrought iron entrance blocking the walkway from the street. It was the gate that I'd used, but I had locked it. I always locked it… safety is an obsession with me. Besides, it had a spring-loaded catch designed to clasp automatically. Even if I had forgotten, the door would have bolted itself. I crept over to the gate and tugged on the bright brass knob. It swung open on well-oiled hinges, and I stared in absolute amazement.

"Did I do something wrong" Russ asked.

"It's not you, but this is just never unlocked…Lucille would pitch a fit." I was picturing my somewhat addled ninety-three-year-old grandmother driving her motorized scooter down the hill, waving a loaded shotgun and screaming "the perimeter's been breached" at the top of her lungs.

I shook my head and guided Russ through the passage. When I let go of the gate, it clicked as the lock caught. But I shoved on the surface to make sure before following Russ to a cherry-red Mazda Miata parked at the curb.

CHAPTER TWO

After depositing Russ's check I spent three hours searching the web for his brother with very limited success. My headache was back with a vengeance when Willa shoved through the plate glass door. I looked up, trying to hide my shock. I couldn't believe it was already time for dinner.

"Whatcha doin'? Oh, Honey, no! God, you're not even dressed yet? You can't possibly go out like that, what are you thinking, jeans and a T-shirt to the theater? Even in Austin that just won't do. No, we need to get you home and into something presentable fast, some nice pants and a button-up shirt, maybe a jacket. Do you want people to think you're from Oklahoma? I have a cousin in Enid and ev—"

"Give me a sec to log off," I said, but the soggy ground was already starting to slide.

"So I said 'well, I like a cutlet now and then—but that doesn't mean I want a romantic relationship with the chicken.' Tell me, Honey dear, did you hear that Dan's talking about replacing Mimi? It's about time is all I can say. Janet Malloy screeches like a banshee and dances like a wolf. Not with the wolves, mind you, like a wolf. Have you ever seen a wolf dance?"

"Nope."

"My point exactly. And besides, she weighs two hundred pounds. Mimi needs to be svelte, not stomping around onstage like a hippo. When she does that song where she sings about having the best ass in the neighborhood, I keep thinking *what neighborhood*? It's got to be somewhere in Mississippi because her butt's as broad as West Texas, in fact she's kind of like the entire desert Southwest—dry and dusty with a hint of cow dung in the air."

Willa is not the best person to have around when you have a headache. I tuned out the prattle and steered her through the doorway with one hand on the small of her back.

❖

After I changed, Willa suggested dinner at the Paggi House and I quickly agreed, smiling over the prospect of real honest-to-goodness food. The Paggi House is a ritzy place, with intimate dining rooms sporting terra-cotta-colored walls and lacy cloths on the tables. We were seated in a small dining room and Willa ordered a field green salad and water. I asked for a thirty-dollar glass of Domaine des Comtes Lafon Clos de la Barre *and* threw caution to the wind, ordering the beef tenderloin rare. If the asterisked warnings were correct, I could expect a rough week dealing with trichinosis and salmonella. I was pretending to listen to Willa while trying to keep from splattering blood on my light gray Ike Behar shirt and hoping that the zipper held on my Sahara twill Ballin pants when in walked Lola.

Saying Lola Riatta and Willa Jensen have "history" is like saying Ryan Seacrest has hair gel. They had been mortal enemies since Lola slept with Willa's ex, Ralph Mason. Now, that might end even the best of friendships, but to truly understand the scope and depth of the hatred between these two women, you need to know three more things:

1. Ralph proposed to Lola,
2. Willa seduced him into sleeping with her on his wedding day, and
3. Willa sent a videotape of the sexual encounter to Lola on her honeymoon.

It was a short marriage.

We watched as Lola strolled up to our table, a brittle smile on her face. Without missing a beat, Willa grinned back and said, "Lola, are you pregnant or did you gain forty pounds?"

"Willa, Willa, Willa—why do you insist on wearing a bra when a couple of Band-Aids would provide more-than-adequate support for those dried-up walnuts?"

"Lola honey, could you stand downwind? The people at the next table ordered salmon and they're thinking it's ready."

"I'd get that rash looked after, darling, stage two syphilis is dangerous."

"I'm sure you'd know."

"You still looking for a job? Surely there must be a pimp down on South Congress who needs another skanky ho."

"Oh? Did you recently retire?"

And they bid each other farewell with this cheery exchange:

"Hope you die bleeding with a broomstick up your butt, crack whore."

"May you cut yourself shaving your oozing twat, ass-wipe."

I watched as Lola strolled off toward the next dining room, trying to ignore the pictures floating through my mind.

Willa said, "I don't like her."

"Really? I had no idea."

We finished dinner in relative silence. The vitriolic flow of nastiness had temporarily dried up the hillside. Willa paid with a credit card and we hurried across Lamar to the theater. As usual we were two hours early for the show. Willa abhorred tardiness.

I watched as she set up the box office, counting the money in the till, checking the comp list, and arranging will-call tickets alphabetically. I always liked the unrushed time at the theater before the patrons arrived. It made a nice reprieve before the doors opened and a bunch of boisterous drunk people pushed forward, jostling each other and asking for tickets and concessions and directions to the bathroom.

Willa's prattle was back with a vengeance. I tried to listen as I kept one eye on the stage door, hoping to catch a glimpse of Matt on his way backstage.

"So I said to him, 'if God had wanted me to make grilled cheese sandwiches I wouldn't have been born lactose intolerant,' and he said 'I want a woman who can cook,' and I said 'I want a man that can buy dinner,' and he said 'get in that kitchen and rattle them pots and pans, woman,' and that's when I hit him in the face with the waffle iron."

I checked my watch—still an hour until show time.

"I don't know why he took it so poorly. The pattern on his face sort of went with his complexion and I had buttered the surface, everyone knows butter is a natural skin emollient."

A group of actors I recognized from other productions jangled through the doorway, and Matt walked in behind them. He was surrounded by this golden aura and dripped sexuality from head to toe. Well, maybe *I* was the one dripping. The point is someone was dripping, and he looked really good. I waved to him in the least nelly way I knew how—which ended up looking kind of like a salute. He grinned back before disappearing through the stage door. Inside my head Etta James began to sing, even though the only music in the lobby was the marimba ringer on my iPhone.

I pointed at my phone to stop Willa's chatter and stepped away from the box to answer.

"Hello?"

"I know where you live. And I'm coming for you."

"Who is this?"

"You better be careful. Be very careful, gay boy."

The caller hung up and I stood in the lobby staring at my phone with the feeling of elation I'd experienced not six seconds earlier escaping into the air like a rancid fart. I wondered if it was just a random prank call, and pictured my mother handing my cell phone number to one of the hundred or so psychotic members of her church. I was shocked and confused and struggling to think what to do next. I checked for a callback number, but caller ID was blocked. I thought it must have been a mistake and deleted the call log.

I was still staring at my phone when the main doors opened and people began to file into the lobby from the parking lot. I sighed in frustration. It pissed me off that some random person could call me at the theater and almost ruin my evening with a childish prank. Well, I wasn't going to let that happen. Matt Kendall was playing Mark in the production of *Rent* I was about to see, and the thought of watching him for almost two hours was the closest I'd come to having sex with an actual other person since…well, since whenever I had last had sex with an actual other person.

It was going to take more than a bizarre and potentially threatening phone call to ruin my evening.

I switched off my cell phone and stepped back inside the box. Willa was yammering away as usual. This time, the flow was directed at a dangerously sunburned patron who had asked about the theater's dress code. Basically, the policy was you have to cover most of your private parts (unless *Hair* was playing, then you were free to swing whatever you had in the breeze). Willa told him this in a way that made the man want to go home and change.

"Yes, you can wear that ratty old T-shirt and those hopelessly undersized shorts into the theater. If you want to look like a refugee from Bangladesh—it's up to you. Personally if I were a man I wouldn't choose to flash my scrotum every time I sat down, but it's strictly your business. And flip-flops are allowed too, though if I sat next to anyone wearing them, I'd be sure to take every opportunity afforded me to step on their feet. Don't you worry about looking like you can't afford a real shirt either, we get people in here all the time that dress like that, mostly people that live under a bridge, for sure, but we're used to it. So if you have a ticket, feel free to ruin the show for the rest of us."

I had to admire Willa; she wasn't subtle but she was effective. I watched the man make his way back to the parking lot.

I found a quiet corner and sat down waiting as Willa meted out tickets. The box office closed five minutes before show time. Willa and I took our seats in the packed theater just as the lights dimmed. The first strains of the opening music filled the room and I was starting to feel titillated in the "wish I had a coat to lay in my lap" sort of way when the first actors made their way onstage in the darkness. The music started up and the magic of theater transported me back to the 1990s.

❖

At intermission, I followed Willa through the theater's exit happy to let her prattle on since I had experienced something akin to an hour-long tantric massage that left me unsure if I still possessed the power of speech. The dark hallway was crowded, but that didn't worry Willa. Her voice was clearly audible above the background shuffle.

"What'd I tell you about Janet Malloy? Worst Mimi ever...an absolute train wreck. I can't wait until they can her fat ass. Jesus, she only hit a few of the notes and that was pure random luck. That scene when she tossed her hair and all the glitter came out—did you see half the audience trying to dodge the sweat? She perspires like a horse at the Kentucky Der..."

We stepped from the darkness into the brightly lit concession area and I spotted a heavy lesbian staring at Willa. I assumed she was a lesbian based on her styling choices—worn jeans, plaid shirts, Doc Martens, facial piercings, and boyish haircut—I mean, she couldn't have been more obvious if she carried a bowling ball. As we moved toward an open area, the woman's eyes followed Willa like a hungry dog watching Lady Gaga in her meat dress.

Willa was beautiful in a flat-chested, ballerina sort of way. She looked like a Russian ice princess when you caught her with her mouth shut (which almost never happened). It was not unusual for men to come sniffing around whenever we were out together, but I found it interesting to see the same reaction in a lesbian.

As usual, Willa was totally oblivious to the attention she drew. The same thing happened with men. As I pondered that, Willa broke up the stream of chatter to find out if I was going to the concession stand.

"What do you want?" I asked with feigned irritation.

"Oh, you're a peach, Honey, I'll take wine. Red, white, or rosé, you choose."

I left her nattering away in the direction of whoever was unfortunate enough to be standing nearby and made my way across the lobby.

I was standing in the concessions line when Russ Buttons stepped out of the crowd. He was dressed from head to toe in orange spandex with his hair poofed out like an early Jackson (probably Tito). He looked like an Oompa Loompa. As he neared, enough Axe cologne wafted through the air to bring down a redwood.

"Don't tell me, pumpkin is the new plum."

"Shouldn't you be working, Honey?"

"Russ, it's nine thirty on a Friday night. Give me a break, will ya? Besides, I've already got a lead on your brother and I plan on following up in the morning." I was a little pissed off and didn't really want to be bothered, so I exaggerated the results of my Internet search hoping he'd back off.

Of course Russ, being an anal-compulsive gay guy, didn't know how to back off.

"It seems to me if you were working tonight you might find him sooner and *then* you can take the rest of the weekend off."

"It seems to me that slavery was abolished a few years back. There was a war, I think."

"I certainly hope you're serious about finding my brother, Greg Honey. If you took my money and now you're thinking you can sandbag the results, I'm here to tell you you don't want to do that."

"Of course I'm serious about finding him, Russ, honest. And if he can be found, I'm going to do it, but no one can work all the time. Even the most hardened detective needs to take time off once in a while." I said all this, thinking it sounded pretty reasonable. I was serious about my job in the I-have-to-make-this-work-so-I-don't-need-to-ask-Mom-for-more-money sort of way. And it wasn't reasonable for Russ to expect me to labor on nonstop.

Russ said, "Right, we'll see what you find by Monday," and stomped off in a pumpkin fury just as I reached the concessions window.

When I got back to Willa, I gave her the plastic glass of cheap red wine (from a box). The flow of prattle didn't even slow as I approached and smiled at the lesbian.

"So I said to her, 'when you need a kidney you shop at the morgue,' and she said to me, 'but he's not dead yet,' and I said 'I know his doctor and that's gonna change'...oh, thanks, Honey."

I handed Willa her wine and she introduced her new friend.

"Greg, this is Doodle." Turning to the woman, she added, "This is my friend Greg. He's as gay as musical theater and available, though smitten."

"Doodle?" I asked, extending a hand.

"My name's actually Dorris, Dorris Brendell, but everyone calls me Doodle or sometimes Bug, but that's a long story involving an exterminator and I don't want to go there."

We shook, and I said, "Are you enjoying the show?"

"For sure, lots of fun. I don't see much theater, so this is a real treat. I'm mostly here to support a friend, though."

"Oh? Do you know someone in the cast?" Willa asked.

"Yes, Janet Malloy...she's playing Mimi."

Willa sort of froze with this inane smile on her face, and I realized she was trying to figure out if Doodle had heard her critique earlier in the hallway. I took the opportunity to say, "We have a friend in the cast too. Matt Kendall, he plays Mark." Just saying his name made my heart flutter.

"Oh, he's great, cute guy, I really love his voice."

I smiled, and feeling like I needed to reciprocate, I said, "Well, your friend is…" but couldn't bring myself to finish the sentence, so there was another uncomfortable pause while I searched for an adjective that wasn't "horrible," "ridiculous," or "headache-inducing." Doodle saved me.

"Lousy," she said with a smile. "There's simply no denying the fact. Janet has the voice of William Shatner and the stage presence of Play-doh."

We all laughed, and Willa said, "Well, she could be better."

With a straight face, Doodle said, "There is room for improvement. Actually, the reason I'm here is Janet's pretty sure the director is letting her go tonight after the performance. If she falls apart I'm supposed to sweep up the pieces."

"That's nice of you," I said. "Might not be easy…you'll need a big broom."

Willa agreed with a nod, adding, "I did hear that Dan Stanley, that's the director, he's considering another actress for the part, someone who can sing better, I mean…and act better…and dance better. If you work in the theater you hear these things. I remember the time Mickey Craig, he's the other box office manager, told me he heard Alice Wilson tell the foundation manager, Joseph, to take his hands off her behind, I heard about it from six different people in like ten minutes. Why Joseph would want to put his hand on Alice's fat ass is a mystery to me because the man is so gay he farts lavender and she's about as attractive as a box of dried prunes, but the story zoomed around the theater like a Formula One racer. Funny thing was, I think Alice was sort of excited by the physical contact. Probably the closest the old biddy ever came to a sexual encounter. My guess is she still dreams…"

The house lights blinked and I led the way back into the theater with Willa rattling on as usual. As we took our seats, she turned back to Doodle and I heard her whisper, "I'll be around after the play if you need help with Janet."

❖

After multiple curtain calls and a standing ovation, the show's refrain kept echoing through my mind as I watched Willa talking with Doodle in the rapidly emptying lobby. I had one eye on the stage door, hoping to catch a glimpse of Matt, when a teary-eyed Janet burst through and made a beeline toward our group.

"I can't believe it, he fired me. Now what am I going to do?"

Tears gushed from her eyes and carved arroyos through the stage makeup on her cheeks. She picked me to cry on, so I patted her shoulder while Doodle did the same and Willa looked on with concern. Janet nestled deeper into my chest, wailing and seeping copious amounts of body fluids onto my shirt. I was starting to feel a little like a Kleenex and mouthed the words "help me" toward Willa and Doodle.

They managed to pry Janet off me, and she started hugging Willa immediately. Doodle shrugged and continued patting Janet's shoulder. I looked down at the image of Janet's face painted on my shirt in makeup. Two black mascara smudges for eyes and a flesh-colored blotch where her nose rubbed against the fabric; below that was a ruby-red gash of lipstick. I didn't even want to think about the source of the dark wet spots dribbling below.

I heard Willa say softly, "Come on, Janet, it's not as bad as all that. This part wasn't right for you, so what? There are others. I'm sure we can find you something that fits your talents better. Maybe a role that doesn't have so much singing or dancing or…acting. Have you ever been a mime or magician's assistant? I wonder if anyone we know is looking for a plus-sized model?"

A voice cut through the background chatter as I scrubbed facial features from my shirt. It said, "This is tough."

I looked up to see Matt Kendall's impossibly beautiful green eyes staring back at me. My mind froze while I stared at him. It took effort to keep from drooling. I said, "Yeah."

He grinned. "You have a face on your shirt."

I looked down, then up, then back down again. "Yeah."

"This is going to go on a while." He nodded toward Janet, who was wailing away on Doodle's shoulder while Willa scrubbed makeup from her blouse with a Kleenex.

I paused. "Yeah."

"Did you come with Willa?"

Pause. "Yeah."

"Looks like she's tied up."

I looked across the corridor as Willa pried Janet off Doodle. All three women hugged each other in a kind of estrogen huddle.

I said, "Yeah."

He asked, "Do you need a ride?"

I nodded and choked out another "Yeah."

It seemed I had lost the ability to form a polysyllabic sentence.

A wicked little smirk broke across Matt's face. When I smiled back, my smile was bigger.

I turned and waved to Willa. She nodded back, a knowing grin flitting across her face when she saw Matt.

As we turned to leave, Matt held the door open as I wobbled through with weak knees and the entire Mormon Tabernacle Choir singing the Hallelujah Chorus inside my head.

CHAPTER THREE

My father used to say that even a blind hog finds an acorn once in a while. I was twenty-two years old when his coronary artery blew and I can honestly say that in all the time I knew him, I never once understood a thing he said. But that magical morning, lying in the rumpled sheets of my sleigh bed with the sun peeking through the blinds and sparkling across the skin of Matt's perfect back, I was feeling like I'd found an acorn.

Matt stirred enough for me to see his face, sandy hair falling rakishly across his forehead, his lips perfectly shaped and totally kissable. I fought with the urge to touch him, letting my eyes feast on his perfection while the angels sang inside my head. As I watched, one eye peeked open. Gently, his hand reached out and touched my chest. I was totally, 100 percent in love when he slowly propped himself up on one elbow and said, "Hi, sunshine."

"Hi."

"You were great last night, mister."

"Wow," I said, trying to keep the corners of my lips from touching my earlobes.

"Yeah—wow. I'm so glad we finally got together. You're pretty amazing, Greg."

That's when my innate insecurity kicked in. I started thinking something had to be wrong. This was a joke or a nasty trick. Matt Kendall could not have possibly said what he just did without there being a punch line in there somewhere. I fought the urge to search the room for the "You've Been Punked" camera guy. That's when Matt snuggled closer and I started to think, *Oh well, if this is going to be on YouTube, I might as well enjoy it while I can.*

I snuggled back and one thing led to another, which eventually led to some pretty amazing and athletic things and then I was drenched in…let's call it sweat…and I had pretty much lost the ability to move my appendages. I was also fairly certain I had done permanent damage to my jaw, but other than that I had never felt so good in my entire life. I looked over at Matt, who was lying in a similar pool of ecstatic muscular paralysis, and I thought, *Well, they can't put that on YouTube.*

As we cuddled, I considered Hindu philosophy and realized they had it right. My experience had shown that union with a supreme being is truly nirvana. I had almost fallen asleep when Matt pushed back and looked at me again with his sea-green eyes.

He said, "In a few minutes I'm going to leave you, because I have to, not because I want to, and when I do I don't want you to think that I'm not coming back, because I am coming back. We have unfinished business here and I plan to take some time finishing it." Then he grinned at me in his naughty way and I waited for an anvil to fall on my head or maybe I'd burst into flames because my life just could not be this wonderful without something going wrong.

I smiled again, though. Maybe I was tempting fate, but I felt amazing. I had never been so happy. Still, I worked hard to stifle the urge to sing a show tune.

No need for Matt to see that on our first morning together.

When the phone rang, I thought briefly about letting the machine pick up, but changed my mind after the thought of my mother's voice spouting a religious tirade with instructions to marry a woman and produce offspring flashed through my mind.

"Hello?"

"Greg, thank God you're there." It was Willa, and she sounded flustered.

"Of course I'm here, Wil, where else would I be?" I smiled at Matt, who had rolled off the bed and was padding down the hallway toward the bathroom.

"I need your help. I don't know how this happened and it's a little…no, make that a lot embarrassing, so I'm asking you to keep this to yourself. We've been good friends for a long time, right? And you know I would do anything for you, right? And I think of you as a good friend, no, make that my best friend, and so as your best friend

I'm asking you to please…no, you have to promise. Please…promise right now, okay?"

She was tripping over her words and talking fast even for Willa, but I was so high on endorphins that I didn't pick up on the note of desperation. Thinking it was a joke, I asked, "This doesn't involve digging a shallow grave in the desert, does it?"

"Greg!" she screamed. "Promise me you will never breath a word of this to another living soul…or so help me, Mr. Honey, I will hunt you down and hurt you in the most disgusting way."

I finally clued in to the desperation.

"Okay. Okay, Willa, I promise. Now just slow down and tell me what this is all about."

I listened to the sound of heavy breathing while she tried to compose herself. There was a moment of actual silence while I waited for her to speak. Finally, she said, "I don't know where I am and I've lost my car and my dignity and my mind…well, most of my mind… and I don't remember how I got here and I don't know where I am and I don't have my panties and I don't know what happened. Do you hear me, Greg? I don't know what happened."

"Wait, you lost your panties?"

"Yes, I lost my panties."

"No way, no one loses their underwear. Where are your clothes?"

"Gone. Well, most of them. I have my blouse and my left shoe."

"Willa, how do you lose your clothes? No one loses their clothes."

"I don't know!" she screamed, and there was more heavy breathing while she tried to calm down. When she continued, her voice had softened. "I can't remember, I'm alone and I'm cold and I need to pee and I don't even have my panties, Greg. I need my panties, everyone needs their panties."

She broke into a fit of sobbing that was so un-Willa-like that for the first time I began to worry. There wasn't an obvious plan of action, so I decided to wing it. Keeping my voice as steady and confident as possible, I said, "We're going to fix this, I promise. But first you need to calm down. I'm going to come get you and we're going to find your clothes and your car and no one will ever know about this. It will all be over soon, so pull yourself together and give me some help. Okay?"

"Okay." She sniffed once and swallowed hard.

"Good, so tell me where you are."

"In trouble." And she started to whimper again.

My voice was sharp when I said, "Willa, look around—are you in a room?"

"Yes."

"Is there a door?"

"Yes, and a bed and a window."

"Good, now go look out the window."

I heard the sound of clanking. When she returned to the phone, her voice sounded stronger. "I see a field and some trees and a road, I think."

"Okay, that's a start."

Just then, Matt stepped out of the bathroom. He was dressed and carrying his cell phone. He made motions as if he were going to leave. I cupped the receiver to my chest and said, "Will I see you again or does the heartbreak start right now?"

"Greg Honey, you are going to have my babies."

I smiled, "Okay then, I'll get to work growing a uterus."

He grinned back and bent down to kiss me. I was having trouble wiping the silly smile off my face. He asked, "You coming to the show tonight?"

"Can't tonight. I have family obligations, but maybe you could come by after?"

"Okay, I'll call you."

"Do you have my number?"

He glanced at my cell phone lying on the bedside table. He picked it up and dialed. When his cell phone rang he peeked at the screen and said, "Now I do."

"Cool."

"Be good," he said, and stepped through the door as the smile faded from my face. I listened to the gate clang shut and was just starting to miss him when Willa's voice squealed through the receiver.

"Greeeeeeeggggg!"

"Okay, sorry," I said, "I'm here. So this is what you're going to do…"

I told her to wrap herself in a sheet and step outside. I waited while she did as instructed. When she came back on the line, she told me there was an alley behind the building and at the end of block she could see another building with a mural on a wall. She described the painting and I recognized the image.

"Okay, I know where you are—it's not too far. You hold on and I'll be there as soon as I can."

"I owe you, Greg."

"Don't worry Willa, this will be okay. We will make it okay."

I disconnected and snuck up to the big house to steal a car—but I intended to tell the cops that I'd borrowed it, if asked.

Twelve minutes later, I spotted Willa's blue Honda angled into the street with one tire perched on the sidewalk. I turned off South First and pulled to a stop beside it. Most of Willa's clothes were piled in the Honda's passenger seat (though her panties had somehow escaped). As I gathered her things, Willa came hobbling out of the alleyway on one five-inch heel with a sheet wrapped around her waist. She lugged her purse onto the car's hood and sighed heavily. The image Janet's makeup had left on her blouse was missing one eye smudge and Willa's hair was sort of wild, like her stylist had been a pack of weasels.

She said, "Thank God you found my car."

"It was here all the time—I just pulled up." I pointed at the Lexus.

"You mean my car was eighty feet away from where I just peed in an alley?"

"Evidently."

"I am never again in my entire life ever going to drink again…in my entire life…so help me Jesus."

"What happened?"

"I don't know." She sighed again in frustration. "We went for a drink. It was me, Doodle, and Janet. We were trying to cheer up Janet, sort of a 'drown your sorrows' girls' night out. The last thing I remember was taking one quick swig at the table and the next thing…the *very* next thing, I was waking up in that nasty shack down the alley." She threw a reluctant glance back toward the intersection and shuddered.

This wasn't making any sense to me at all. Willa could hold her liquor. She was anything but dainty when it came to alcohol, and while she'd been known to overdo, it was the exception, not the rule. Of course, people black out from alcohol all the time. I once knew a guy in college who went on a weeklong bender—he woke up on Sunday and couldn't recall Monday through Saturday. But that certainly wasn't

Willa. She was a happy and controlled drunk, sort of like a boozy Mary Poppins. I was starting to suspect something stronger than alcohol had been in her drink. As I watched, Willa's face blanched and she hurried toward the curb.

"I'm gonna be sick," she said, bending over and following through on her promise.

I held the tag ends of the sheet out of the way while she emptied the contents of her stomach on the side of the road. When she'd finished, I found a garden hose to wet my handkerchief and handed it to her. She wiped her face. Angry tears started flowing from her eyes. "I just don't understand what happened."

"You were probably drugged."

She looked up at me and shook her head. "Why? Who would do that? I was with Janet and Doodle."

"I don't know, Wil, but we're going to find out."

Willa swung her legs into the car and said, "Right now I just want to go home." Her voice was full of defeat, but I knew it wouldn't last. Willa was never one to stay down for long.

I followed in Mother's Lexus as she drove slowly back to her place. Understandably, she was not up to company. I saw her inside and sat for a few minutes in the Lexus trying to figure out what had happened to her. As the sun peeked over the top of Willa's complex, the temperature in the car began to feel uncomfortable. I decided it was time to go to work. I dropped Mother's Lexus back at Lost Wind and hopped on a bus.

I arrived at my office to find the cat had deposited the unrecognizable remains of some unfortunate creature at my front door. It was a gruesome collection of feathers and fur, probably hacked up on my porch as a show of gratitude or payment or pure boastfulness. Briefly, I considered the ominous implication of a day that started off with so much regurgitation. Then I shuddered and nudged the blob aside with the toe of my shoe.

My night had been a little light on the sleep side, so I decided to kick-start my system with a Red Bull before turning on the computer. I usually avoid caffeine, but the day had already started off strange, and even though I was still floating on a postcoital cloud of endorphins, I felt like I needed the caffeine to help me focus. Today, I had to find a line on Milton Buttons.

The day before, I had tracked down an online court record from the fall of 1999. A parking ticket had been issued to the driver of a silver Toyota Corolla registered to Martin in the downtown section of Houston. Luckily, he had failed to pay the fine, so the court had initiated proceedings and issued a summons. The record listed a Houston address and phone number.

I'd called the number and got a recorded message—the phone had been disconnected. The plan today was to find someone who knew Milton, or knew of Milton, and might have an idea of his current whereabouts. I would start by making a few calls, canvassing businesses and residents in the area of his old Houston address. It had been twelve years since the date on the ticket, and the apartment building listed was no longer there. My guess was that it had been razed during one of Houston's periodic downtown renovation efforts. From my rudimentary knowledge, the address looked to be in the Westchase district, a rather seedy part of downtown. Chances were slim I'd find anyone willing to help. Still it was worth a shot.

I spent an hour compiling a list of hopeful phone numbers before picking up the receiver to dial. The first call went like this:

Pause…
Me: Hello, is anybody there?
Him: Depends, what the hell do you want?
Me: I just have a couple questions about someone you may know.
Him: *Click, buzz.*

I wasn't particularly disappointed, reasoning he was probably busy or just antisocial. You run into all kinds of people in this line of work. I was sure to have better luck with the next call.

It went like this:

Her: What the hell do you want?
Me: Ma'am?
Her: If your lousy ass is calling to sell me something, you better hang up now 'cause I swore to Jesus that I would gut the next telephone solicitor who called my number… and I never lie to Jesus.

Me: I promise, I'm not selling anything.

Her: And if you're calling 'cause you work for someone I owe money to, then you're a sorry sack of shit that better hang up now 'cause I swore to God I would hunt down the next loan shark that called and rip his testicles off with a pair of pliers…and I never lie to God.

Me: Look, I swear, it's nothing like that.

Her: And if you're bothering me with a survey or asking a bunch of dumb-ass questions, I'll tell you right now that you better kiss your sorry ass good-bye because I'll be there shoving a garden rake up—

Me: *Click, buzz.*

This was going to be harder than I thought.

I went at it diligently until five thirty, figuring seven hours of work on a Saturday ought to be enough. I'd had very limited success. Only one person would actually speak with me. She gave me a forwarding address and mentioned a possible alias for Milton: Gene Spleen.

I vowed to follow up on that in the morning. As I filed away the notes I'd taken, I started dreaming about the things I planned to do with Matt later that night. Most of them involved flexibility, so I began stretching my quads as I checked the bus schedule. I had been lulled into complacency by a pleasant afternoon of work and had managed to totally forget what day it was.

But the bus schedule brought me back to reality and I felt my stomach clench in anticipation. Saturday meant dinner with Mother, and the last thing in the world I wanted to do was spend my evening at Lost Wind. But the price of being a Honey is Saturday night dinner with the circus troupe I call family. I grabbed my cell phone and kicked through the door determined to survive the encounter.

CHAPTER FOUR

There comes a time in almost every gay man's life when he gets tired of the dance. When he realizes he doesn't care anymore about what others think because he's so sick of hiding and pretending or bargaining and questioning or being judged and pitied and hated that he wants to scream or punch something or write a screenplay. It's the universal "coming out" experience, a systematic letting go of all the social niceties when everyone hopes the hamper is big enough to hold all the dirty laundry. That time came for me when Mother said, "Please pass the peas," at our weekly family dinner.

It wasn't the words so much as the way she said them, sort of cold and distant…like she preferred composting the baby to changing the diaper.

The entire mealtime conversation had bubbled with unresolved issues and innuendo. I knew something was brewing from the moment I saw the seriousness in Mother's eyes as I stepped through the ornately carved and delicately arched doorway into Lost Wind.

She waved away her butler, Chin, and grabbed my arm like an eagle capturing a salmon. She pulled my head downward to whisper in my ear. It was impossible to miss the grave intensity in her raspy voice as she said. "Greg dear, you are a Honey and tonight you're going to act like one." I looked at her in confusion but she swept past, leading me onto the marble floors of the gallery and down the long, richly paneled passage (with the stained-glass windows and expensive artwork) into the solarium.

The rich hues of sunset splashed across the marble floors and painted Grandmother's bald head an eerie burnt orange. She was sitting on her motorized scooter, dressed in a ridiculous lime-green frock with what looked like Easter eggs where her breasts had once been (now they hung somewhat lower). A waifish figure stood in front of her wearing a coral-seashell prom gown in rippling chiffon. This vision in pink pivoted her head my direction on a swanlike neck with the slow, stately precision of royalty.

Mother said, "Cicely dear, this is my son, Greg Honey. Greg, Cicely is from the Philadelphia Wessleys." Then Mother shoved me forward like she was feeding a chicken to the gators in the swamp.

Cicely nodded and offered a daintily bejeweled hand. I looked down at it, unsure if I should kiss it or polish the rings sparkling on her fingers. I settled for a firm shake and a sideways glance toward my mother that I hoped would burn forever in the deepest part of her soul.

"Your mother tells me you play the piano."

The comment came so completely out of the blue that it left me wondering if I had somehow stepped through the looking glass into in a strange new universe. I neither own nor play a piano. I'm not musically inclined, have never learned to play an instrument, and the sum total of my experience in the area was that I had heard Billy Joel's recording of "Piano Man" on the radio. I wondered what could have brought my mother to make up such a ridiculous lie when she broke back into the conversation.

"Cicely dear, I told you how truly shy Greg is regarding his playing. I'm sure he'd rather talk about you than his talent."

Since my talent on the piano is at the "maybe I could pick out Chopsticks" level, it would have been a short conversation anyway.

"Yes," I agreed lamely, and Cicely smiled.

"Well...there's not much to tell, really. My family is from Philadelphia, but you already know that. I've just finished a literature degree at Brown and I'm in Austin visiting my aunt Berta. Your mom asked if I'd come to dinner when we met at Berta's ladies' tea yesterday afternoon."

A little voice inside my head said, *Uh-oh, this cannot be good.* Mother never did anything on a whim. A picture began to form in my mind as I looked around the room, noticing that Chin was the only other male present and all of the jewelry glittered from Cicely's right hand. Whether Cicely Wessley knew it or not, this was meant to be a date. Cicely was probably a perfectly nice girl, regardless of her propensity to believe the most horrendous lies, her obvious princess fixation, and her questionable taste in clothing, but I had absolutely no interest in taking this maternal hallucination any further. There was a lull in the conversation as I composed an appropriate response meant to let everyone know that this was not going to happen when Grandmother broke the silence as only my grandmother can.

"That Anderson Cooper's one hot piece of man flesh. I wonder if he's available, 'cause I could really use a little lovin' from a stud muffin like that."

The look on Cicely's face was about what you'd expect, but Mother just rolled her eyes. I grinned, knowing Grandmother Lucille, though capable of occasional flashes of lucidity, was one Corona short of a six-pack. With advancing dementia had come a relaxation of moral standards that occasionally produced memorable moments. I found them refreshing; Mother less so. A few months back, dear Lucille had even tossed her panties onstage at a Sha-Boom concert. Of course, she wears the biggest knickers in Texas, so they just about blanketed the stage.

Mother said, "You have to excuse my mother-in-law, Cicely. The doctors are having trouble balancing her medication."

Grandmother said, "What? You don't think he's sexy? 'Cause I could ride that baloney pony all night long."

Silently, I agreed with Grandmother. Anderson was both hot and gay—a winning combination if ever there was one. The thought sent my mind following a bunny trail. I figured if it doesn't work out with Matt, maybe I could become a correspondent at CNN and work my way up to Anderson's stable of friends. I followed this flight of fancy mostly because that was how my mind worked, but partly because reality was not so *real* for me at that moment.

As I pondered life as a correspondent, Chin stepped out of the hallway to announce dinner and we followed Grandmother's scooter to the dining room. As we shuffled along, the thought came to me that the best way to deal with the upcoming meal might be to toss a grenade in the salad bowl and run for cover. I was searching my pockets for an explosive device when Mother seized my arm again and whispered in my ear, "She's a nice girl, don't you think?"

What I really thought was she'd be better with a penis, but I held my tongue as we all sat down.

Conversation was stilted and awkward as we fiddled with our cutlery. My mother worked to block Grandmother's interaction with the lovely Cicely, and this did not go over very well with the nonagenarian.

She snapped, "Livia, you're in my way."

Mother totally ignored her. "So, Cicely, I'm so sorry you visited during our horrendous Austin summer."

"I can't see." Grandmother leaned forward from her chair.

"It is hot," Cicely replied with a smile.

"I hope you stay until the fall when it's so much nicer." Mother's tone was inviting.

"Move aside."

"And our winters are absolutely lovely."

I watched, thinking *this could be fun* as Grandmother picked up her salad plate.

"I said move, damn it."

"Of course, you probably have lovely weather in Philly too."

"Yes, usually."

"Well, you can't say I didn't I warn you."

As I fought to keep from laughing, Grandmother gave new meaning to the term "tossing a salad" and the service staff looked away in horror. Fine china shattered on the floor and a soggy wad of romaine lettuce smacked Mother in the face. Chin hurried over with a hand broom to sweep up the pieces. Mother calmly wiped drops of olive oil from her forehead. Without missing a beat, she said, "I hope to visit the East Coast soon. As I told you earlier, I met your mother in the eighties. She's such a lovely person."

Evidently the Philadelphia Wessleys upheld the same rigorous social standards as the Honeys, and the conversation continued without pause as Mother plucked a bit of radish from her hair and a fugitive olive rolled across the table.

Cicely said, "That would be lovely. My mother speaks very highly of you too, Mrs. Honey."

I was still following the olive's plaintive progress when Mom turned her steely gaze in my direction. "Greg dear, tell Cicely about your little business venture."

I cringed. "Little business venture" was her way of saying "waste of time and money." I hurried through a brief explanation, hoping to avoid details.

"I own a private detective agency. Most of the work so far has been for insurance companies, but I have a few individual clients too. It's mostly background checks and locating people."

"How exciting," Cicely said coldly. It was obvious she wasn't impressed. I began to think that I didn't like her. In general, I tried to give Mother's acquaintances the benefit of the doubt. They were, after all, people too (most of them), but Cicely's patronizingly superior attitude was starting to rub me the wrong way. Who was she to ooze condescension, anyway? I looked at her sitting there in her tiara and prom dress, her lips pursed, and that excessively glossy complexion, smirking at the salad as if fresh vegetables were beneath contempt. For God's sake, how I-want-to-be-the-princess could she be?

"It can be," I replied, wondering what punching her in the face would feel like.

Quite pleasing, probably.

I was saved from a possible aggravated assault charge by Dolores's arrival, followed closely by the rest of the kitchen staff bearing steaming dishes. Dolores's expertise was Southern cooking, which meant something was fried, something was baked and everything was smothered in butter or lard or bacon fat. In other words, comfort food—which was what I needed because comfort, in any form, was sadly lacking at that table.

As the food was served, my gaze trailed across to Grandmother, who'd been noticeably silent since the salad-throwing incident. A look of distracted amusement played across her face while she fiddled with the Easter eggs on her dress. Or maybe she was rearranging her mammary parts—it was hard to tell from across the table. Her eyes lit up when a basket of cornbread was set in front of her. Within seconds, she had crumbs scattered across her lap and trailing down what used to be her cleavage.

The forced conversation lulled while we tucked into our fried chicken and mashed potatoes. As we ate, my irritation grew. This wasn't the first time I'd been led unwittingly into social interaction with a prospective marriage partner by my mother. I fumed at the idiocy of the situation. I was twenty-eight, after all, certainly old enough to pick my own partners, but how to get Mother to back off? I'd avoided social occasions, pretended to date Willa, and dropped more hints than a flirty teenage girl. On a whim, I decided to try something truly unique: candor.

I cleared my throat. Everyone looked up at me with stuffed mouths. I said, "Cicely, I want to apologize for this little farce. I'm afraid my mother has asked you to dinner under false pretenses. I want you to know I had nothing to do with this, but I believe Mother owes you an explanation."

Cicely swallowed roughly, confusion playing across her bejeweled forehead. She wiped her mouth and turned to look at Mother.

For once Livia Honey was flustered. Her face softened, and I could almost see the wheels turning inside her head. The uncomfortable silence was finally broken when Mother dropped her fork. It clanged on her plate and she patted her lips nervously with her napkin. Then the flinty sharpness returned to her eyes and I knew she'd regained her composure.

"Well, Cicely dear, Greg is correct, I do have ulterior motives. But I also have the best possible intentions. The truth is I was hoping to put together a little party for the very finest of Austin society in your honor and hoped you would allow Greg to be your escort. Would next Saturday evening work for you?"

Cicely smiled demurely, and I glared at Mother, who flashed a wicked grin of victory before picking up her fork.

Cicely said, "That would be lovely, Mrs. Honey. I would enjoy meeting Austin's society. Thank you very much."

I fidgeted nervously, my mind racing. I needed to find a way out of this mess before plans were set in stone. I stammered, "I don't particularly like 'Austin society,' and I'm not sure I'm the one you want—"

But Mother barged right over my objection. "Nonsense, you're the perfect escort for Cicely. It will give you two a chance to spend some time together."

"Yes, that would be nice," Cicely agreed and a huge grin broke across her face like she'd just been elected Homecoming Queen. I wasn't sure if she was happy because Mother was throwing a party in her honor, or if she actually wanted to date me. Either way, I needed to find a way to avoid this impending train wreck. So I decided to bring in the big guns.

"But there's another thing you may not be aware of. You see, I'm—"

Mother cut in with the immortal words, "Greg dear, please pass the peas."

Okay, I'm not usually one to make a scene, but if there ever was a time for a scene to be made, this was it. Mother had cut me off in the middle of my coming-out statement. I was furious and determined, ready to spit nails.

I said, "Here are your precious peas, Mother." I slid the bowl across the table and turned to Cicely.

"My mother is trying very hard to keep me from telling you I'm gay, you know...homosexual, a friend of Dorothy, an Irish creamer, queer as a three dollar bill...She doesn't want you to hear I'd rather style your hair than sleep with you. You see, I've done things to men that would draw a murder sentence in most Muslim countries. And they liked it...well, most of them...the point is I loved it. Those things require parts only men have. Mother doesn't want you to hear that I'm in love with a man, truly in love, and I worship him. And for the first time in my life I can honestly say I'm happy."

I turned to Mother, who was staring at me in stony silence. "I'm sorry if the truth is uncomfortable for you, Mother, but it's my life to live, not yours."

The room was hushed as I finished my speech. Somehow the hatred and anger I'd felt only seconds before had melted like a snow cone in a sauna, and I felt great. I'd freed myself from all the unspoken obligations my mother had tried to foist on me since childhood. Never again could she imagine I'd outgrow this phase, and never again could she pretend all I needed was to find the right girl. It was over. Because I had found the right girl and she was a gloriously beautiful man.

The footmen looked away in embarrassment and the mood in the room was shifting into darkness until my grandmother said, "What exactly do you do with this guy in bed? 'Cause if it was me and I had a penis I'd be sticking it in all sorts of places, but mostly I can think of one place and that could be a little uncomfortable...and messy."

I ignored the question. Despite the surreal appeal of discussing sexual technique with my grandmother, it was not the appropriate time or place.

Mother slid her chair back from the table slowly. When she looked up I could see most of the color had drained from her face. She turned away and said, "I apologize for this scene, Cicely. It appears you've been dragged into the middle of a family crisis. Perhaps you'll excuse me, I'm not feeling well."

And she left the table without another word. Chin held the door as she sailed through with her head held high. I realized she was hurt and angry and things between us would never be the same.

❖

Back at home I decided to call Willa, partly because I wanted to make sure she was okay but mostly because I needed to hear a friendly voice.

"Hello."

"Hi, Willa, how are you doing?"

"Lousy."

"Still worried about last night?"

"Yep."

"Anything I can do?"

"No."

"You sound depressed. What's wrong?"

"Worried."

Willa had never been like this. I didn't think she was capable of giving only one-word answers.

"What is it, Willa? Why are you worried?"

"Someone has my panties, Greg, I think that speaks for itself."

"You don't know that. Maybe they're just lost, maybe you dropped them somewhere and they're lying under a bush or a table or something." Even as I said it, I realized how ridiculous it sounded.

"No one just drops their underwear, Greg."

"Okay, you have a point, but it's just panties, for God's sake. It's not like you lost a friend or a pet or your dignity."

"I lost my panties, Greg, there's not much dignity in that."

"But it's just panties, Wil."

"No, it's not *just panties*."

I waited for her to tell me what it was, but she remained silent. My apprehension deepened—her reticence was definitely un-Willa-like. Finally, I said, "I think you're upset because you don't like losing control."

"Bingo."

"Well, how did it happen? What do you remember?"

"I don't remember *anything*. That's the point. I followed Doodle and Janet to a bar on Red River. We went in, ordered a drink, and the rest...all the rest...is a total blank."

"You realize this doesn't sound credible—I mean, I accept what you're saying, but something is not right with this story. People don't black out after one drink. Twenty, sure, but not one."

"I swear that's what happened—except it wasn't after, it was during."

"I trust you, I don't believe it was just a drink...I think someone put something in it."

"Who would do that?"

"I don't know, Willa. Someone wanting to take advantage, maybe."

"You mean Doodle or Janet? But that doesn't seem right. Janet was a weepy mess and Doodle was just glad to have my help with her. Why would either of them want my panties? They were just looking to get by. That doesn't make sense."

"No, it doesn't make sense. I'm really sorry, Willa."

"Yeah, well, what's a girl to do. Anyway, what are you up to tonight?" She sounded sad, and I realized she wanted to change the subject.

I decided to fill her in on my evening.

"Oh, man, do I have something to tell you." And I launched into a description of dinner and my coming-out speech. I could feel her getting caught up in the drama and she actually laughed when I told her about the salad incident.

She even sounded happy when she told me she was proud to be my friend. That's when I heard the tone telling me e-mail had arrived at my computer. I took the phone to my desk and clicked on the icon.

"Give me a sec, Willa, I've got e-mail."

There was total silence for a few seconds as I read the message. Finally, Willa got tired of waiting and said, "You still there?"

"Yeah, I'm here, but, Willa, we've got a bigger problem than my mother and your panties."

"What are you talking about?"

"Check your e-mail—I just forwarded you something."

I waited while she fired up her e-mail program. After a moment, I heard the low sort of growly sound a pit bull makes just before it rips someone's throat out. She said, "I will crucify her, I will surgically remove her tits and attach them to her forehead, I will sand the skin from her torso and spray her down with rubbing alcohol."

The e-mail on my screen showed a series of carefully posed pictures of Willa removing her panties; the last shot had Willa straddling the Texas cowboy statue at the Capitol building with her pale pink panties covering the rider's face. The e-mail had been delivered to about two hundred people, including the manager of Zach Scott Theater and the pastor of Hyde Park Baptist Church. It was unsigned, but both of us knew who had sent it.

"What are you going to do?"

"Not sure yet, but whatever it is, it will be painful and humiliating."

"I don't know, Wil, you really think that's smart? Maybe it's time to rise above the situation."

"Greg, my panties…these pictures…" She sighed in frustration. "This e-mail went to my mother."

"Luckily, your mother doesn't know how to open her e-mail."

"But Lola didn't know that. She humiliated me. She abused me. She wants to destroy me. But I survived, and now I'm going to unleash the hounds of hell. This is war!"

"I don't know, Willa, you should be careful that—"

But I was talking to dead air. Willa hung up, presumably to prepare plans for Lola's torture. I was going to warn her vengeance only begot vengeance. And whatever she did, Lola would only retaliate—but she didn't want to hear it. I realized I hadn't even told her about my evening with Matt. That made me smile again and I checked the clock; it was nine thirty. The show would last another half hour. Give him fifteen minutes or so to change, and he'd be on his way.

I looked toward the door expectantly and fidgeted in anticipation. I picked up the paper to peruse the news while I waited. It was full of what you'd expect—photos of natural disasters showing massive forest fires, a draught of biblical proportions in the west, and drenching rains and hurricanes in the east. The south was sweltering and it was locust season in the northern plains. Wars raged on in Afghanistan, the Congo, and South Sudan. North African dictators were under siege and it seemed like the whole of the Middle East was ablaze. One article pointed out a prominent Democratic senator had proposed eliminating tax breaks for people with annual incomes over two hundred and fifty thousand dollars, and a prominent Republican congressman countered with a proposal to eliminate taxes altogether for people earning over two hundred and fifty thousand dollars. Locally, an education organization was complaining about the low test scores of Texas schoolchildren, and a Texas politician was working on a bill to remove all references to radicals like Thomas Jefferson and John Adams from Texas schools. In a related story, the state legislature was considering a proposal to replace high school evolutionary studies with genealogy curriculum designed to trace each student's ancestry back to Adam and Eve. (The father of two Hindu students threatened to sue if the measure ever became state law.)

Nervous energy made it impossible to sit still for long, so I got up and walked to the bathroom. My insecurity was mounting as I stood in front of the mirror and tried to inventory my features. On the up side, I had the standard Honey strong chin and aquiline nose, my eyes were bright, and my ears were relatively small and well placed. My eyebrows and nose hair were trimmed, and my on-again-off-again relationship with the gym had given me a chest that looked like I had pectoral muscles instead of man boobs. On the downside, my hair was wild and strange with cowlicks and swoopy parts. I appeared to have corners on my head and my abs were less rippling than rolling.

I stepped away from the mirror, more convinced than ever I wasn't worthy of Matt and that he was just playing with me like a cat batting around a mouse before dinner.

And then the phone rang, and it was Matt. He was on his way over, and my heart started singing *Tosca* arias, the upbeat part before Mario gets shot and she leaps to her death.

CHAPTER FIVE

On Sunday morning again I woke before Matt and took the opportunity to peruse his sublime excellence while he slept. He had this way of snuggling with the covers that looked cute and cuddly and made the world a better place. I was feeling like a toasted marshmallow, warm and creamy in the middle with a sugary crust. It wasn't that I'd stopped worrying about Willa, or that I was no longer concerned about my finances, or that I had forgotten the nightmare of dinner with my family—that was going to take copious amounts of therapy and alcohol. But it seemed, with Matt's absolute perfection lying next to me, those things just didn't matter as much.

He stirred a little and one eye popped open. He said, "Hi, sunshine."

"Hi, yourself."

"Did you have a good night's sleep?"

"My entire night was good, sleeping and otherwise."

"I want to stay here forever."

"Good, then I won't have to chain you to the bed."

He grinned again and rolled over. "But I have to go."

"Hold on a minute while I find my handcuffs."

"Wish I could stay, but you have things to do and I have a show this afternoon."

"Ah, the rigorous life of a talented regional theater actor."

"And the exciting exploits of a private detective."

"Busy guys, barely have time for their private lives."

"Which they share."

I smiled. "So tell me something, all this lovey-dovey stuff, is it for real? Or—"

He reached over and touched my lips with a finger. "Hush, Mr. Honey, 'cause I have something to say and I'm only going to say it once, so don't freak out. I've been in love with you since the first time I met you. There, I said it, so try to hold it together until I get out of here—then you can panic or scream or practice self-immolation or whatever it is you're going to do, in private."

He sat on the side of the bed and stuffed his legs into his jeans. I snuggled beside him and said, "You've got some time, the gas can's in the garage and I'm out of matches."

He kissed me and stood, pulling his jeans up. I watched him walk toward the bathroom with the angels singing in my head. He stopped at the doorway and asked, "Will I see you at the matinee?"

"I'll call Willa, she can probably get me in for free." I spoke with volume so he could hear me over the sound of running water.

"I can get you in for free," he yelled back.

"But then everyone would figure out that we're a couple."

"What's wrong with that?"

"Hey, I'm cool with it if you are. I just don't want to rush you." I was grinning again.

"I'm cool," he said as the toilet flushed. The water started running in the sink again. He poked his head through the door and said, "How about an honest-to-God date tonight, dinner after the show?"

"You bet." I'd need to stop at an ATM to try to bleed a few dollars from my woefully anemic account.

Matt walked out of the bathroom slipping into his T-shirt. He flexed his chiseled chest, and I tried not to swoon as the shirt conformed to the contours of his immaculate torso. He moved to the bed and sat next to me.

"You know what this means, right?"

"It means I have a date?"

"It means you have a lover."

I couldn't wipe the obnoxious grin from my face as I said, "And it means you have a lover."

Now he was smiling and the chorus of angels was belting out hallelujahs in my head.

❖

About an hour later, I stepped into my office and the cat shot out through the gap between my legs before I closed the door. The light blinked on my answering machine. I punched the Play button and listened to Gary Weiss at Texas Insurance Purveyors ask me to call him back. I keyed in the number and waited while the connection was made. He answered on the first ring.

"You're working on a Sunday," he said.

"You're working on a Sunday," I parroted.

"We've got to get lives."

I smiled to myself, thinking *I've got one, thanks,* while he told me about a task he needed my help with. On Friday, he'd received a heads-up from an underwriter that an employee of the Williams Construction Company was planning to file a possibly bogus worker's compensation claim. According to the underwriter's source, the guy, Bradford Collins, alleged to have been injured while lifting a load of bricks at a construction site downtown. Gary's underwriter was suspicious because Mr. Collins had asked some pointed questions about the company's sick leave policy less than twenty minutes before being injured. Gary wanted me to run a background check and surreptitiously follow Bradford around for a day or two to see if I could come up with any evidence they could use to prove the claim was phony.

I'd been trying to get some of Texas Insurance Purveyors' business since I first met Gary at an Austin bar named Charlie's last fall. The bar had shut down recently, but used to run a weekly drag show I showed up to watch back in October. That evening, Gary was frantically searching the audience for help. His partner was stuck in Houston, and he needed someone to play Sonny to his surprisingly authentic Cher. I volunteered, of course, hoping the effort would yield future dividends. When we took the stage I wore a pageboy wig and warbled a passable rendition of "I've Got You Babe" from my knees as Gary flicked long black hair over a shoulder, licked his teeth and leaned an elbow on my head, all the while looking oh-so-bored. He proceeded to turn around and slip his glittery gown to the floor, flashing the audience with the flame tattoo coming out of his butt.

At the time I was sure I'd reached a new low point in my search for success, but now the performance was paying off. The thought that maybe I should spend more time on my knees at drag shows flashed through my mind. I jotted down the information Gary gave me and asked him to meet me in the office on Monday with a five-hundred-dollar advance check.

I hung up and sat down at my computer, planning to give my full attention to the search for Russ Buttons's brother, but it was not to be. The phone rang again and I answered, "Honey Detective Agency, when you need a dick, please rent this one."

"Catchy slogan." Russ's voice dripped sarcasm.

"I kind of like it too. If you called to nag at me, you should know I'm working on your brother's case right this moment."

"Good, but that's not what I called about. I have another job for you."

"What's up?"

"I think Billy is seeing someone on the side." His voice caught on the words and I listened to a few seconds of rather dramatic sobbing.

Billy Crenshaw, Russ's boyfriend, was a tall and muscular guy with more style than hair. He was quiet and faithful, not the kind of guy to be dragged into the bushes by his gonads.

I said, "Russ, that doesn't sound like Billy."

"Find out!" he screamed and more sniffling followed.

"What do you want me to do?"

"You're the detective, how the hell am I supposed to know?"

"I can ask around, I guess but first you need to come by the office so we can sit down and talk about it."

"Jesus, Honey, I'm at the salon and Jerry just dyed my hair."

Jerry worked for Russ at the Blow Job Salon, an upscale beauty shop that catered mostly to West Austin ladies with more money than taste and an addiction to pedicures, manicures, and herbal-tea colonics. Russ was relatively famous in stylist circles for inventing the Bolivian Blowout—a hairstyle I'd seen advertised as "a cut, a dye, a tease, and a tickle."

I said, "Well, pull on a shower cap and come on over."

He hung up with all the fury of a powder puff, and I turned back to the computer.

The forwarding address I had for Milton Buttons's alias was in a little town named Enid, Oklahoma. I used an online cross-link look-up directory to find a phone number for the address and made the call. A young female voice answered.

Her: Wilson residence, this is Matty.

Me: Can I speak to one of your parents?

Her: Um, maybe—gimme a sec. (Background sounds of steps and a distant scream: "Mama! Telephone!" "I'm on the toilet—tell 'em to call back." More steps.) She's on the can, you want I should call Dad?

Me: Please.

Her: Okay…gimme a sec. (Background sound of steps and distant scream: 'Daddy, telephone!" "Jesus, Matty, can't you see I'm sleeping? Take a message." More steps.) He's sleeping, you wanna leave a message?

Me: I wonder if you can help me? I'm looking for someone named Milton Buttons, you might know him as Gene Spleen.

Her: I don't know no Milton, but Gene lived upstairs. She's gone, though.

Pause…

Me: "You mean he. *He's* gone, though.

Her: Um, no, Gene's a lady.

Me: Really?

Her: Well, I didn't do a strip search but yeah, she looks like a lady to me. I mean, she's soft and smells like flowers and she's got lady's parts. Maybe the biggest lady's parts I've ever seen.

Pause…

Me: You said he, um, she's gone. When did she leave?

Her: Jesus, mister, you ask a lot of questions, I dunno, maybe a couple of weeks ago.

Me: Do you know where she went?

Her: Somewhere in Texas, I think. You wanna know more, you're gonna have to talk to Mom, and she's in the can.

I thanked her and hung up, making a mental note to call back in an hour.

❖

I was trying to get my head around Milton Buttons's alias, Ms. Gene Spleen, when Willa walked into my office with a big smile on her face.

"Hi, Honey, isn't life beautiful? This is just one of the most beautiful days ever. It gets like this in Austin sometimes, all sunny like the gods sprinkled it with glitter and shit. I saw Russ Buttons pulling his pickle-colored Cadillac convertible into your parking lot. That queen was wearing a shower cap, for God's sake, so I said to him, 'what's with the cap,' and he said 'I just dyed my hair,' and I said 'why'd you do that,' and he said 'I have to keep up with fashion,' so I said 'Russ, you and fashion parted a long time ago,' and he said 'Willa, you'd be pretty if you just had tits,' and I said..."

The old Willa was back, which made me wonder what she'd been up to. That's when the door jangled open and in walked Russ, followed closely by the cat. Russ wore leopard skin pants, knee-high riding boots, and a deep green salon apron.

The cat wore muddy white fur.

A disposable bouffant cap covered Russ's tresses, and dark smudges ran down his forehead. Evidently, he was going for an Elvis look.

Willa said, "Russ honey, that color is not going to work with your complexion, it's much too dark. You're going to look like a licorice lollipop."

"I have to get back to the salon to add the highlights. It'll look earthier with the highlights. I'm using carrot."

Willa said, "If you wanna look earthy, I'd go for turnip highlights. You can't get more earthy than turnip."

It was hard to argue with that. I turned to Willa. "I've got some business with Russ. Do you need anything in particular, or are you just here to spread your own unique brand of cheer?"

"No, nothing in particular, just floating through. Maybe we can do lunch later."

"Okay, give me a call."

"Okey dokey," she said, and off she went, pushing through the door as the cat jumped up to his regular perch on the window ledge.

"Nice cat," Russ said, dripping sarcasm. The cat looked like it had been in a fight with a wet-vac; its fur was matted and sticking up in tufts and swirls. He stared directly at Russ, then lifted a leg and proceeded to lick his private parts.

Personally, I thought the cat understood sarcasm.

"He came with the office," I said.

"You should call animal services, he could have rabies."

"I'm not going to have him put down, Russ, he brings me presents."

"Like what? An iPad?"

"More like fur. An occasional dead mouse or half a squirrel," I answered, figuring half a squirrel was probably superior to an iPad in a cat's view of the world.

"Ewww."

"Once he brought me what looked like the head of an eagle. You know, precious things like that. The point is he likes me."

"I'm sure you're flattered. I'm going to watch where I step around here."

"Probably a good idea. So what's up with Billy?" Russ's eyes were red and puffy. He'd obviously been crying.

"I told you he's sneaking off to see someone else." With that, his eyes teared up and he was having trouble breathing through his nose.

I handed him the box of Kleenex from my desk and asked, "Do you have any evidence?"

"That's what I need you for." He blew his nose and said, "Jesus, Honey…you want me to spell it out for you? It's adultery, it's cheating… it's murder of a marriage." Mud-colored dye seeped from under the shower cap and tears began streaming down his face. He was one of those criers who balled up his face in a nasty squint. It was comical and sad at the same time.

"But what makes you think he's sneaking out on you? Come on, Russ, give me something to work with here. Did you find a love note in his wallet? Is he coming home smelling of Aqua Velva? Did you catch him humping the pool boy?"

"Look, he leaves every night after dinner and he won't tell me where he's going. He comes home late, exhausted, and just falls straight into bed. We haven't had sex in forever, at least two days…two whole days…in a row!"

And with that he broke into a fit of sobbing so long and loud I wondered if he was having intestinal distress.

"When did this start?"

"Well, we didn't have sex last Sunday. I guess it started then. Can't you just follow him, you know, without him knowing? See who he's sleeping with and leave the rest to me."

"And then what? You don't want any trouble, Russ." He didn't strike me as the vindictive type, but you never knew where love was concerned.

"Jesus, Honey, do I look like I'm going to hurt someone? I'd talk to them, make them see that Billy is a married man."

"And that's all?"

"Yes, that's all. But first I need to know. You need to find out who it is that he's seeing. Will you follow him?"

"Okay, I can do that, but I'll have to start tomorrow."

He looked at me with sad eyes and said, "I can't live another day without closure on this."

"I have a date tonight, Russ."

"Can't you please just follo—"

"It's not negotiable. I have a date," I interrupted.

Russ huffed a little and sat back in the chair with his arms folded. "I have a date," he mocked. "Some detective agency this is."

"Look, Mr. Buttons, I have a personal life just like you. I said I can start tomorrow—I don't work twenty-four hours at your beck and call. If that's good enough, fine. If not, I guess you can look for another agency."

"Okay, okay, Jesus, no need to get all lay-down-the-law-y on me."

"Good, now I'll need a check. This time let's make it five hundred since you're a repeat customer."

I handed him the standard agreement form and tried to keep from smiling because I had three jobs on the books…a record for the Honey Detective Agency.

After signing the check, Russ hurried back to the salon, presumably to add carrots to his hair, and I decided it was time to call the Wilsons back. This time, a woman with a very Southern accent answered.

Her: Hello.
Me: Mrs. Wilson?
Her: Yes.
Me: My name is Greg Honey. I called earlier and spoke with your daughter. I'm trying to locate Gene Spleen.
Her: You know, you're the second one calling about her this week? I'm sorry, darlin,' but Gene's gone off to Austin.
Me: Austin? When was that?
Her: Let's see, it must be two or three weeks past now.
Me: I wonder if she left a phone number or a forwarding address. I really need to speak with her.
Her: Hold on, darlin', I wrote it down here somewhere.

I heard rustling sounds before she came back on the line and gave me an address and phone number. I thanked her, hung up, and dialed Milton's new number. I let it ring ten times before I gave up.

I wondered if Russ could have been the one to call about his brother and decided that was unlikely. Why would he hire me to find him if he already knew he was in Austin?

I smiled to myself, thinking about my good fortune. Milton Buttons lived in Austin now. That would make my search a lot easier. I pulled up the cross-link directory site on my computer and verified that the phone number matched the address.

Things were certainly looking rosy over at the Honey Detective Agency.

CHAPTER SIX

Willa called at eleven thirty, and I arranged for her to pick me up at noon. I brought up Google Maps and located the Austin address Mrs. Wilson had given me for Milton Buttons alias Gene Spleen. It was just south of the river on Lamar, a condo project perched on the hill overlooking restaurant row. I wanted to take a look at the place and planned to ask Willa to drive me over after lunch.

She pushed through the doorway as I was printing an aerial view of the condo's parking entrance.

"Whatcha doin'? Oh, I see, copying something. I hate secretarial work...I'm not good with office machines. Did I ever tell you about the time I set the Xerox on fire at the theater? How was I supposed to know you're not supposed to use kerosene to clean toner cartridges? We had to handwrite playbill inserts for a month. You hungry? I'm so hungry I could eat a horse, but I'd rather have couscous or maybe some baba ganoush. What do you think about Marrakesh?"

"It's my favorite Imperial Moroccan city. A little out of the way, though."

"Not the city, silly, the restaurant. I went there once with Wilber Johnston, you remember him, don't you? He's the guy I dated with the great body and bad hair who smelled a little like dog poo and drove a Mercedes convertible. Great in bed, though...as long as you could stand the smell. They serve a mean lamb souvlaki and that stuff they wrap in grape leaves is heavenly, though definitely not kosher, and they brew mint tea too, which makes me pee and maybe gives me the runs a little but I love the taste."

I held the door, and Willa prattled all the way to the car.

We drove six blocks downtown to Congress Avenue. A man in a tasseled Fez seated us at a table near the window with a view of the bus stop across the street. The interior space of the restaurant was a rug-covered wooden floor where belly dancers did things with their midsections that had to be bad for digestion. I took advantage of a breathing pause in Willa's nonstop chatter to interrupt.

"So you want to tell me what you've got going?"

She looked at me, feigning confusion. I stared back and sly smile broke across her face.

"What are you talking about? This is lunch. I ordered the Greek special."

"Don't try to play stupid with me, Willa Jensen. Yesterday you'd lost your panties and a picture of you simulating sex acts with a bronze cowboy was e-mailed to just about everyone you know. That made you mad enough to rip the alimentary canal from Lola Riatta. But this morning you come into my office all happy and airy...smiling like you'd douched with daisies. You did something to Lola, and we're going to sit right here until you tell me what it was."

Her smile widened.

"I'm waiting."

She looked at her fingernails, pretending disinterest, and said, "Well, if you must know, I got even."

"Tell me Lola is not tied up and bleeding in your basement."

"No, she's not in my basement...and the skank will live since only the Japanese commit hari kari."

"What happened?"

"Well, if you must know, I followed her to the gym this morning and added a little Veet depilatory product to her conditioner bottle."

I looked at her with disgust. "You didn't."

"Yep, it came off in clumps. When she left the gym her comb-over looked worse than Donald Trump's."

I pictured Lola's patchy head and realized there was little chance retaliation was not on the horizon. I asked, "Did you at least talk with Doodle and Janet before you destroyed Lola's hair? I hope to hell it was Lola who messed with you, or this thing will get even more ugly. How did she do it? How did she get to you?"

"Of course I talked with them. It was Lola, I didn't know it then, but it turns out she bartends at the Red River Ale House. Doodle described her to me. She was the one who went to place our order. My guess is Lola spotted me when we first arrived and was staying low, looking for an opportunity. No doubt she slipped something into my drink. Later when I'd passed out, she came over to the table and offered to help get me home. Doodle, of course, doesn't know about my history with Lola."

Willa seemed a little too willing to believe Lola was the only one to blame here—probably to reduce the number of targets she'd have to get even with. I was a little less certain, but kept quiet.

"Doodle said Janet went all weepy when I hit the floor. So Doodle was overwhelmed. She told me she was so relieved when Lola offered to help out that she accepted immediately. Doodle took Janet home, and I guess that's when Lola lugged me to the Capitol for a few candid pictures sans my panties."

"You realize, of course, that your little payback session will only escalate the level of violence."

"Let her come, this time I'll be ready."

"I just hope I'm not sitting next to you if she comes with a flame-thrower."

Her head pivoted in my direction and a smile broke across her face. "I can handle it. So what about you? You're glowing like a newly minted penny. I haven't seen you this happy since they aired Sarah Palin's interview with Katie Couric. Spill."

I felt a rush of excitement and said, "If you must know, I'm in love."

"You sure it's not just gas?"

"It's the real thing, Willa."

"With Matt?"

"Of course with Matt."

"So your date went well on Friday night."

"Matt spent the night and came over last night too."

"Two dates in a row with the same man. Isn't that a record?"

"And we've got plans after the show this afternoon."

She dropped her voice conspiratorially and said, "So it's not gas."

"It's love, Willa." I said the words slowly while staring at her eyes.

"So you've finally found someone to diddle your thing."

"Definitely."

A tentative smile painted her face, and she said, "Greg darling, I'm so happy for you. Matt seems like a great guy—but please be careful. It's a long way down from that cloud you're floating on, and I don't want to see you hurt."

"He loves me too, Willa."

"Of course he loves you, Honey, everyone loves you. I'm just saying go slow, for me. Okay?"

I stared at her, wondering why her words were so—*lukewarm* at best. Worry began darkening my mood. I pictured heartbreak and pain. But then I remembered Willa had pierced more hearts than Cupid. Enough emotional flotsam and jetsam floated in her wake to sink a battleship. Without a doubt, she had a lot of experience in the seamy underside of love, and she'd view the world through that prism of misfortune. So I couldn't bring myself to take her fears seriously. Sometimes love makes you foolish, and sometimes it makes you fearless.

As we ate our lunch, I slowly worked the conversation around to Milton Buttons, building up the interest level until Willa offered to drive me over.

I felt deliciously devious controlling the situation like that until Willa said, "You realize you could have just asked me to take you there."

The drive was harrowing; stop-and-go angry traffic full of honking cars and oversized buses. When Willa finally pulled her Honda into the lot and parked, I was ready to get out of the car. We hiked up the hill searching for directions to unit 3D. Willa spotted a sign before I did.

"It's over here. Man, what a dump, I know cockroaches who keep a cleaner place. What's that? No, don't tell me. A blow-up doll, for God's sake? No one keeps a blow-up doll on their front porch. That's like advertising for sexual predators. I'd watch where you step; it's kind of sticky over here...I don't even want to know what that is."

She pointed at a strange-looking blob of red goo that may or may not have been beating.

I picked my foot placements carefully and said, "Willa, what are you doing?"

"I'm just going to knock on the door. I want to meet Russ Buttons's brother. Wonder if he's as nelly as the pope in tights too." She tiptoed around the pseudo-beating mass and climbed the mold-encrusted steps to the porch.

"Willa, no," I rasped, trying to stop her. I wanted to take it slowly. We had no idea how Milton Buttons would take our unexpected presence at his door, and I didn't want to spook him. But Willa is nothing if not determined. She pounded on the door and it swung open, squeaking on un-oiled hinges.

"Hey, it's not locked." As I scrambled to catch up with her she stuck her head inside the doorway. "Anyone in here? Yoo-hoo, your door's open, is anyone home?"

I froze midway up the steps as the sound of movement came from a back room. A deep rough voice called out, "Gimme a minute, will ya?"

Willa looked at me, and I motioned for her to back away from the door. I pulled out my iPhone on the off chance of catching a candid shot and listened to the grunts and scuffling sounds of a sleepy person getting dressed. After a few seconds, an unshaven face popped through the door. Milton's head was mostly bald and he squinted in the sun with a sour expression; otherwise he looked like a big, burly version of Russ.

"What do you want?"

"Are you Milton Buttons?" Willa asked, and I snapped a quick shot with my phone. The guy looked at me before squinting at Willa.

"Who's asking?"

"Oh, sorry, where are my manners, I'm Willa Jensen and this is Greg Honey, we're friends of your brother Russ and we want—"

At the mention of Russ's name, the man stepped backward and slammed the door hard.

Willa said, "Well, that was rude."

"We obviously interrupted his sleep." I was satisfied. The photo on my cell phone was all I needed to prove to Russ I'd found his brother. "We should go."

Willa wavered on the porch, torn between the need to find out what was going on, and my request. My request was ignored, of course. She climbed off the porch and walked around the side of the building pressing her face against each window, shadowing her eyes with hands cupped against the sides of her head.

At the third window she yelled, "Here he is, what is that? Uh-oh," then I watched her duck and run toward me as the window jerked open. Milton's bald head poked through the threshold. The barrel of a shotgun flashed in the sunshine and I ducked too. We ran back to the car in a zigzag pattern as Willa huffed and said, "That went well." She inhaled quickly and we jumped in her car. We drove three blocks before she added, "What do you think set him off?"

I looked at her with disbelief. "You're kidding, right? Jesus, Willa, you're about as subtle as a cruise missile."

"What? What did I do? I only wanted to meet the guy. Who would have thought he would turn out to be so rude and inhospitable."

"I guess there's bad blood between him and Russ."

"Evidently. Still, he tried to shoot me, and I was almost totally unarmed."

I looked at her and she pulled a small pistol from her side pocket. "This is Texas, a girl's gotta protect herself."

"Jesus, Willa, what the hell is that?"

"What, this little thing? Just a puny little .38 special, barely big enough to bring down a linebacker."

"You want to put that away?"

"Why? You afraid of guns?"

"A little."

She looked at me in disbelief, but slid the gun back in her purse.

I shrugged. "Well, at least everyone survived and I got a picture. Russ can tell us if it's his brother and then I get paid."

"Why do you think he's so touchy? Obviously they have family issues. I had a neighbor like that once. If you asked about his mother he'd flip out. Of course, she used to keep him in a refrigerator and spank him with a shovel. Families can be like that. I know my mother won't be happy until I'm a prairie wife making my own clothes from feed sacks and slaughtering chickens with an axe. Chicken plucking holds no…"

She yammered on as she drove and I tuned her out, checking the photo on my iPhone. It was a grainy shot showing Milton in the doorway. I hadn't noticed what he was wearing, but in the photo I could clearly see a lacy dressing gown and white women's shoes. I e-mailed the photo to Russ with a note explaining that it might be his brother and letting him know I'd call in the morning.

I checked my watch. It was one thirty, just an hour and half before the show, so I asked Willa to drive me home to change. We zipped north on Lamar, avoiding the downtown traffic. She pulled the Honda up to the curb and parked a few feet from the gate. I was pulling out my keys when I noticed the gate hanging open.

"What the hell?"

Willa said, "Your gate's open? Your gate's never open. Your grandmother would blow a gasket if she saw this—a flaw in the famous Honey line of defense. Reminds me of the time I tried to drop by unannounced and ran into Lucille before I could call your number. She frisked me at gunpoint. If you've never been frisked by a ninety-year-old woman holding a loaded Glock with shaky hands, well, let me tell you, it's not as much fun as it sounds. Thank God you came out when you did, she was planning on doing a strip search."

I said, "This is weird, same thing happened a couple of days ago."

"A strip search?"

"No, the gate left open."

We walked through and I pulled it shut, but this time the latch didn't click, so I opened it again and stared into the strike plate. A piece of clear cellophane tape covered the latch hole.

"Will ya look at that? Someone's been fiddling with this."

Willa said, "Weird…and you know what else? Whoever did that did it when the door was open, which means it was someone with a key."

"Maybe one of the staff at the big house?"

"Maybe, or maybe Lucille doesn't want your mom to know she's bringing in supplies to make a bomb."

"Willa, you have an overblown impression of the threat posed by my little grandmother."

"That happens whenever someone frisks me. It leads to a suspicious attitude and overwariness. It's like the time I was dating Ronald Slickwilli, you remember him, don't you, the one with the bubble butt and nice hair that spit when he talked and squeaked when he sat down? I was never sure what caused the squeak, for a while I thought he carried a mouse in his pocket."

Willa was squirting her own unique brand of verbal diarrhea while

I tugged the tape from the lock. The gate swung shut and I heard the latch catch before I led the way into the gatehouse. We needed to hurry because I didn't want to miss the first act.

❖

"So I said 'your children are like toe fungus, impossible to ignore and just won't go away,' and she said 'what, you don't like children,' and I said 'I love children, it's your children I don't like,' and she said 'I've never been so insulted in all my life,' and I said 'stick around because I have a few more things to tell you.'"

Willa's nonstop chatter continued as we made our way to our seats in the theater. I took a moment to check out the other patrons while trying to follow the gist of her incessant blather. When I glanced toward the stage, I spotted Matt's beautiful head poking through the side curtain. His eyes scanned the audience, and I found myself hoping he was looking for me. He spotted us and a big smile broke across his face. I grinned back. He blew me a kiss and I felt my heart swell as the group of queens seated stage left sighed audibly. They glared at me with that special touch of envy mixed with hatred usually reserved for someone wearing a prettier dress.

I waved and Matt pretended to catch an arrow aimed at his heart before disappearing behind the curtain.

Willa said, "What the hell was that?"

"Love, Wil."

"I'm happy for you, Greg, I really am, but that was so sickly sweet it makes me want to barf…right here…all over you. How about you put that lovey-dovey stuff away for a while?"

I shrugged and sat back just as the lights went out. The warning announcement played, reminding me to turn off my cell phone. I pulled it out of my pocket and noticed I had a message. It was too close to show time to listen to voice mail, so I switched off the phone and popped it back into my pocket.

An uncomfortable twinge of fear edged into my consciousness as the band played the introductory music. But the stage lights came on, and I was transported to New York in the 1990s by the magic of musical theater.

❖

At intermission, Willa led the way out to the lobby, and as usual, the constant babble was gushing.

"Well, thank God for small favors, the new Mimi can sing...but do you believe that ghetto hair? If she was any nappier we could use her to change a diaper. Still, it's a big improvement, I mean, at least her ass would fit inside a bus, they'd have to strap poor Janet to the roof. Still, I wish she was prettier. I keep looking at the mole on her forehead and wondering if she's Hindu. It's like a third eye, for God's sake."

We were standing in line for drinks in front of the concessions window when I spotted Cicely Wessley weaving through the crowd in our direction. She was wearing a full-length gown in purple tulle with a beaded sweetheart bodice and a contrasting pink ribbon cummerbund that emphasized its empire waistline—I swear, Cicely could overdress at the opera.

As she neared I said, "What, no tiara?"

"Hi, Greg, I was hoping to see you here, your mom told me you spend a lot of time at this theater."

"Sometimes I play piano with the band."

Willa shot a look at me like I had just sprouted another head before turning her eyes on Cicely. I could tell she was dying to ask me about this vision in shiny fabric.

I said, "So, are you alone, or is the crown prince signing autographs in the bathroom?"

Cicely chuckled. "I have to tell you, I do love the Honey sense of humor."

Beside me, Willa began to radiate energy. She fidgeted and vibrated with unsuppressed interest, but I was determined to ignore her.

"Did you need something?" I asked Cicely. "Directions to the prom, perhaps?"

She chuckled again and said, "Well, there is one thing."

She paused to collect her thoughts, but Willa had finally had enough. She elbowed me out of the way, stepping forward with a hand extended.

"Hi! I'm Willa Jensen, I don't think we've met."

Cicely looked at me first, then down at Willa's hand like it had three fingers missing and leprosy was still raging. Finally, she shook it, sort of, grasping Willa's knuckles with the tips of her fingers. With a voice as cold as the Arctic she said, "Cicely Wessley." Then she turned her back to Willa, leaning forward to whisper in my ear, "I wanted to tell you that your mother is going ahead with the party."

It might have surprised someone with less experience with Mother's ways, but this was not news to me. I'd expected Mother to follow through on her invitation, despite the ridiculous circumstances of its inception.

"Have a ball," I said to her.

"And I was hoping you would come."

I looked at her with the eyes of a dead fish on the sushi tray, but Cicely didn't pick up on the disgust and loathing. Instead, she barged ahead with a proposition.

"I don't really know anyone here and it would be nice to have at least one friendly face at the party. Look, I know you're gay. You can bring your friend if you want."

I wasn't interested in attending the train wreck of a party and said, "Cicely, I don't run with Austin's elite. They're not really my peer group."

"But you're a Honey."

"Yes, it's my cross to bear."

"So you know these people."

"Well, I know them, but…"

"Then you can introduce them to me. Come on, Greg, you're the only person close to my age I know in Austin. And after dinner at your house last Saturday I feel like I *really* know you, if you get my meaning."

I could see Willa's eye's light up when she heard this.

I'd rather drink sulfuric acid than attend one of my mother's parties, and Cicely was pleading in that whiny way that makes me wonder how straight men put up with some women. The thought of Matt meeting Livia and Lucille caused a host of weird images to play inside my head. I pictured Mother trying to snub Matt, then saw her welcoming him into the family with open arms. I wondered if Lucille would query him about sexual technique or try to bed him. I pictured a hundred different scenarios that all revolved around themes of humiliation and disgrace.

I was lost in thought when Willa nudged me out of the way again. She turned to Cicely and said, "When you sloshed up in that ridiculous ball gown, looking like a float in a parade celebrating cranberry day, I pegged you for the debutante wanna-be Greg told me about this afternoon. Sounds like I was right. You know, I'm surprised you're still interested in the party, given the humiliating circumstances of Mrs. Honey's offer, but if you have the *huevos* to go through with it, the boys and I would love to attend your coming-out event. We support anyone who wants to come out."

I stared at Willa. *What the hell was she thinking?* There was no way I was going to that party. Before I could kill the abominable notion, Cicely smiled and said, "That sounds marvelous."

She looked past Willa directly into my eyes and added, "I'll make sure you get the formal invitation, see you all there."

"Bu…I'm not…well you see…" I stammered, but she had already turned away and was striding across the lobby. I watched her sail into the crowd as it parted like a herd of zebras eyeing a lion.

"You can't possibly want to go to that party," I said to Willa.

"Are you kidding? Austin's elite pretending not to stare as your grandmother propositions the waiters and your mother meets your lover? Now, that's my idea of entertainment. Maybe we need to see if we can fit a bulletproof vest under your tuxedo."

"Mother is usually unarmed. Lucille is another matter."

"Matt will go, don't you think?"

"Not if I have anything to say about it."

"Come on, Honey, why the hell not? He has to meet that pack of wolves you call family sometime. Might as well make it a public event. It's safer. There will be others around to douse the flames when you spontaneously combust. I mean really, it's not going to be as bad as you think."

"And you know that based on what, exactly?"

"Based on the fact that I know you and I'm pretty sure you've already decided that it's going to go something like Carrie's prom."

She had me there. We finally arrived at the concession stand and Willa ordered a glass of red wine in a plastic cup. I asked for a Dr Pepper and we returned to our seats to wait for the second act.

Willa asked, "So you really don't want to go to the party?"

"Of course not."

"Why not?"

"Well, apart from the obvious, the crowd's going to be a bunch of fossils from the Triassic period, mostly blue-haired ladies and cigar-chomping Republicans. They will drink too much, talk too loud, and try to out-snub one another from fifteen paces. To add to that, the music will be lame, like watching Lawrence Welk conduct a polka."

"I bet it's better than that. For one thing you can count on your grandmother for entertainment. And I've always wanted to meet the governor. I have a few things to say to him."

"You'll never convince me to go, Willa, so get that thought right out of your head."

"Never say never, Honey."

The house lights flashed as an image of flames flickered through my mind. But that was probably just terror blazing in my soul.

❖

After the play ended, I hugged Willa good-bye in the parking lot and made my way backstage to wait for Matt. When he stepped through the door looking freshly scrubbed, I felt a flush of excitement. As we walked toward his car I pretended to interview him.

"So, Mr. Kendall, tell me about life as an actor, off-off-*off* Broadway?"

"Drama, it's full of drama and angst too, so hard being everything to everyone all the time."

"I see, and so the rigors of performance are starting to wear on you, are they?"

He emoted, "Life as a major star in a minor production has its limitations. I can't, for example, call the queen. That's the English monarch, mind you, there are plenty of local queens I could call."

"And why exactly do you want to call her majesty?"

"To find out why I never received an invitation to the jubilee, of course."

"An oversight, no doubt."

"No doubt." He reached over and mussed my hair. "How was your day?"

"I gained a lover and two new jobs, found out just how vindictive Willa can be, located Russ Buttons's long-lost brother, dodged shotgun fire, received a disturbing invitation, and saw a stellar theatrical production of *Rent*. You know, the usual. How was yours?"

"Found a lover, the rest was downhill from there, but things are looking up again."

We arrived at his British-racing-green Mazda Miata. The top was down and I sat in the passenger seat. He asked where I wanted to go to eat, and I suggested a hamburger joint up Lamar called Austin Java. He started the engine and we pulled out of the lot, turning north at the light and trundling over the bridge.

It was a clear night and stars sparkled above our heads. I yelled to him over the sound of rushing air, "I need to tell you what's going on with my mother."

I watched as he mouthed, "Okay."

He pulled the Miata to a stop at the light on Sixth and I continued, "To start with, I had a high-drama moment last night at dinner. It was the big 'I'm gay' speech with Mother."

"How'd that go?"

"It could have gone better." He glanced over at me and I shrugged. "For one thing, we weren't alone. My grandmother was there and so was Cicely Wessley, she's a Philadelphia Wessley—evidently that impresses Mother. She was trying to set me up with Cicely."

He looked at me in confusion. "What?"

"Anytime Mother runs into a single female from a prominent family, her first thought is would she make a suitable match for me? And Cicely comes from money, has good teeth and, presumably, a functioning womb. That makes her appropriate to give birth to the Honey progeny. Mother can be like that, constantly pressuring me to spawn."

"I see, and I assume Cicely's presence was what prompted your coming-out speech?"

"Yes and no. Yes, because I'm not above playing the G-card to keep Mother from forcing me into another pseudo date and no, because you're mostly what prompted the speech. To be fair, my being gay should not have been news to Mother."

A small smile flickered across his face as the light changed and we sped northward. The air roared by and he hollered in my direction, "So you told your mother about me?"

"Sort of," I yelled back. He glanced at me with a look of

bewilderment. I waited to speak again until we pulled to a stop at the light at Twelfth.

"You came up obliquely. I didn't plan on mentioning us at all. I had hoped to keep them from knowing about you for a while." I could see uncertainty in his eyes and smiled. "At least until you had met them and could decide for yourself if and when they should know. But last night I was trying to be dramatic, I guess." I looked down at my lap. For the first time I considered my intentions and didn't like what I was starting to understand about myself. *Did I really tell her I was in a relationship just to cause pain?*

We watched the traffic turning onto Lamar, and Matt said, "So how'd she take the news?"

"Stoic. I think she was embarrassed about the whole affair. More so because she was trying to force me to escort Cicely to a party."

"And your grandmother? How did she react to your declaration?"

"Very well. Mostly she wanted to talk about the mechanics of our sex life."

He looked at me with his eyebrows raised and I realized I needed to explain.

"She's ninety-three, and inhibition was the first of her mental faculties to go. Now if she thinks it, she says it."

"I like her already."

"Yeah, she's fun. Mother is wound tighter than a watch, but Lucille is looser than diarrhea."

He looked at me with a sour expression, and I apologized. "Sorry, I've been spending too much time with Willa."

The light changed and we pulled ahead, turning left into the restaurant parking lot. It was about half-full of beat-up foreign cars. Matt parked and we wound our way through picnic tables sprinkled with college-age kids, their faces turned down, clicking away on laptop computers.

I led the way inside. At the counter, we both ordered salads and pasta. I followed Matt to a table next to a window overlooking the parking lot. He set the laminated number card on top of the napkin holder and looked up at me with a smile.

"What's it like being a Honey, anyway?"

"Frustrating usually...full of angst and poverty. Mother is fiercely opposed to charity, above all handouts to her son, which means money is more of an issue than I would like to admit. Other than that, it's probably not much different from anybody else's life…well, anybody who lives in an asylum."

The smile faded slowly, and Matt said, "It doesn't sound all that bad."

"I'm just getting started. There's also the pressure. You see, I'm the last of the Honey line. According to Mother, if I don't figure out how to subdivide and generate offspring, the whole world will come tumbling down."

"And how are you planning to manage that?"

"I've been looking under cabbage leaves."

"I take it biology was not a strong subject in college."

"Not so much. And what about you, are there any deep hidden secrets in the Kendall clan?"

"To my knowledge there are surprisingly few bodies buried in the basement. I came out to my parents in high school. It wasn't much of a shock. I'm pretty sure they'd already figured it out, given my interest in musical theater. I've got a sister who's in Arizona and a brother in the army. Both are straight and married. Neither is particularly interesting. They both have oodles of children, which takes the pressure off me."

"I wish I had a fertile sibling with a passel of sticky-fingered children crawling over the artwork at Lost Wind. Maybe then Mother would back off."

"I think I want to meet her."

"My mother?"

"Sure, I can be charming if I need to."

"You are charming without any effort at all, but—"

Just then, the waiter arrived to serve our food. After he left, Matt asked, "But what?"

"Huh?"

"You said *but*. I told you I wanted to meet your mother and you said I was charming *but*. You're not ashamed of me, are you? I can play it straight if I have to."

"It's not you. I'm just worried that Mother can be…um…well, unpredictable. She has this snotty sense of entitlement and likes to act imperial. I don't want her to lay into us, or you at least, without adequate preparation."

"I can take care of myself, Greg."

"I didn't mean that, it's just that she's…well, she's a Honey…and she knows it."

On that sour note, the conversation stifled while we tucked into dinner. I mentally began to debate the pros and cons of Matt meeting my family. On the one hand, if I was really serious about this relationship, what was the hold-up? It had to happen sometime. On the other hand, Mother couldn't live forever. I was trying to figure out what I was really worried about when Matt said, "Don't sweat it, Greg, I'm not going anywhere. I'll be here when you're ready for us to meet."

Something about the sweet way he said it almost caused me to throw caution to the wind and ask him to go with me to the party. I caught myself before I opened my mouth, but just the thought of it made my palms sweat.

All of a sudden I'd lost my appetite.

CHAPTER SEVEN

I woke the next morning blinded by sunlight streaming through the window in Matt's apartment. I squinted and could make out Matt's form sitting back against a pile of pillows. I realized he'd been watching me, and I prayed I hadn't been snoring or drooling in my sleep. I pulled my head off the pillow blinking and looked down at the wet spot—so much for the power of prayer. I smacked my lips. My mouth tasted musty and my tongue felt thick and furry, like it had morphed into a small rodent overnight. I turned my head and caught a glimpse of my image in the mirror hung on his closet door. My hair was wild and windblown, like I might have discovered the theory of relativity in my sleep.

And I had a morning woody.

Matt, of course, looked beautiful.

He said, "Hi, sunshine."

"Hi." I smacked my lips again.

"How did you sleep?"

"Good." I sat up and tried to pat down my spiky hair.

"It's eight thirty. Are you in a hurry, or can we do breakfast?"

I blinked. "Eight thirty, damn…I've got an appointment with Russ at nine. I've got to go."

"Love me and leave me," he said, smiling.

"I do love you and I will never leave you."

"Be still my heart," he said, tousling my hair. I rolled out of bed and padded softly to the bathroom, trying to halt the metronome motion of my erection. Urination was difficult and uncomfortable. It required bending forward at the waist and pressing down to guide the stream into the bowl.

I washed my hands, brushed my teeth, and sighed at the hopeless condition of my hair in the mirror before sliding into my jeans and T-shirt. Matt dropped me at my place. I had to hurry or I'd be late for Russ's appointment, so I pushed through the gate and hustled up the walkway. I pulled up short, confused to find my back door unlocked. There wasn't time to consider the cause, so I chastised myself for leaving it open and hustled inside. Showered and dressed, I rushed through the gate. Pausing to check the lock, I noticed an envelope sticking out of my mailbox. I grabbed it and stuffed it into my pocket, then scurried on to the bus stop.

Maurice Williams nodded at me as I flashed my pass and stepped onto the downtown shuttle. "Good morning, Mr. Honey. How's that feisty grandmother?"

"She's as naughty as ever, and Lakisha?"

"Just the way I like her, jiggly." He shot me a wicked grin.

Maurice's wife Lakisha had a body type that changed shape in the water…bits and bobs seemed to move independently as they reached for the surface. I had the pleasure of running into the pair of them on South Padre beach one summer. I was trying to keep Lucille from getting in trouble, and they were spending a lazy afternoon wading in the surf. When Lucille spotted Maurice's muscled frame she made a beeline toward the water screaming, "I'm coming, Kunta Kinte, ravish me with your big black muscles!"

I had to pry her off Maurice and hose her down with cold water. Luckily he understood the vagaries of an addled mind and refused to press charges. Lakisha thought it was hilarious.

I made my way back to the rear of the packed bus and had to stand, leaning against the metal railing. A yellow pickup truck darted in front of the bus as Maurice pulled away from the curb. Maurice slammed on the brakes and I was momentarily airborne. On my way down my face caught someone's knee, and it stunned me. I sat on the floor for a few seconds while a couple of guys hovered above me, asking if I needed help. I could feel my face starting to swell and waved away the other passengers as Maurice pulled over to the curb. He walked back to where I was sitting in the aisle and said, "I'm so sorry, Greg. That truck pulled right out in front of me. Are you all right? Can you stand?"

"Yeah, I'm fine, I just need to find a place to sit down for a minute. I'll be fine."

In truth, I was pretty shaken, but survival was never in doubt. As the other passengers made room for me on the bench, Maurice ambled back to the front of the bus. I tenderly probed my eye socket as we pulled back out into traffic, thinking there had to be a better way to get a seat on a crowded bus.

Twenty minutes later, I was sitting at my desk, an ice bag pressed against the growing goose egg on my forehead. I was frustrated and sore and wanted to feel like I'd accomplished something, so I pulled my iPhone out to peruse Milton Buttons's photo. I had a message, and remembered the call I received at the theater the day before. I played the message. All I could hear was the sound of someone sighing. I checked the call listing, but the number was blocked. I deleted the notice and turned off my iPhone. My office line rang just as I settled back in my chair with the icepack.

"Hello."

"Whatcha doing?" It was Willa.

"Waiting for Russ."

"My sister called yesterday, she's trying to lose weight. You remember Donna, right? Mother always said she was big boned, but the truth is her bones are normal sized, it's the rest of her that's big. She's on the Atkins Diet and at first she loved the fact that she could eat ribs and steaks, but after three months of barbecue she wants to strangle a pig."

Willa was even worse on the phone than in person. It would be a while before I could participate in the conversation, so I tucked the receiver against my ear while hooking my iPhone to the USB port on my computer. It took a few seconds to download Milton Buttons's photo. My plan was to fiddle with it a while to see if I could enhance the image. There were some shadowy objects in the background I wanted to make clearer.

"So I said 'a baked potato is not allowed on Atkins,' and she said 'how about a rice sandwich,' and I said 'well, if you're talking about a three-way with a couple of Asians then yeah, otherwise nope,' and she said…"

As the image loaded, I carried the receiver and my ice bag to the bathroom to check the damage. This was my fourth trip to the mirror since arriving at the office, and just like the other three times, I could tell I was getting a black eye.

"So she said 'to hell with it, if he really loves me he should love my wobbly bits too,' and I said 'there can be too much of a good thing,' and she said 'true, but outside of hacking them off with a cleaver, what's a girl to do,' and I said 'there's liposuction, lap band surgery, and bariatric bypass, of course—my understanding is that tapeworms don't really work as a weight loss strategy,' and she said 'that's a shame because I ate some dodgy pork chops for lunch.'"

"Speaking of lunch," I said, seizing my opportunity, "would you mind terribly if we canceled our plans today?"

"Why?"

"I fell on the bus and now I've got a black eye. I'm feeling kind of crummy and am starting to look like Joan Rivers after surgery."

"You what?"

"Fell, but it's not that bad. Still, I think I'm just going home for lunch."

She let out a long sigh. "Tell me he didn't hit you, because I swear to God if he laid a finger on you I will slap him so hard they'll find teeth in three counties."

"What?"

"So help me God, if Matt laid a hand on you…"

"No, Willa, no…it's nothing like that. I fell on the bus. Well, sort of fell. It was crowded and I was standing and…" I noted the stony silence on the other end of the line. "You still there, Wil?"

"Don't lie to me, Greg."

"I'm not."

"Please don't do it. Lying will only make things worse. Tell me the truth, right now…tell me the truth."

"I am telling you the truth—honest. No one did this to me, it was an accident on the bus."

But Willa had already made up her mind. "I'm coming to see you, we need to talk. Don't leave."

I heard the click of Willa's hang up and stared at the receiver. *This cannot be good.*

Willa, bless her soul, could be a little like a dog with a bone—especially when it came to protecting her friends. She'd decided Matt had beaten me and I was lying out of embarrassment. Now she was on her way over to force me to see the light. Getting Willa to pull back when she was wound up was like stopping a speeding train.

It was going to take a *lot* of friction.

I padded back into the bathroom to have another peek in the mirror. The face staring back at me looked confused and worried, and a little like it had gone a few rounds in the ultimate fighter ring.

As I was scowling at the mirror, the door jangled open. I stuck my head out of the bathroom. Russ Buttons froze, staring at me from across the office floor.

"What the hell happened to you?"

"I like your hair," I said. Russ's hair could best be described as *bizarre*. It looked like someone dropped chocolate sauce and candy corn on a Chucky doll. He was dressed like a *Solid Gold* dancer in skintight gold lamé pants, glittery Doc Martens chukkas, and an aquamarine wifebeater T-shirt. He was also carrying a purse.

"Thanks," he said, totally missing the sarcasm. "But what the hell happened to you?"

"I fell on a bus, long ridiculous story. Nice purse."

He floated past and took the chair opposite my desk, crossing his legs like Maggie Smith in *The Prime of Miss Jean Brodie*. "It's a man-bag, the latest thing from Paris. You really need to get with the times, Honey."

If "getting with the times" meant carrying a shiny golden clutch, wearing a hairstyle that probably needed to be composted, and dressing like a Hollywood hooker, then I was happy being out of step. I said, "I'm planning to follow Billy tonight. So I assume you got the photo I e-mailed?"

"Yes, and that was definitely Milton. How did you find him so quickly?"

I sat down at my desk and turned the computer monitor so he could see the enhanced image of his brother's picture. I said, "I tracked down an acquaintance who knew him in Houston, and they gave me an address in Oklahoma. It turns out he'd moved but, luckily, someone there had a forwarding address."

"Damn! You're really an investigator, aren't you?"

"At the Honey Agency, we strive to please our customers. Remember us whenever you need a dick."

"Is that your new motto?"

"You like it? I'm still wrestling with a few options."

He grinned at me. "I'm a gay man, Honey, of course I like it. So what do I owe you?"

"Let's see."

He watched as I clicked on a document to pull up his account record. I summed up the hours logged and added the labor cost to the balance due. I printed his invoice and gave it to him with a copy of the report I'd typed up earlier. The report contained Milton's address.

Russ spent a few minutes reading through the report before pulling a checkbook from his tiny clutch. I watched as he wrote my check. He grinned again as he gave it to me and said, "You know, you almost look butch with that shiner."

I smiled back, but my smile was brittle. Willa jangled through the door.

"God, look at that eye, you poor baby."

"I'm all right, Willa."

"I swear I'll kill him," she said.

"Kill who?" Russ spun around in his chair, sensing gossip.

I said, "No one. It was an accident on the bus, Willa," but as usual, she was off on a rant.

"This is unacceptable, violence in a relationship is unacceptable and if you don't put a stop it now, it will only escalate. Next time you may not survive."

"Willa, you're jumping to the wrong conclusion."

"What relationship?" Russ asked.

"If you think it will end with this, you're wrong. I can tell you from experience, I was in a violent relationship once, you remember Joey Palmer? He tried to lay a hand on me…"

"He was six years old."

"I really fell for the guy, then he tried to punch me."

"He tried to punch everyone on the playground."

"But it was different with me, he wanted to hurt me."

"If I remember correctly, he was the one who ended up with the broken nose."

"Yeah, and it served him right for trying to hit me. The point is he would have hurt me if I had let him, but I didn't let him and you shouldn't either."

"Willa, no one hurt me. I fell on the bus."

Russ's voice sounded incredulous when he said, "Greg Honey is in a violent relationship? I thought you were celibate."

"It's not a violent relationship, why won't anyone listen to me? I fell on the bus."

Willa said, "It's natural to want to cover this up. No one wants to be a victim. but you have to speak up, Greg. You need to tell the police about Matt."

"Willa, you're wrong and I've had enough of this." I could hear the strain in my voice.

"Matt who?" Russ asked.

"If he gets some help now, maybe we can stop the violence before he ends up in prison. I know a lawyer that will handle the whole thing."

I'd had enough. I yelled, "You aren't listening to me, Willa. I fell on a goddamned bus!" She started to speak again, but I didn't give her the floor. "I'd be the first one to tell you, but Matt Kendall did not do this to me." I pointed at my black eye. "He dropped me at my house this morning, I cleaned up and boarded the bus, it was packed, I had to stand in the aisle and fell when the driver slammed on the brakes to avoid some fool pulling out in front of us. No one hit me. I fell and bumped my face on something on the way to the floor, and that's all there is to it."

Russ let out a long, slow whistle and said, "You're seeing Matt Kendall? That hot guy playing Mark in *Rent* at Zach Scott Theater?"

I looked at him in stony silence, and he said, "Honey, Matt must be a size queen and your penis must be as big as a salami, because he's at least four levels above you on the gay-boy food chain."

My voice was flat when I said, "Thanks for the vote of confidence, Russ."

Willa said, "I don't care how hot he is, if he lays a hand on you again I'll gut him like a fish."

I sighed in frustration. Willa had made up her mind and wouldn't listen to reason. I shrugged and picked up the ice bag; I leaned back in my chair and pressed it to my face, hoping they would get the message.

After a few minutes, I managed to escort them both out of my office and spent the rest of the morning searching the Internet for information on Bradford Collins—the Williams Construction Company employee—and his pending worker's compensation claim. I performed a criminal records search and located a Bradford Phillip Collins of Waco, Texas, who'd been convicted of failure to pay alimony back in April. The associated court record listed a Peggy Lee Maloney as the spouse seeking maintenance. I tracked down a phone number for Ms. Maloney and gave her a call.

Her: Hello,

Me: Hi, Ms. Maloney?

Her: Call me Peggy.

Me: Okay, Peggy. My name is Greg Honey. I'm a private investigator.

Her: Hot damn, what can I do you for, mister?

Me: I have some questions about Bradford Collins and was hoping you would give me a few minutes of your time.

Her: What do you want to know about the cheating, lying scum sucker?

Me: So I have the right person, you know Mr. Collins?

Her: I was married to the pencil-dicked weasel for ten years, and believe me, it was no picnic.

Me: When did the marriage end?

Her: I finally got rid of the bottom-feeding slime sucker two months ago.

Me: It sounds like it was a difficult relationship.

Her: I helped the goddamned greasy little toad through trade school, working three jobs to pay his tuition, and it turns out the son of a bitch was porkin' a waitress at Hooters the whole time.

Me: I take it you divorced him?

Her: Only because murder is illegal. Filed in January, like I said, it came through in March.

Me: When was the last time you saw Mr. Collins?

Her: About five minutes ago. The urine-soaked little tree sloth is across the street. My guess is he's banging his wee little pickle dick against Mary Moody's silicone tits right now.

Me: Excuse me?

Her: What can I say, she's a slut, he's a dog. For all I know they're over there swapping STDs, it's just like him to walk out of a clinic and into a whorehouse…and I've got a lifelong herpes infection to prove it.

Me: Ms. Maloney, can you tell me how he looked?

Her: Peggy. Call me Peggy. What do you mean, how'd he look? He looked like an asshole. A sweaty, balding armpit of an asshole.

Me: I'm wondering if he was limping when you saw him this morning, or if he was having trouble getting around?

Her: Nah, the snot-encrusted fly-eating lizard looked the same as he always did, a little more hair on his back maybe. I was bringing in the groceries from my car when he jogged up the street, flipped me off, and slithered through Mary's door like a king snake slipping into a rat hole.

Me: You say he jogged up?

Her: You hard of hearing? Yeah, he jogged up, sweating like a pig.

There appeared to be no love lost between Peggy and Bradford, so I decided to play it straight.

Me: Thank you very much for the information, and I don't want to take much more of your time, Ms. Maloney, but I was wondering if you would be willing to sign a deposition stating the facts you just told me?

Her: What kind of deposition?

Me: It could lead to criminal charges against Mr. Collins.

Her: Hot damn, you bet, mister! There is nothing I'd like better than seeing that asshole go to jail.

I thanked her and made an appointment to drop by later that afternoon. Then I hung up and called Gary Weiss. I explained the situation, and he agreed to go with me up to Waco to witness Peggy's signature. He offered to drive before hanging up. I was grateful since it meant I wouldn't have to steal my mother's car. Then I typed up the notes I'd taken during my conversation with Peggy Maloney.

When I finished, I printed the document and decided to deliver my rent check to LL Properties before heading home for lunch. The LL office closed early on Mondays, and there was no way I could make it back from Waco in time. I pulled out my checkbook and wrote the check. When I folded it and placed it into my pocket, I found the letter I'd stuffed in there on the way out of my house that morning.

I examined the envelope. The surface was bare. No postage, return address, or postmark. I ripped through the sealed flap and opened the single sheet of white paper. The note was written in black ink with a childish hand. It said, *I'm watching you, gay boy. Be scared, be very, very scared.*

I read over the note a couple of times. I remembered the phone call I'd received at the theater on Friday night. Should I take the message seriously? The whole thing seemed so juvenile. There were no demands. It certainly wasn't an explicit warning—just a vague, taunting request meant to frighten me.

I gave up, stuffing the note into my desk drawer.

The building management office was in the same building, just four doors down the hall. LL Properties was owned and operated by Larry Lawson. Since I knew it was a sleazy one-man operation, I was surprised to be greeted by a gum-popping vision in leather sitting at the desk. She was lacquering what had to be a third coat of teal-green polish on her two-inch fingernails as the door swished shut behind me. She blew on her fingers as her dead brown eyes looked my direction.

She said, "You need something?"

"You work here?"

"Nah, just keeping an eye on my husband. What can I do for you?"

I shook my head in disbelief. I found it hard to picture Larry married to this woman. I would have bet money he'd never been with a woman—unless you count inflatable ones.

"Uh, yeah, I need to see Larry, is he in?"

Mrs. Lawson pivoted in her chair and yelled through the back office, "Larry, you got a visitor." She turned her attention back to her nails and blew some more.

Larry Lawson waddled through the doorway and frowned when he saw me. He turned to his wife and said, "Will ya use the intercom, Viola? Like I told you before."

"Okay already, sheesh! All the time with the intercom."

Larry rolled his eyes and turned his reptilian smile in my direction. "Mr. Honey, what happened to you?"

"I fell on a bus," I said, wondering if I should have a T-shirt printed up so I wouldn't have to repeat myself all day long.

"I'm sorry to hear that, won't you come in?" He gestured toward his office, and I followed him past Viola. I chose the folding chair opposite his desk, opting to avoid the red leather beanbag in the corner. I watched, transfixed, as he squeezed his bulky frame past an open file cabinet in a maneuver that defied the laws of physics.

"I just came by to drop off the rent check." I handed it to him. He studied the check closely before folding it and stuffing it into his wallet.

He asked, "Are you a Christian, Greg?"

I was flustered by his question. "Excuse me?"

"Are you a Christian? Have you found Jesus yet?"

It was the second time I'd been asked that question in less than a week. I sighed, thinking, *Christ, why don't they just send out a search party?* I fidgeted and searched my mind for an appropriate response, one that said "back off, asshole, that's none of your business," but came out sounding more like "thank you for caring."

Larry took my silence for reluctance, and added, "I prefer doing business with Christians, I find them more reliable...except maybe Methodists who are prone to depression and Catholics who drink too much. Of course, I knew a couple of Lutherans from back in college I wouldn't trust with the party keg either, if you know what I mean. But give me a good old-fashioned Baptist any day of the week. Now, there's a religion you can count on to teach the power of prayer and instill good Christian fear in its followers. It's that fear of Satan's temptations that keeps us on the straight and narrow, Mr. Honey. Fear of the everlasting fires of hell, that's the basis for the truly, faithfully, spiritually religious Christian. Do you have that fear, Greg? Will you renounce Satan and live forever in His grace...or will you go the way of sin and have the flames of hell devouring your flesh for all eternity?"

Is this guy serious?

"You must attend Sunrise Baptist Church," I said, recognizing the skewed vision of Reverend Ray's church. He taught a very dark version of Christianity that blamed the problems of the world on loose morals and Democrats. Sunday sermons taught a black-and-white view of the world, charging everything from dandruff and acne to earthquakes and AIDS on insufficient prayer and progressive politics. In Reverend Ray's view of the world, everyone was born a sinner and the tortures of hell awaited anyone who died before being baptized and joining the NRA.

"Why, yes, I do," he said, with a wide smile. "And I know your mother too. She is very concerned for your immortal soul. On Sunday, she added your name to the list of sinners we pray for, and so I ask again, Greg, are you a Christian?"

I was on the spot. I definitely did not want to debate theology with Larry, and that was where this conversation was headed. I was searching for an elegant way out when my cell phone rang. I held up a finger and answered.

"Hello."

"Guess who just came into the bank?"

It was Matt, and he sounded a little flustered.

"No idea, who?"

"Willa. She burst into my office and accused me of being a raving maniac who beat you half to death this morning. I had to have a security guard haul her out of the bank. So I'm calling you to ask two questions. First, are you okay, and second, what the hell was that all about?"

"I can't believe she did that. Can you hold on just a second?" I put my hand over the speaker and told Larry I was sorry for leaving so abruptly but this was an emergency. As I walked to my office, I apologized to Matt and explained about my black eye and Willa's errant assumptions.

"I've tried to explain that it was just a fall on the bus about fifty times, but she won't listen. I'll try again, I promise."

He sort of chuckled and said, "You have to admit, she's got your back. Okay, I get it now, and the truth is, I kind of like the fact that she's such a good friend that she's willing to make a scene in order to protect you."

"I'm so sorry about this, Matt."

"Stop apologizing, really, it's okay. So, how about you? Are you okay?"

"Yeah, just a little bruised and sore. Russ Buttons says I look manly."

"Who's Russ Buttons?"

"A client. That reminds me, I'm glad you called, I have to go to

Waco this afternoon and then I have some night work, so I'll be out late."

"Oh...night work?"

"Yeah, it's business. Sometimes a dick's needed in the dark."

He chuckled again. "A dick is always needed in the dark. Save some for me, will ya? You want to drop by my place after your dick work's done?"

"There's no telling when I'll get there, and I'll need to shower and change first. Maybe I should just head to my place and we can get together tomorrow?"

"Oh."

I heard disappointment in his voice and it made my heart do a little happy dance, so I added, "Or...I could drop a key for you at the bank and you could head over to my place when you're ready for bed. That way you'll be there when I arrive."

"Really?"

"Sure, if you want to."

"I want to, but not if this is going to freak you out."

Now I was smiling. "It would have if you'd said no. I'll be over around one."

"I can't wait to see your newly enhanced manliness."

"Yes, be prepared for extreme manliness."

I hung up and sailed into my office full of joy. The cat looked up from cleaning his private parts, blinked in feline ennui, and went right back to work licking fur. I tried not to take it as judgment but there was just no denying the fact he was less than impressed.

CHAPTER EIGHT

It was turning into a busy morning. I needed to take Russ's check to the bank before Larry cashed my rent check, so I endorsed it, made out a deposit slip, and headed out of the office. The tellers at Seamen's Bank could be pretentious, and gave lousy service to customers from affiliated banks. Occasionally I thought about switching institutions because in truth, Seamen's had larger-than-average fees and few amenities, but there was just something thrilling about making a Seamen deposit.

I stepped into the frosty atrium a few minutes before noon, overheated and wondering what I was thinking walking three blocks in Austin in August. As usual, there was a line in front of the only open teller's window. I joined the queue and tried not to drip sweat on anyone. The lady standing in front of me was holding an unhappy baby. The squirming bag of fun let the rest of us share the discomfort by screaming at the top of his lungs. His mother tried to soothe him, babbling baby talk while sorting through a handbag the size of a bushel basket.

She handed him her keys, which he threw on the floor. Then she handed him her cell phone, which he also threw on the floor. She handed him a brightly colored toy that was probably made in China and might be toxic; he stuffed it into his mouth and began chewing. I could see flecks of paint chipping off, but held my tongue.

Maybe the toy was actually a vitamin supplement.

She made it to the teller's window finally and set her child on the counter. The teller must have been at least seventy-five years old. He was wearing a bow tie and thick glasses that made him look owlish.

His ears were the size and shape of waffles, and he had a comb-over reminiscent of Rudy Giuliani when he was a US attorney. He glanced at the baby like it might be radioactive. The baby was still happily chewing his toy. I imagined a clock counting down IQ points as the infant ingested lead.

The teller's voice was noticeably cold. "Welcome to Seamen's Bank, how may I help you?"

"I need to make a loan payment, but I seem to have left my checkbook at home."

"I can transfer the payment from your account, but I'll need some identification."

"Uh, sure." She sorted through her bag once more, this time pulling out items and placing them on the counter as she searched. I inventoried a curling iron, a pair of men's boxer shorts, a half-eaten Whataburger, and an assortment of feminine hygiene products rivaling the selection at a well-stocked pharmacy.

"I seem to have left my driver's license at home," she said as the baby tore into a package of Stayfree mini-pads. The little imp tossed the pads to the floor and looked at its mother with a drool-enhanced smile.

The teller said, "I can't make the transfer without some sort of identification."

She bent to retrieve the pads and yelled back up to the teller, "But I came all this way…can't you please make an exception?"

A rather sour look appeared across the baby's face and I guessed it was a signal that he was summoning the necessary concentration to fill his diaper. The teller said, "Without ID, there's nothing I can do."

"Fine," she snapped at him and stood, shoving all the items back into her purse. She hiked the-now smelly infant onto a hip and stormed toward the doorway, his diaper leaking bits of sewage across the atrium.

I watched her jostle through the revolving door and turned back to the teller. Without missing a beat, he said, "That bitch's baby is evacuating its bowels."

I smiled. He smiled back, and said, "Welcome to Seamen's Bank, how may I help you?"

❖

I grabbed a burger at Hickory Street on the way back to my office and wolfed it down as I walked. I brushed my teeth in my office bathroom and tried to mop the sweat from my armpits with a paper towel. I took one more look at my black eye. *Very manly.* I was still striking rakish poses when Gary Weiss came in through the plate glass doorway.

He was wearing a stylish notched-neck pantsuit in turquoise, complementing his complexion, and a pair of matching Manolo Blahnik pumps that had to have cost eight hundred dollars. His long golden hair was pulled back in a ponytail. The only jewelry was a tasteful silver necklace and matching silver hoop earrings. Even with a protruding Adam's apple and rather large hands, Gary looked every inch the lady.

"Are you ready for a road trip? Whoa, there, mister, what happened to you?"

"I was mugged on a bus."

"Oh, Honey…what were you doing on public transportation? Don't you know that most of the State Hospital patients moved onto Capital Metro vehicles when the state legislature cut mental health funding? Now Austin buses are literally Bedlam."

"I have to get around somehow."

"Don't you have a car?"

"Nope."

"Why the hell not?"

"Money, mostly."

"But you're a Honey. I thought Honeys used federal currency to blow their noses."

"That would be Mother, the only one with assets…and she doesn't believe in sharing. Well, not with her son anyway. Look, buses aren't that bad, I wasn't actually mugged, there was an accident and I fell."

"But a Honey on a bus is like a Kardashian in the DAR, just not natural."

I shrugged. "Shouldn't we be on the road?"

There wasn't much I didn't know about how unlivable Austin was without a car. I had heard all the arguments before and none of them changed the fact that, short of winning the lotto or building one out of bottle caps, the chances of my owning a car anytime soon were slim indeed.

I held the door. Gary sailed through, waiting while I flipped the

Gone Fishing sign and locked up. As we marched down the corridor I asked, "Can we stop by Frost Bank on the way out of town?"

"Sure thing."

I peeked through the glass doorway as we passed by the LL Properties office. Viola Lawless sat at her desk, peering into a handheld mirror. She was applying thick black eyeliner, grimacing as she pressed the telephone receiver to her ear with a hiked-up shoulder. Even from this distance I could see the dusting of face powder on her cheeks and a smudge of pink lipstick on her front teeth.

Gary's silver Mercedes coupe was parked at the curb. He started it up, and the air conditioner blew cool instantly. I called Matt on my cell phone, and he agreed to meet me in the lobby.

When we arrived at the bank, Gary idled in the commercial parking space while I stepped across the sidewalk, my extra house key tucked in my jeans pocket. Matt stood just inside the doorway. He was wearing a dark gray suit, crisp white shirt, and a navy-blue Hugo Boss silk tie. He looked very handsome.

He also looked worried.

"Man, look at your eye. That's quite a shiner. Does it hurt?"

"What, this little thing?" I pointed at my eye with my chin stuck out à la Robert De Niro. "This is nothing, you should see the other guy."

He grinned. "Manly, it's definitely manly."

"Your key, sir." I handed it to him with a flourish. He stepped closer and hugged me. I sort of freaked a little and looked around for prying eyes. I wasn't used to showing affection in public. I whispered into his ear, "Aren't you worried that your coworkers might see us?"

"They know I'm gay, so no, I'm not worried." He stepped back and looked me over. "Now tell me the truth, you are okay, right?"

"Piece of cake. Don't forget, I'm a manly man." Gary's car horn beeped outside. "I got to go."

"Be careful out there, mister."

I turned to leave, and Matt grabbed my hand. It jerked me a little off balance and he caught me before I fell. He kissed me. It was a long, serious kiss and I sort of lost myself in it. When it ended, I felt my face flush as my boy parts started to engorge. It was a strange and exciting sensation, and I turned away, embarrassed to show my emotions.

And that was when I bumped into Mother.

"That was vulgar, Greg," she said icily while clutching my arm in a vise-like grip.

"Mother, what are you doing here?"

She ignored my question, focusing a withering gaze on Matt like a laser-guided bomb. "You must be the young man my son told me about." Her voice was as cold and brittle as Arctic ice.

Matt offered his hand. "Matt Kendall. It's good to meet you, Mrs. Honey."

Mother stared down at Matt's hand with a sour expression that reminded me of the kid at the bank just before he soiled his diaper. I tried to summon the power to mentally force her to shake his hand. After what felt like an eternity, she took Matt's hand with both of hers and stared directly into his eyes.

"Mr. Kendall, I won't lie to you, when Greg mentioned you in his little outburst the other day I pictured someone different, someone older perhaps."

Matt said, "I hope you're not disappointed. I can play older."

Mother ignored the joke. "Not any more disappointed than is to be expected under the circumstances." Her voice dripped venom.

"I'm sorry you feel that way, Mrs. Honey," Matt said, and I could tell he was confused by her anger. We both stared at her. She clenched her jaw. The scene played out in front of me in slow motion. It was like watching two trains approaching each other on the same track. Disaster was imminent, but there was nothing to do but watch, and eventually help bury the bodies.

"You see, it's difficult for a mother when her child is confused and unable to see what's best. As a parent, one wants to protect him from everything, but especially the dangerous and unsavory elements in this world."

"Mrs. Honey, I want to assure you that all I want is what's best for Greg."

"And this?" Mother said, pointing at my face. "This is *not* what's best for my child, Mr. Kendall."

"What? No…Mother, please, you have it all wrong." I pleaded, but she ignored me completely.

"You will find that I can be a very dangerous adversary, young man." It might have been my imagination, but everyone in the atrium seemed to freeze as if time stood still.

"For God's sake, Mom, I fell on a bus, it was an accident and Matt had nothing to do with it. He wasn't even there." I glared at her. I needed to draw her attention back to me the only way that ever worked—confrontation. I played hurt and defiant, like a mother bird feigning a broken wing hoping to entice the cobra from her nest. But Mother was full of poison and ready to strike. She ignored me completely, still holding Matt's hand she peered into his eyes and said, "I assure you, Mr. Kendall, I am not without resources and I will not stand by and watch as my son is harmed. If you hurt him again, you will answer to me. I hope we understand each other."

"I understand you completely, Mrs. Honey."

"Good." She let go of his hand and pivoted *en pointe* like a Kirov dancer, bolting through the revolving doorway without another word.

"I'm so sorry, Matt. She's, well, she's evil. It's no picnic being the spawn of Lucifer."

"Hey, it's family. I get it. We can choose our friends and our loved ones, but…"

"We can't choose our family," I said.

"Exactly."

Gary beeped his horn again.

"Okay, now I've really got to go. Can we talk about this tonight?"

"Sure," he said, smiling.

But as I turned to leave, anger and frustration bubbled inside my head like Mentos in a Diet Coke bottle.

Soon I would need to have a serious talk with my mother.

When I got back to the car, Gary watched as I buckled my seat belt. He said, "So you have a boyfriend."

"Yes, I have a boyfriend."

"It's good to have a boyfriend."

He started the car and backed out of the parking slot.

"It's very good to have a boyfriend," I agreed.

"Do you want to talk about that scene with your mother?"

"No."

"Just so you know, I have one just like her."

He was trying to sympathize, but the truth was there was no one like Mother.

As he pulled into traffic he said, "And don't get me started about my mother-in-law. I think Wally wants her to move in, but I'm afraid she'll steal my makeup. She has a little kleptomania problem since her husband left. That was a year and half ago, and now I have to pack up the medicine cabinet whenever she drops by."

I wasn't in the mood to talk, but Gary felt the need to fill the silence with mindless chatter, so I sat back and pretended to listen as we turned onto the highway entrance ramp.

About an hour later, Gary had just finished explaining his plans for an upcoming Austin drag show involving a Barbra Streisand song and a nose prosthesis. I was barely listening; my mind still going over the scene at the bank. It didn't take long to figure out how my mother had heard about my black eye, but I was stewing over the appropriate response. We were exiting Killeen's city limits when I pulled out my cell phone.

> Willa's Machine: If you want it, I got it. *Beep.*
> Me: Willa, it's Greg. If you're there we need to talk.

Almost immediately I heard the jangled sound as Willa picked up.

> Her: Hi, whatcha doing?
> Me: I heard you went to see Matt at the bank.
> Her: Yeah, I went down there to talk some sense into him. I knew you'd freak out if I told you my plan. Did he tell you he called security on me? He hates me now, for sure.
> Me: He doesn't hate you, Willa.
> Her: Sure he does, but that doesn't matter.
> Me: Tell me why you called my mother?
> Her: Because you need protection.
> Me: First, Matt doesn't hate you, he kind of admires you. You're actually on the same side of this but you're just too bullheaded to see it. Second, the only one I need protection from is Mother. Third…seriously? You called my mother?
> Her: She was the only one I could think of that would get

your attention. Violence in a relationship is dangerous and I'm not going to stand by while—

Me (louder now): Willa! Greg did not hit me. I fell on the bus! You're not listening to me.

Her: And pretending it didn't happen won't make things right either. You need help, and I'm going to get it for you.

Me: No, you're the one who needs help. I swear, Willa... what will it take for you to back off? I know you have my best interests at heart, but this is getting out of hand. You won't even entertain the idea that I'm telling you the truth.

Her: Because I know what it's like to be in an abusive relationship.

Me: Jesus, Willa, will you let it go? Joey Palmer was six years old. You weren't in an abusive relationship—you were in grade school. It was a playground fight and for all I know you picked it. I've had it with this crap... here's what you're going to do.

I explained my plan to her and got her to agree to meet me later for dinner. I was angry because of her mulish attitude. Why wouldn't she see the truth? But I found myself smiling when I realized that it was much better to have Willa as a friend than an enemy.

Now, *that* would be dangerous.

After I hung up, Garry looked at me with a furrowed forehead and raised eyebrows.

I answered the nonverbal query. "A very confused friend."

"I assume Matt was the guy I saw you lock lips with at the bank."

"Yeah." I smiled sheepishly. "Willa thinks Matt gave me the black eye."

"But Matt didn't give you the black eye, right?"

"You've got the picture."

"And Willa..."

"Is as stubborn as a mule."

"Sounds complicated."

"Like Middle East politics."

"Or my mother-in-law situation. What're you going to do?"

"Make Willa see the light, then maybe I'll publish my plan for a viable Palestinian state."

"While you're at it, could you help me figure out what to do with my mother in-law?"

"That's simple, she needs to find a man."

"Did I mention she smells funny and looks a little like Ed Asner?"

"A desperate man."

"With hammertoe and a big nose."

"A desperate, blind man."

"She's also got a surly attitude."

"Of course."

"But other than that she's a peach."

"No problem, here's what we do. First, we'll need a tranquilizer gun and some rope."

"Nothing is easy, is it, Honey my friend?"

"Amen to that, sister. Amen to that."

Peggy Maloney's address turned out to be a run-down apartment complex with a moldy brick façade and rusty metal stairwells. A kiddie pool festered in a concrete slab surrounded by a paved parking lot strewn with used condoms, syringes, and broken glass. The pool looked like it needed to be flushed.

Across the potholed street and backing up the freeway on-ramp stood a row of cinderblock shacks with all the allure of a Soviet-era housing unit. Judging by their look, they most likely housed hookers, drug addicts, and refugees from third world countries. The place could have been Chernobyl—the only thing missing was an encased nuclear reactor.

We located Peggy's unit on the ground floor near the front of the complex. She invited us inside when I knocked. Gary shuddered as I followed him through the doorway. The place smelled like old gym socks and crème de menthe. There were a few dozen cats around the front room, and I could see others trailing off toward a rear hallway. Sandboxes were scattered around the floor in a haphazard pattern, and

I vowed silently to take care where I stepped. From the revolting odor, it was obvious the sand hadn't been changed in weeks.

I introduced myself as Peggy sat down on a wooden bar stool tugging a cigarette from the package of Kools on the countertop. She took a long swig from a can of malt liquor and lit the cigarette, exhaling a blue cloud of smoke as she spoke.

"Who gave you the shiner?"

"Detective work is dangerous."

Peggy squinted at the two of us through the smoke, sizing us up. She wore a muumuu and house slippers, her hair looked like a skewed stack of pancakes, sort of piled on top but sliding off to one side. She leaned back against the countertop and took another long pull from the malt liquor can. "Y'all want something to drink? Fresh outta these, but I got a six-pack of Falstaff in the fridge. It might be a little skunky, though."

We both declined.

She wiped foam from her upper lip, burped, and nodded toward a row of sticky-looking bar stools.

We shook our heads. Standing was safer.

She said, "Gary? That's a pretty name for a pretty girl like you."

Gary said thank you, and I pulled the notes I'd printed out in my office from my backpack. We both watched as she scanned the pages, her lips working hard to form the words as she read. I pictured her mind sort of sloshing over the letters. It was obvious she'd been drinking for a while…my guess was since January of 2005. After a few minutes, she looked up and said, "So what do you want me to do with this?"

"If you agree it's what you told me on the phone, then I'd like you to sign it."

"Sure, sweetie. You got something I can write with?"

She made the word "write" sound like "rat." I pulled a pen from my pack and got her to sign and date the final page. Gary watched as I took her through the document, getting her to initial each page. When she was done, he looked at me with a frown on his face. This was not what he had hoped for. It would take a few months in rehab before Peggy might make a credible witness. Chances were good even then that a rookie attorney would destroy her in the courtroom. Gary dutifully notarized the signature, entering the time and place in his notebook along with Peggy's driver's license number.

I thanked her for her help. She followed us out of the apartment, tossing a steady stream of questions at me.

"When will they charge Bradford? I want to be there when the police haul his ass off to jail."

"It's not like that, he has to file the compensation claim first and then we bring a motion with the court."

"But there will be a trial, right?"

"I'll let you know when we get to that point."

As we approached Gary's car, I noticed he was staring at the cinderblock structure across the street. I glanced over just in time to see a heavyset man shove a key in the lock and jostle the door open. When the chain caught, he yelled, "Damn, Mary, why is this fucking thing latched? Open up, will ya?"

Around the corner of the building, a window slid open and a pudgy man wearing jogging shorts hiked his hips up on to the windowsill. I grabbed my iPhone in time to capture thirty seconds of video as he climbed out of the window and sprinted up the alleyway before rounding a distant corner.

I turned to Peggy. "Please tell me that was Bradford Collins."

She smiled as she spoke. "Mister, that was none other than the little bird turd himself." She gestured across the street as a bleached blonde with huge breasts appeared at the door.

Peggy said, "It looks like Mary Moody's husband got home a little early."

She took another long slug from her can and tossed the empty toward the street, wobbled unsteadily on her feet, and shook her head slowly, singing, "Mammas don't let your babies grow up to be cowboys."

Then she burped and swaggered toward the apartment complex, swinging her ass in time to an unheard rhythm.

Gary deadpanned, "Such a lady."

We looked at the video on my cell phone in the car before Gary turned the key in the ignition.

"Well, I'm no expert, but that sure doesn't look like someone too injured to work to me."

Gary grinned as he said, "I have to agree with your assessment, Mr. Honey."

Bradford's image on the video was shadowy, but there was a split second where his face was unmistakable.

We watched the video again before I sent a copy to my business e-mail account. Gary pulled away from the curb and both of us were buzzing on adrenaline all the way back to Austin.

CHAPTER NINE

I watched *American Idol* last night. What a stupid show. Ninety seconds of off-key warbling followed by three and half minutes of mindless chatter and ten minutes of acne treatment commercials. Ryan Seacrest preens and struts like a peacock while trying to act straight in an Armani suit and enough stage makeup to spackle a wall. You ever notice how he manhandles the female contestants like melons at the grocery and slaps the male contestants on the back like he's trying to dislodge a piece of sausage from a windpipe? And then there's Randy Jackson, wearing what looks like a Glad bag and sounding ghetto, which isn't easy for a guy who makes two hundred thousand dollars an episode and lives in Brentwood. And where do they dig up those butt-ugly teenagers—it's just painful watching them trot onto the stage, stare soulfully into the camera, and then murder an eighties ballad. Honestly, it's enough to make you want to slap Stevie Nicks."

Willa was her chatty self as she drove to the bus terminal. I'd decided my only chance at getting her to believe me was for her to meet Maurice the bus driver. I was banking he'd convince her my black eye was a result of a tumble on his vehicle. If that didn't work, plan B was to move to Mexico—but that had me worried because my Spanish sucked and I always got the runs in Mexico.

We parked at the curb and sat watching the terminal building. I'd called Maurice as we left Waco and caught him taking a five-minute break at the turnaround point of his route. He explained he was working a double shift but agreed to meet with us if we could make it to the terminal by 8:30.

"Never heard so many unwarranted compliments in my entire life. The judges gush over every song like Sally Fields accepting an

Oscar. Their strategy, which must be to hype the mediocre talent, would probably work better if at least a few of the contestants could hit a note once in a while—one that humans could hear, I mean. And what's up with Steven Tyler's mouth? I swear he could wrap his lips around a Buick."

She blathered on as I caught sight of Maurice walking across the parking lot.

"Let's go, Willa," I said.

I opened the door, and called to Maurice. He waved back as I crossed the street with Willa in my wake. When we got close enough for Maurice to see me clearly, he said, "Oh my, you've got quite a black eye there, Mr. Honey."

"It looks worse than it feels. And it's Greg. Please call me Greg."

He smiled. "I apologize again for your fall, Greg, but I'm sure if I hadn't slammed on my brakes the bus was going to hit that truck."

I glanced at Willa to make sure she'd heard. She looked a little uncertain.

I said, "I totally understand, Maurice, and I don't blame you at all. These things happen, and it was as much my fault as anyone's. I wasn't holding on tight."

I nodded toward Willa and said, "This is my friend, Willa Jensen."

"Maurice Williams," he said, offering his hand. They shook, and the image of her hand inside his made me think of a canary in a bear's paw. Maurice said, "Did Greg tell you about his fall this morning?"

Willa nodded slowly. "Well, yes, he did mention it."

"Tough way to get a shiner, that's why we always tell riders to sit or hold tight to the handrail."

"Yes." Her voice softened.

Maurice asked, "Was there something you needed, Greg? Not that I mind meeting this young lady, but you were so insistent on the phone."

I shook my head, still smiling. "Not really, Maurice, I just wanted to bring Willa by. She's never met a bus driver."

It sounded lame even to my own ears, but Maurice smiled. "Well, that was nice. It's nice to meet you, Ms. Jensen."

Willa smiled back. I shook Maurice's hand, and we murmured good-byes before crossing the street to the car.

"Okay, I get it," she said as we pulled away from the curb. "I guess I was wrong."

"Yes, you were."

"And I owe Matt an apology."

"Yes, you do."

"And I owe you an apology."

"Accepted." I grinned.

On a whim, I decided to press my advantage and see if I could get her to take me to Russ's house. I wanted to follow Billy Crenshaw on his nightly disappearance. But before I could ask, my cell phone rang.

"Hello."

"I know where you live, gay boy."

"Who is this?"

"Be frightened, be very, very frightened."

"I haven't been afraid of a phone call since *Dial M for Murder*. I don't know who you are or what you want, but I think you need to get a life and leave me the fuck alone!"

"Don't forget to check the closet."

I hung up and slipped my phone back into my pocket. Willa was looking at me, bewildered. I said, "Wrong number."

"Sounds like someone you don't want to talk to."

"Pretty much."

As we pulled into traffic, I tried to keep from worrying about what I was going to find in my closet.

"I had a phone call like that once," Willa said. "It was nasty and threatening, full of innuendo and criticism. Just like you, I didn't want anything to do with the caller. Of course, my call was from my mother."

❖

Russ Buttons and Billy Crenshaw lived in the Hyde Park section of central Austin. Their home was a Victorian McMansion with gables, dentils, and transoms above the windows. It had a cornice, an entablature, and a portico. There was a turret rising above a corner and a gaudy five-tone-on-tone paint job of mostly lavenders tending toward pink. An intricately sculpted wrought iron fence surrounded a neatly trimmed yard overflowing with pink and white azaleas all summer and pink and white pansies all winter. In the fall and spring, the begonias took over.

As we drove past, I noted a green Mercedes sedan parked behind Russ's pickle-colored Cadillac in the driveway. The blinds were open, and I could see Billy moving around in the kitchen.

"What now?" Willa asked.

"Now you park, and we wait."

She pulled a K-turn and edged to the curb across the street, one lot down from the house. I monitored the activity inside while Willa filled me in on theater gossip. The current buzz was all about the artistic director's pointy shoes.

"It's not like he lives in a tree and bakes cookies, for God's sake. I say if you're not building toys for Christmas, you shouldn't dress like an elf. I mean, the toes even curl up at the ends—when he bends his knees he looks like he's skiing. It reminds me of the witch under Dorothy's house. And there's no way that can be comfortable, unless he's got the oddest-shaped feet since hairy humanoids skulked the northwest forests. All he needs is sleigh bells glued to the points and he could star in the Santa-land Diaries. Speaking of Santa-land, Craig thinks Dave would look good in candy-cane tights and I have to agree, some legs were just born to be swathed in red-and-white Lycra."

The lights went out in the house, and a shadowy figure exited through the side door. I watched it creep across the grass toward Billy's Mercedes. The car's interior light drew yellow patches on the ground, and I recognized Billy's balding head as he slid into the driver's seat.

I gestured to Willa.

"There he is…now wait till he backs out, then start up and follow slowly. But hang back and don't be obvious. Remember, we just want to find out where he's going. If it's somewhere embarrassing he may change his plans if he knows he's being followed."

"There's not a lot of traffic to hide behind, what do you want me to do?"

"Wait until he gets a few houses away and then pull out. Try to match his speed. You don't want to sneak up on him, or heaven forbid, lose him."

Willa idled the car until the Mercedes moved through the

intersection and turned onto Duval Street. We followed at a snail's pace. The street was dark, and Willa kept the Honda's headlights off, navigating by the slim light cast by Hyde Park's moon towers.

"So why are we following this guy anyway? He's not a murderer or a rapist or a drug runner, is he?" I could tell she was thrilled to be part of this little excursion.

"Nothing like that, I just want to find out where he's going."

"Do you have a gun?"

I shot her a look of irritation and said, "Of course not."

Willa was a big proponent of lethal weaponry and would arm the world if she could. I dreaded what was coming. In the sketchy moonlight, I watched her rummage through her shoulder bag as the car rolled slowly down the tree-lined lane.

"Here, take this one."

She pulled a snub-nosed Smith and Wesson .38 from her purse. She set it in my lap. "I'll use the magnum."

She reached over and took the biggest handgun I'd seen out of the glove compartment.

"What the hell? Willa, put that away. We don't need guns."

She shook her head. "Isn't that just like a Democrat? You're not scared of these little guys, are you?"

"Little?"

"Well, they aren't exactly what you'd use to bring down an elephant...except maybe the magnum."

"No guns, Willa."

"Even that little ole thing?" She nodded to the gun in my lap, waving the magnum around like she was stirring pancake batter.

"Hell, yes."

"It's just a scrawny little .38, for God's sake. I use guns bigger than that to swat flies. This one's a little more substantial." She pointed the magnum at me, and I felt my testicles retract.

In a higher-pitched voice than usual, I said, "I swear, Willa, if you don't put that away..."

"Okay, okay already, Jesus!" She shoved the gun back into the glove compartment.

"This one too." I nodded to the .38 still lying in my lap. She snatched it up, dropped it back in her purse, and I exhaled slowly.

She said, "Do I need to pull over so you can change your shorts?"

"Very funny."

"It was just a .38." She sighed in frustration. "I have friends who send their children to school better armed. You realize this is Texas, Greg. Everyone carries a gun."

"Not me, and neither will you when you're with me. I don't do guns, Willa, no guns."

"I swear, sometimes gay boys can be such pansies when it comes to firearms."

When we turned south on Duval, Willa flipped on her lights. The Mercedes was a couple of blocks ahead of us, just crossing Thirty-eighth Street.

"What if he's a member of a mob and figures out we're following him...I'm just saying I'd be more comfortable with a gun."

"You don't need a gun."

"But can you be sure? He could have spotted us already and..."

"Willa, it's Russ Buttons's boyfriend. He's not dangerous, he's not even dodgy. Just follow the car."

"Yeah, but it's nighttime and it's dark out here, kind of spooky."

"It's Hyde Park at ten thirty on a weeknight, not Mogadishu, for God's sake. Relax, will ya?"

She sighed again. We pursued the car as it headed toward the university. We missed the light at Thirty-second Street, but caught up with Billy as he waited on traffic at Twenty-ninth Street. Willa lagged back and we followed across campus, slowly sighting glimpses of his car as we looped around Waller Creek, trying not to get too close. He sped through the intersection at MLK Boulevard, but the light turned red before we got there.

"Run the light, Willa."

"Are you crazy?"

"There's no one coming."

"But it's red."

"We're losing him, run the damn light."

She panned her head both directions, then gunned the motor. The tires chirped and we darted across the street. Up ahead, the green Mercedes turned right on Fifteenth Street.

"He's heading toward the Capitol. What do you think he's up to?"

"No idea. Maybe he's meeting a state worker?"

"But everything's closed."

The Mercedes drove past the Capitol complex, picking up speed as it whipped by vacant buildings. Its taillights glowed red as it slowed and turned left on Guadalupe. One block away, he curled left onto a side street.

Willa said, "He's parking, what do you want me to do now?"

"Turn and drive on. We can park up ahead around the corner."

When we passed by the Mercedes, I caught a quick glimpse of Billy in the driver's seat. He was talking on his cell phone. Willa drove through a light, and I kept track of his movements in the side mirror. He was just getting out of his car when Willa turned onto the next street. The closest parking slot was a half a block away. She pulled into an angled slot, and we jogged back to the intersection in time to see Billy disappear into a building.

From the side street, it looked like an apartment complex. But as we approached, I spotted a marquee with framed photos of women in skimpy costumes posted alongside a happy-hour menu of drinks. *Les Furieux Chat*, scrawled in curlicue letters, glowed in pink neon tubing above the door.

"A strip club? He went into a strip club?"

"Sure looks like it."

"But you said this was Russ Buttons's partner." She drew double quotes in the air around the word "partner." "I don't get it. He's gay. Russ said he was gay. I mean, Russ Buttons is really, really gay. So his lover has to be gay too…right?"

I shrugged, as baffled as she was. I turned my attention to the building. It was brown brick, at least six stories tall, with trimmed hedges. Cement steps led to a pair of tinted glass doors.

My experience with strip clubs was strictly limited. I'd been in one once for a meeting with a potential client. I remembered it being dark and smoky and smelling like a stockyard. The drinks were watered down, the ambience seedy, and the entertainment depressingly creepy—mostly forty-year-old women onstage and topless, pretending to be schoolgirls or cowgirls or cheerleaders. And the only thing they did was hump rhythmically to the music and pout at the dirty old men stuffing sticky bills into their G-strings. It was sleazy and sad, and I felt ridiculous watching it.

I followed as Willa pushed through the glass doors. A high counter dominated the carpeted entrance hallway. To our left, the sound of heavy bass thumped from behind a curtained doorway. Pictures of women with big hair and huge breasts scowled at us from the wall behind the counter, where a burly guy wearing a T-shirt stretched so tightly I could see his nipples glared at us with dead fish eyes.

"Les Furieux Chat is a private club. I can't let you in because you're not members."

Willa stepped aside as I cleared my throat.

"Actually, I just need to have a word with the guy who came in before us. You know the bald guy? I think I may have dinged his car." It sounded like a lie even to my ears.

He nodded and said, "Okay, just wait here."

When he disappeared through the curtain, Willa looked at me fidgeting in anticipation and whispered, "Come on."

She pushed through the curtains after him, and I rolled my eyes, sighing. Entering the club was a bad idea. Still, I ignored the warning voice in my head and followed.

After the brightly lit entrance, the room behind the curtain was so dark it felt like I'd entered a closet. I could just make out shadowy movement behind the bar to my right, but my attention was immediately pulled to the brightly lit stage forty feet in front of me.

A raised platform painted white sat in the middle of the room. It was harshly lit by a couple of overhead spotlights angled inward from the corners. A scantily clad woman sparkled in a shower of glitter body paint. She moved fluidly in a pulsating motion. I stared at her, mesmerized. She had melon-sized breasts and was doing things to a pole that had to be illegal in the state of Utah.

As eighties-era music thumped from the corner speakers, she wriggled and writhed onstage, occasionally flickering her tongue like a snake ready to strike. I found myself transfixed by the spectacle of pendulous sagging flesh on metal for a moment until Willa grabbed my arm and tugged me back into the shadows.

Both of us scanned the room for Billy. The club smelled sour, a mixture of spilled liquor and vomit. As my eyes adapted slowly to the darkness, I began to detect movement in the shadowy spaces. Men sat at tables, mostly in small groups, drinking. Willa elbowed me and pointed. To the right of the stage, the bouncer from the front leaned over a table, speaking to a couple of guys. From where I stood I could only see the back of one guy and the bald head of the other. The bouncer's head pivoted between the two men as they spoke. As we watched, the bouncer left the table and strolled toward a doorway on the other side of the stage. I studied the bald man still sitting at the table. He was punching keys on a small calculator and entering numbers onto a sheet of paper in front of him. He smoked a cigar as he worked, totally ignoring the action onstage.

"What do you think is going on back there?" Willa's voice strained to be heard over the music.

"Don't know."

"You think Billy's boyfriend could be back there?"

"Well, he's not out here." We both looked over the room once more and turned our attention back to the door. It was just beyond the stage, past the hallway with signs pointing to bathrooms.

"Come on," Willa said. I followed her with a sinking feeling in the pit of my stomach. Something was telling me to tread carefully. The atmosphere had turned edgy with a hint of danger, or maybe that was the smell coming from the bathrooms…the point was my confidence was starting to lag.

We crept past the stage furtively. The door was closed, but when Willa turned the knob, it opened. I stood behind her. Manliness was one thing, but this felt dangerous. I wasn't above hiding behind a woman in a dangerous situation. The door swung inward. I caught a quick glimpse of two people sitting at a table in the center of the room. The one facing us was Billy, and the other one was a large female with big blond hair and a nurse's cap. I only saw her back before the bouncer blocked the doorway. He crowded us back over the threshold and pulled the door shut.

Willa said, "I thought you wanted us to follow you? Didn't you want us to follow you? I could have sworn you said follow me. Didn't he say that, Greg?"

I nodded meekly.

The bouncer stepped closer to Willa and yelled, "What the fuck are you doing in here?"

I could tell Willa was revving up to tell him off, which, I felt certain, would not end well. I stepped between them and said, "It's just a simple mistake, we'll go now."

Willa, however, was not one to be mistreated.

She shoved me out of her way. With her legs firmly set, she stuck her index finger in the bouncer's chest and yelled back, "Look, buddy, you can put that tiny little weenie back in your shorts because this pathetic show of testosterone-enhanced dominance doesn't scare us, okay? You can pee in the corners after we're gone."

The bouncer tried to grab Willa's finger. I knocked his hand away reflexively, and the next thing I knew I was lying on the floor looking up at Willa, who was wiping my face with a grimy dish towel. I tried to sit up and saw stars so I lay back, and soon another face floated into view. It took me a moment to recognize the bald-headed guy I'd seen working the calculator.

He said, "Now, there he is, I think he's going to be okay. You going to be okay, buddy, ain'tcha? Yeah, see, no harm, no foul."

Willa said, "What do you mean? Look at his face…that face is a mess, an absolute mess. I'm calling the police. Your goon decked him without cause. He's going to jail, they'll probably shut the whole place down." She reached in her purse for her phone.

The bald guy said, "You could do that, and then, of course, we would have to have you arrested for trespassing. This is a private club, you see, and you were supposed to wait out in the lobby."

I raised myself up on an elbow and said in a raspy voice, "Willa, just let it go. Give me a hand and let's get out of here."

The bald guy said, "That's the ticket, that's the ticket." They both helped me stand, and I hobbled past the bar, leaning on Willa. We wove through a few tables with guys fixated on the action onstage.

I caught a glimpse of a bartender looking in my direction. He turned away quickly when the bald guy sneered at him, but something about him was familiar.

The bald guy escorted us through the double doors and left us standing on the sidewalk. As we walked back to her car, Willa kept looking over at me.

"What?"

"I think you're probably gonna have two black eyes, and maybe a fat lip to go with it. This has not been one of your better days."

"One of these days your aggressiveness is going to get us into some real trouble."

"What are you talking about? A girl's gotta stand up for herself, you know." She added, "What do you think we should do now? We could hang around and wait for Billy, if you want."

I shook my head. "I'm feeling lousy. Just take me home. I want to go to bed."

On the way back to Lost Wind, I realized who the bartender looked like—Bradford Collins, the guy I'd filmed in Waco. The more I thought about that connection, the less likely it seemed. Why would an insurance scofflaw be tending bar at Les Furieux Chat?

CHAPTER TEN

Tuesday morning, Matt let me sleep in. I pried my eyes open at nine thirty. I must have twisted something when I was knocked to the floor, because my lower back felt tight and sore. I sat up and bent over slowly, trying to touch my toes. The stiffness released gradually, but returned as soon as I stood and gingerly crept to the bathroom. I switched on the overhead light. There was a bruise on my left hip and scrapes on my torso. My upper lip was swollen, and both eyes were circled in deepening color, making me look menacing and cartoonish.

I scowled into the mirror. My eyes were bloodshot and watery, and my face felt hot and inflamed. I opened my mouth. My teeth were all present and accounted for. I felt along the ridge of my cheekbones and checked my nose, which was puffy and swollen, but unbroken. All in all, I was in amazingly good shape...considering.

I flashed back to the phone call I'd received in Willa's car. I'd completely forgotten to check my closet. I poked my head out of the bathroom and looked at the closet door. It seemed normal. No glowing iridescence or questionable reddish fluid seeping through the transom, no ticking bomb or hissing snake sounds. The ominous pounding noise I heard was just my heartbeat.

I schlepped slowly across the hardwood floor in my boxer shorts and sniffed the air. It smelled like ripe gym socks—much better than the fetid odor of a decaying corpse. I stepped closer and caressed the doorknob. My mouth was dry and my mind raced. I took a couple of slow breaths, trying to calm myself.

The doorbell rang and I almost peed myself.

I grabbed a T-shirt and a pair of sweatpants from my gym bag and padded to the front door, dressing en route.

Willa's distorted image stared back at me through the fisheye lens. I opened the door. She stood on my porch, iPod earplugs stuck in her ears. She was holding a box of chocolates and dancing to the beat of music I couldn't hear. Her eyes widened, and she tugged out the earplugs.

"Oh my God, you're a mess. Does that hurt? That has got to hurt. It looks like you've been playing tetherball with your head. That guy really whacked you. I wonder if it caused a concussion. Do you feel dizzy? If you feel dizzy you should go to the doctor." She stepped through the doorway and handed me the chocolates.

"I'm okay. How'd you get in?"

"The gate was open again."

"Damn! Maybe I need to say something to Mother. What's this?"

"Thought you could use some cheering up, and dark chocolate is very healing unless you're allergic…you're not allergic, are you?"

I shook my head.

"It has medical effects too. I think it lowers your blood pressure and increases your metabolism. Or maybe it raises your blood pressure and decreases your metabolism. Whatever…the point is it tastes good. Speaking of mothers, if you're not busy maybe I can tempt you to go on a little adventure. I gotta go see my momster and I could use a shoulder to lean on. She's gonna ask me about church attendance and boyfriends. Then she'll criticize my hair, insinuate I've put on weight, and express her disapproval over what I'm wearing. She'll follow that up with questions about when I last bathed, when I'm going back to school, and why I haven't been over to see her in more than a month…That one's easy. It's because she's a bitch."

"Sounds lovely." My voice dripped sarcasm. "But first I need to check my closet."

She squinted at me, mystified. "Got some new shoes?"

"Nope."

"Reorganize your socks?"

"Nope."

"Want help changing the vacuum cleaner bag?"

"Uh-uh."

"What's there to see in your closet?"

"Don't know."

"Okay, guess you're a little nostalgic for your childhood years."

"Something like that."

We walked to the bedroom. I set the chocolates on my dresser and jerked the closet door open.

"What's that?" Willa asked.

"It looks like a pincushion."

I grabbed the black cloth figure from the floor. When I held it up, Willa said, "That's got to be painful."

It was a voodoo doll with two large pins stuck in the groin area.

"How very Prince Albert."

"What's it doing in your closet?"

"Someone's trying to scare me."

"With a pincushion? I guess that would work if you had a sewing phobia maybe, but I think if you really wanted to scare someone you'd drop off an item that was a little more macabre, like a severed head."

"Willa, where does one get a severed head?"

"Maybe on eBay. A pincushion's not scary. Now, a pig's heart, that's scary."

"A pig's heart is not scary, it's messy."

"Maybe a dead pigeon?"

"Again, Wil, more messy than scary."

"Oh, oh…I got it, how 'bout your senior prom picture?"

"Hey, it was a bad hair day."

"Trust me, it wasn't the hair. You wore a lime-green tux! Lime-green formal wear is almost never appropriate."

"It was fashion forward."

"It was Kermit the Frog."

"Hey."

"Remember the mullet? You had a mullet, for God's sake, and a face with more craters than the surface of the moon. I love you, Greg babe, but you were not a pretty man in high school."

"So sue me, I had acne."

"That picture pretty much curdles milk."

"I was a teenager."

"With Wham! hair and a face like a Petri dish."

"You really want to go there? Because I remember you were a pretty unfortunate teenager too, dressing like a goth Joan Jett in bowling shoes and a leather poodle skirt. You drove the softball team mad with desire."

"It was a statement."

"Yes, it was…it said 'desperate to be different.'"

She frowned. "So who sent you that?"

"Don't know for sure."

I explained about the phone call. Willa's face wrinkled up. When I finished, she said, "There's some weird stuff going on here, Mr. Honey. Threatening phone calls, the unlatched gate, and now this, and what is it anyway?"

"It's a doll."

"I know it's a doll, but what does it mean? Is it a curse or a warning or just a gift of bad art?"

"I have no idea, it's just stupid." I kept my voice steady. I was trying to bluster through, but the truth was I was more than a little unnerved. Willa saw right through me.

"Still, it has to make you feel anxious. Whoever put it there broke into your place, and that's unsettling by itself."

"Yep, it's not cool."

"Maybe you should do something like…call someone…or arm yourself…or move."

"I'm not moving, Willa, and I'm not getting a gun. It's just a doll, for God's sake. Besides, who'd want to hurt me? I'm kind, I don't have enemies, people like me. I'm a good guy."

"Maybe, but you've made an enemy of someone."

"So it would seem."

Willa checked her watch and said, "We need to hurry. It's never a good idea to keep Mother waiting."

"Give me a minute."

I limped off toward the bathroom. She waited, thumbing through my DVD collection while I showered. I considered shaving, but decided the stubble fit my new manly persona…and besides, shaving would probably hurt. I tugged on fresh jeans and a T-shirt. We made our way out to the gate.

"So this was open again?" I asked.

"Weird, huh? I swear something is going on."

"I know."

We climbed into Willa's Honda. Twenty minutes later, we pulled to the curb outside her mother's house. On the way over, I could tell Willa's mood was darkening. Now she stared straight ahead through the windshield and took a couple of deep breaths, trying to calm her nerves. The house was a split-level ranch with trimmed grass and a garden bursting with color. It looked innocent enough, but I was anxious too. No telling what awaited us up the walkway. Saying Janice Jensen was a controlling mother was like saying the priesthood drew perverts. Willa was worried with plenty of reason.

The first time I saw Janice, she was lugging a Tupperware container full of frosted cupcakes through the metal detectors at East Side Elementary. A year earlier, Mother had decided a six-year-old was sufficiently mature to handle intense humiliation and hard-core violence and enrolled me at East Side, the poorest and most dangerous elementary school in Austin. The first day of classes, I wore khakis— and since khakis are flammable, I spent most of recess trying to extinguish the flames. By second grade I was relatively inured to the place and felt quite at home dodging bullets in the hallway. That year, the school threw a party celebrating something unexpected (like a week without bloodshed), and Janice was our Homeroom Mother. One could question the wisdom of bringing sugary treats to a bunch of underfed juvenile delinquents, but that simple act had endeared Janice to all the sticky-fingered booger eaters in Mrs. Clayton's class. All except Willa, who was given a carrot because Janice didn't want her daughter eating junk food. I waited until Mrs. Jensen left and made a friend for life by letting Willa dip her carrot into the icing on top of my cupcake.

Willa sighed and opened her car door. I followed her up the walkway, giving her plenty of room as she progressed in a series of starts and stops, talking to herself.

"God, I don't want to do this. Forget it, I'm going home…but she'll just call again, or worse, she'll come over. No, I've got to go in. Damn, this sucks…To hell with it, I'm going home. Come on, Willa, you might as well get it over with. Shoot me now, please. In the forehead…Maybe I'll shoot her in the forehead…I wonder how long I'd be in prison… She'd look lovely in a casket…No, mustn't think of that."

The door opened before we got to the porch, and Janice stepped out with her hands on her hips.

"Oh, Willa, what have you done with your hair? That cut is very unattractive. You should have parked in the garage so the neighbors wouldn't have to look at your dirty car. Hi, Greg, what happened to you? Come inside. Willa, get the door for Greg—why do I always have to ask you to do these things, can't you think for yourself?"

Willa looked at me. She gestured like her finger was a gun and she was shooting herself in the head. Janice herded us inside, a sour expression on her face. A twelve-piece tea service was laid out on the table in a sunny alcove. A teapot steamed in a cozy next to a tray of biscuits with toast and jam. I saw a pot of clotted cream and a honey bear.

Janice said, "Willa, pour for us, and don't make a mess. There are napkins stacked next to the cozy. I know how clumsy you are. Now, Greg, tell me what happened to you?" She said this while watching Willa's every move. I knew she wasn't interested in my story; what she really wanted was to find fault with her daughter. I didn't like Janice, but she didn't seem to mind me. For some strange reason she liked me. Perhaps she thought my family's status somehow validated my presence in Willa's life. Boy, did that make me want to laugh.

I answered her question with a bold-faced lie. "I was attacked by a group of hoods. They've beaten me half to death, and we decided to stop by here on the way to the hospital."

"I see…Willa, the cream goes in first. Don't you know anything? And the pot is dripping—be careful!"

"In fact, I may be bleeding internally, so we need to leave soon."

"That's nice…Willa, sit up straight and serve Greg before yourself, he's the guest…pour the tea, then offer the tray, and be careful with the condiments."

"In fact, I'm feeling a little weak and sort of dizzy, so if I happen to pass out, please call EMS."

"Uh-huh…now offer Greg a napkin and pour for me."

Willa shot a sly glance my direction.

"I'll try to struggle through. But if I do happen to die, you should call Lost Wind."

"Call Lost Wind? Whatever for, dear? Willa, I swear, give me that pot…you can't do anything right."

Willa handed over the teapot and shrugged. It was how their mother-daughter relationship worked. Willa was the bumbling underachiever who never succeeded in her mother's eyes, and Janet was caught in the role of meddling, nagging mother unable to accept that her daughter was a fully functional adult. It was sad and unsatisfying, but I learned long ago not to try to solve the problems of the world.

Besides, it wasn't like I was in a position to judge the family relationships of others.

We sipped our tea, and I tried to steer the conversation to something that would drag Janice away from her incessant need to nag at Willa. I was markedly unsuccessful. After a while, I explained that I had to hurry to work. When we got back in the car, I gave Willa a quick hug.

"It's a shame your mother doesn't realize how great you are, Willa. I hope you know I love you and I'm glad you're my friend."

"You gonna sing 'Kumbaya' next? Maybe give me a medal or write me a check? Jesus, Greg, she's a bitch and I know it. She tries to push my buttons and I go along because this is Texas and capital punishment is almost mandatory for a murder charge, but that doesn't change the fact she's a nasty old lady."

Willa dropped me off at the office. I climbed the steps and pushed through the doorway to find Russ Buttons pacing the hallway. He was dressed in head to toe in sienna: tight brown jeans, a long-sleeve mocha T-shirt, and cordovan penny loafers. His skin looked darker than usual (no doubt from time spent on a tanning bed) and his hair had been re-dyed a brunette shade matching his clothes.

If he were standing next to a UPS truck, he would have been invisible.

"Finally, where the hell have you been?"

"Good morning to you too, Russ. You look like a Hershey bar."

"Very funny. And you look like you walked through Williamson County in a dress. What the hell happened to you? No, don't tell me, I don't care. What did you find out about Billy? Where did he go? What did he do? Who did he do?" He spoke fast, tripping over some of the words.

The corridor was hot, and we both were sweating by the time I managed to unlock my office door. He swung through ahead of me and slid my guest chair in front of my desk. I edged past him and we sat down. He fidgeted nervously, crossing and uncrossing his legs, one uncontrolled eyebrow twitching occasionally. He leaned across the desktop.

"Well?"

"Well, what?"

"Jesus, Honey, tell me what's going on with Billy."

"Honestly, I don't know."

"Then what the hell am I paying you for?"

"To find out, but I'm not there yet. Look, I followed him when he left your place last night. It's a little complicated and I haven't figured it all out yet. There was an incident."

"Incident? What kind of incident? Where did he go?"

"He went to a private strip club near the Capitol building, I think he met a woman, but I didn't get a good look at her and I'm not even sure they were together."

Russ shook his head. "A strip club? He was with a woman at a strip club? A stripper?"

"I don't think so."

"Are you saying he's seeing a woman?"

"I don't know. All I know for sure is I found him sitting with one, but I don't know why or even *if* he went there to meet her. It may have been a chance encounter. I barely caught a glimpse of them before we were thrown out."

"We?"

"Willa was with me."

"Willa Jensen?"

"The one and only."

He was starting to get angry. "Why was Willa with you?"

"She works with me sometimes. Detection can be a dangerous business. Sometimes I need a partner."

"Well, she better keep her mouth shut, you both better. If this gets out, I'll sue you for every penny you own."

That would be a lot of work for a very small payoff. I said, "I plan to follow Billy again tonight."

"I should hope so. What can you tell me about this woman he was with?"

"Not much, she was dressed like a nurse, that's really all I know, but the investigation is just starting. I'll find out what's going on. Of course, it would be faster to just ask Billy."

"I can't do that, he would think that I don't trust him."

"Obviously you don't trust him. If you did, you wouldn't be hiring me to follow him around all night."

"Of course I don't trust him, but that's not the point. Look, it's really simple…you know I don't trust him and I know I don't trust him, but the trick is to keep Billy from knowing I don't trust him."

"I see your relationship is built on honesty."

He missed the sarcasm. "Like every successful gay relationship, ours is built on kinky sex, shared skin care products, and a color-coordinated wardrobe."

"What are you afraid of, Russ? You may end up learning something you don't want to know. Talk to Billy." I couldn't afford to lose this job, but Russ was a friend…sort of.

"Are you insane? When it comes to love, honesty is highly overrated. No wonder you've never had a long-term boyfriend. Take it from me, Greg, successful marriages are founded on lies, duplicity, and misdirection."

I stared at him. Russ was cynical and mistrustful, but he and Billy had been together for years. At least outwardly they were as happy as any couple I knew. Maybe it did take a little subterfuge to make a relationship work.

"You need to find out who this hussy is and why Billy is seeing her, if he's seeing her. And if not, I need to know what the hell he's up to. That's what I'm paying you for, isn't it?"

"Of course it is, but I'm not sure you've really thought this all the way through. This is something Billy wants to keep hidden. It's probably embarrassing, or worse. If he's been living a double life or has a shameful secret, you finding out could hurt. Are you willing to risk everything just to know the truth?"

"I didn't come here for marital advice. Just do your job."

My smile was brittle. His nastiness was annoying, and I needed to get back to work. I said, "Okay then, I'll give it another shot tonight."

He sighed, but didn't make a move for the door.

"Have you met with your brother yet?"

"No. But that's really none of your business, is it?" He curled his upper lip.

"I'm just asking. Jesus! Don't bite my head off."

"I'm sorry." But there was no contrition in his voice. "Just do your job. Do what I'm paying you to do…please." For the first time, he looked directly at me. "You're not looking so good—even worse than yesterday."

"Thanks for noticing."

"Now you've got two black eyes."

"Yes, I do."

"Is this your new boyfriend?"

"No."

"You want to tell me what happened?" I could tell he wasn't really interested.

I said, "Not really. Suffice it to say sometimes being a dick is dangerous."

"So is loving a dick."

He dropped his head onto my desk and made soft, blubbering sounds.

"Amen to that, brother." I reached across and patted his back. "Amen to that."

CHAPTER ELEVEN

It was almost ten thirty when I finally managed to maneuver Russ out of my office. I spent a few minutes cleaning mucus from my desk pad and put some kibble in the cat's bowl. I looked around for the cat, but he was nowhere to be found. Probably gone off somewhere to add to the feline gene pool or munch on a mouse. He appeared as if by magic as I turned on my computer.

As I listened to the sounds of crunching, I thought about Milton Buttons. I was perplexed over Russ's reaction to my question. It seemed odd that both brothers seemed to dislike each other, yet Russ felt the need to reach out. I brought up Milton's picture on my computer screen and tried to enhance the image. I wanted to see if I could make out the shadowy objects in the background. When I zoomed in, I picked out a familiar form that initially confused me until I remembered my phone call to the Wilsons and ten-year-old Matty's words. She had told me the person she knew as Gene Spleen had the "biggest lady's parts" she had ever seen. The enlarged image on my computer screen showed a contraption holding a pair of volleyball-sized breast prostheses. Milton Buttons's fake breasts were lying on the soiled carpet between his feet.

And they truly were enormous.

I took it for granted that Milton was living in Austin as a woman; he'd clearly lived in Oklahoma as a woman. But if that were the case, why would he answer Willa's knock without first putting on his female persona? Maybe he was expecting someone else—but that didn't make sense either. It was obvious we'd caught him sleeping. Maybe arriving at the door out of face was just a mistake because we surprised him.

My mind wandered around that point a while until I started to think about his animosity toward his brother. Milton apparently didn't want anything to do with his brother. Russ didn't seem very concerned with Milton, either. He wanted to know where his brother was, but had no interest in actually making contact. My nascent detective sense told me something was going on with roots much deeper and more mysterious than an old family spat.

The sound of my office phone broke through my musings. I answered on the third ring.

"Honey Detective Agency, this dick's for hire."

"Do you really think that is an appropriate greeting for a business?"

My stomach muscles tightened. In the eighteen months since the Honey Agency's grand opening, Mother had never called my office—until now.

"Yes. Assuming you're a private detective." I paused before adding, "Or a rent boy."

Silence.

"Sorry." I wanted to take it back immediately. Mother was constantly looking to press her advantage, and I needed to be strong to keep her at bay. I tried to cancel out my momentary weakness with a snarky comment. "This is an unexpected pleasure. Is there something I can do for you, Mother? Run a background check on the household staff? Drum up some dirty laundry on a rival in the Junior League? Poison someone, perhaps?"

Mother's tone was imperial. "I don't like your attitude."

"And I don't like your hairdo."

"Let's not be ugly, Greg."

"That ship sailed when you thoroughly embarrassed me in front of Matt yesterday. I plan to be angry and unpleasant with you until you apologize to Matt."

"I was wrong, Willa called and explained her mistake. I shouldn't have jumped to conclusions, but you must realize it wasn't all my fault."

"You should have talked with me first."

She paused. The silence lasted long enough to be uncomfortable and I began to suspect Mother hadn't called to alleviate her conscience. Finally, she said, "I'm sorry for that."

"You should be talking to Matt. I'm not the one you offended."

"I know, and I *will* speak with him. In fact, I'm heading to the bank soon. But first I wanted to remind you we aren't having our family dinner on Saturday. Of course you remember Cicely's coming-out party."

"How could I forget?"

"And I want to stress that as a Honey, you are expected to attend."

There it was again. Mother used the *as a Honey* line on me at least once a week. It seemed to me nine months of space to gestate and four hours of (what I hope was painful) labor was a small price to pay for the years of obligation she had heaped on me already.

She continued, "I doubt Matt would enjoy the party. In fact, I think it might be uncomfortable for him, he really doesn't know any of these people."

And there it was, the true purpose of her call. Assuming I was going to the party, she wanted me to arrive sans my lover—she didn't want to broadcast her son's gay relationship to Austin's contingent of Republican elite. Well she didn't have to worry about that. The chances of either of us attending were infinitesimal.

Mother said, "You'll probably need a new suit. I'll send Roscoe over this afternoon."

Roscoe was Mother's personal tailor. I smiled. She was trying to bribe me, offering to pay for a new tux. Well, two could play at this game.

"Okay then, I guess I'll see you at the party." I said good-bye and hung up, feeling a twinge of guilt. Maybe I shouldn't have accepted the suit under false pretenses. I considered calling her back, but I pictured all the times I would need to dress formally at other Honey affairs and figured she owed me a new suit.

Regardless, I was more determined than ever to avoid Cicely's party.

❖

"So she said 'I'm tired,' and I said 'you look it,' and she said 'I can't even remember what I was saying and it's pissing to me off,' so I said 'well, that makes you Sleepy, Dopey, and Grumpy—if Disney had named one of the other dwarves Gassy you'd be a quorum,' and she said 'it must have been something I ate,' and I said 'next time have a salad instead of the horse that pulled the plow,' and she said 'I did overdo it at lunch but did you like my story,' and I said 'it was stupid,' and she said 'why,' and…"

Matt shot a sly smile my direction. This was the first time he'd experienced the full force of the Willa mudslide.

"I said 'the witch gave Sleeping Beauty a poisoned apple, not a Xanax and a beer,' and she said 'I'm updating the storyline,' and I said 'maybe, but don't you think replacing the prince's soft kiss with what is essentially the rape of a drugged woman changes the tale significantly,' and she said 'well, this is a different era,' and I said…"

We were sitting at a table at La Traviata with glasses of wine and steaming plates of pasta.

Willa blathered on. "And it was a pea in the princess's bed, not bedbugs, for God's sake, that doesn't even make sense, otherwise she'd be calling for an exterminator, not another mattress."

Matt laughed, and I took the opportunity to hold up a glass. "How about a toast…to strong women and pretty boys."

Willa raised her glass. "To gracious acceptance of apologies and the end of mistaken accusations."

Matt nodded amiably. "To no more bruises."

"I'll drink to that."

We all drank. Willa set her glass on the tabletop with a click and smiled. "Are we going to follow Billy tonight?"

"I'm game if you are."

"You betcha, mister."

Matt said, "I still don't understand why you don't own a car."

"Yeah, Greg, why don't you have a car?"

I frowned, irritated by her feigned ignorance. "You know why, Willa." I looked at Matt. "I never really felt like I needed one—well, not until lately. I've always gotten along just fine with my bike and the buses and stealing one of Mothers car's in an emergency."

"But grand larceny aside, with your job, it has to be inconvenient."

"Surprisingly not until recently. Most of my work is looking up information on the Internet. When I meet with clients, they usually want to come to my office. But things are changing. It's not like I can follow a car on a bike. There's not much joy in running a private investigation agency via public transportation, either."

"So buy a car."

"Can't."

"Why not?"

"Money, mostly."

Willa said, "Oh come now, surely the Honey Detective Agency can afford a car. You're making a profit, right?"

"Not so much, the business is running on a shoestring. I barely make ends meet."

Matt asked, "Why is that?"

I'd never really considered the source of my financial difficulty. As a Honey, I'd always taken money for granted. But since moving into the gatehouse and opening the agency, I'd struggled. Still, the answer was easy. I said, "In a word, jobs. I don't have a lot of them. I wish I had more, but mostly it's been one or two a month, and that barely keeps the lights on."

"Surely you can turn that around. What you need is a little self-promotion, some sort of marketing. Find a way to get your name out to the hordes of Botox-enhanced West Austin ladies with big houses and wayward husbands. Let them know you'll track their spouse's movements, document dalliances, and help them score big in divorce court."

Willa said, "Oooh, oooh, I've got it. You should take out an ad in *Austin Monthly*. That rag is on every coffee table in Pemberton. And you even know the head of their advertising department. You remember Jenna Bulldog from high school?"

"Was she the girl who weighed like four hundred pounds and sat in the back of Humanities class chewing on her hair?"

"No, that was Jonnie Bulldog, Jenna's twin sister. Jenna weighed in at about three fifty and sat in the back of the class chewing on Jonnie's hair. They were close. I bet I can get Jenna to cut you a deal, seeing as how you're a Badger."

"A badger?" Matt asked.

I nodded. "That's the East Side High mascot."

"I guess that makes you a honey badger." He grinned and I rolled my eyes at the lame joke.

Willa said, "He hates that name. In high school the pep squad used to chant it at rallies. How'd it go, Greg? 'Honey badger, honey badger, what's the matter with the honey badger?'"

I glared at her over my wineglass.

Matt said, "Not much of an athlete, I take it. That's kind of sad."

Willa, never one for prolonged expressions of pity, added, "Yeah, yeah, yeah—it scarred him for life, can't enjoy nature shows and gets weepy at the zoo. Cry me a river. So what do you think about placing an advertisement in *Austin Monthly*?"

"You really think it would work?"

They both nodded enthusiastically.

The thing was, it *sort* of made sense. Besides, if it didn't cost too much, what could it hurt? And as an extra bonus, it would really piss off Mother. I pictured her opening an issue and seeing a picture of me topless, holding a smoking gun above a tagline: *The Honey Agency will strip down to the truth*. Obviously I needed new clients. Russ Buttons and Gary Weiss aside, the flow of potential jobs coming my way was hardly a gusher. Maybe a little notice was all I needed to be successful.

"Okay," I said. "If it doesn't cost too much and Willa sets it up, what have I got to lose?"

As I spoke the words, the room seemed to grow darker. I'm sure someone was just fiddling with the dimmer switch, but the timing was suspect. I tried not to read it as an omen.

Maybe I *should* have.

❖

I spent most of the afternoon being fondled by Mother's tailor, Roscoe Conti.

Roscoe's method of fitting a tux involved checking and rechecking the inseam measurement to the point where my inner thigh chafed from all the friction. I'm pretty sure his inability to get it right had more to do with personal enjoyment than sartorial accuracy. When he finally left, I wondered if I should press charges with the police.

The phone rang. It was Willa.

"Howdy. Whatcha doin'? I just ran into Wilber Wiley. You remember him, right? We dated a while back, had a bad hairpiece and questionable dental work but sexy as hell in a bald-headed toothless sort of way. I ran into him. He's finally lost the toupee, which is a good thing because it smelled like two-week-old fish and looked so much like road-kill vultures would circle whenever he walked outside."

"Didn't he leave you to join a monastery?"

"So he said, evidently his religious calling didn't stick because he was shopping for condoms and soft porn at the pharmacy. Or maybe they're planning a party at the priory. Isn't that just like a Catholic?"

"Kinda busy here, Willa, what do you need?"

"I called Jenna and you're all set at *Austin Monthly*. She even offered to run your ad for free if you're willing to be interviewed for an article they're planning about shunned children of the obscenely rich. But here's the deal, you need to get in touch today because that article is scheduled to run this week."

The story sounded ridiculous, but I figured I could use the discount and jotted down Jenna's contact information.

"Guess what I just did?" I asked.

"Does it involve small farm animals?"

"Not this time. I got fitted for a new tux."

"I assume your mother sprang for the cost on account of the big party."

"Yep."

"Livia's pulling out all the stops."

"She even called earlier to tell me not to bring Matt."

Willa paused before saying, "So you're bringing Matt—right."

"I'm not going."

"Of course you're going. We're all going. I wouldn't miss this party for a heart attack."

I sighed in frustration. "No, Willa, I'm not attending, and neither are you."

"Why the hell not?"

"You can't be serious."

"Sure I am. Look Greg, it'll be a hoot. Cicely even extended the invitation personally, remember? Don't you want to see the freak show? Bring Matt and piss off Livia…you always enjoy that."

"Willa, I don't want to go."

"But you're getting a new tux."

"Right."

"So you should go, for that if nothing else. Livia will spit nails if you don't show up."

"Look, I'm not going and I don't have time to debate my reasons right now. I'm busy."

I said good-bye.

❖

At one thirty, I called Jenna's office from my kitchen phone. She was out, but her assistant seemed happy to set up a meeting. We scheduled the appointment for later that afternoon, giving me a couple of hours to come up with an appropriate advertisement slogan. My first idea, *Honey Agency—discreet inquiries handled professionally*, might be misleading since discretion was not a strong point. *Private Eyes, a Honey of an Agency*, was a little too cute, but *Honey Agency, World's Greatest Detective*—was definitely false advertising. Unfortunately, honest approaches like *Honey Agency, we'll make a reasonable attempt before we give up* or *Honey Agency, if we can't find it, we're sorry*— didn't inspire much confidence.

I was still musing on the subject when I heard a muffled squeak coming from outside. I looked up to see a shadowy figure shoot past my kitchen window. Someone was scurrying along the walkway toward the big house. I sprinted to my back door in time to catch a glimpse of Larry Lawson's enormous butt as it squeezed through a gap in the magnolias.

I stared at the wafting foliage in confusion. I had no idea what Larry was doing on the property. It wasn't likely this was a social call. He didn't run in Mother's circle. The only connection I could think of was church. They were both members of Reverend Ray's congregation. Maybe he was here for some church activity, like embroidering scarlet letters or building a cross—it being a little late in the season for burning witches.

I checked the gate, and as I'd expected, the latch had been taped open. I followed the trail of broken limbs through the scrub. I heard panting. I stopped when I caught sight of Larry struggling to push through a tangle of vines about forty feet in front of me. I watched him struggle and move forward; when he finally broke through, he sprinted across the lawn toward the Lost Wind service entrance. From the shadows, I could see the kitchen door open, but I couldn't see who'd opened it. Larry gave a worried look back over a shoulder as he slipped inside. The door closed behind him.

I was contemplating my next move when the sprinkler system kicked on.

"Crap!"

I was soaking wet by the time I made it back to my place.

❖

I was captivated, watching Jenna as she spoke.

"You must tell me how you stay so slim, Willa."

"You're so sweet. Well, part of it is luck. Good genes, I guess."

"But your sister is a big girl, surely she has the same genes."

Jenna's face rested on a roll of fat that looked like an Elizabethan collar, and when she moved her chin, mesmerizing wavelets rippled outward.

Willa said, "Well, if you must know, I do have a method. Something I figured out years ago. As far as I'm concerned, there really is only one dieting rule to follow."

"Do tell, what's your secret?"

"Simple really. I just follow the rule religiously."

"What rule?"

"If it tastes good…spit it out."

The waves around Jenna's face intensified as she laughed. The three of us sat around a coffee table in Jenna's office. From the couch I turned to peruse the stunning view across the river and up Congress Avenue, all the way to the Capitol. I could tell Willa was itching to leave. She sat on the edge of her seat with one knee vibrating like an unbalanced spin cycle. She had a hair appointment in ten minutes and didn't want to be late.

Jenna smiled, and her cheeks ballooned out beyond her ears.

"Well, Greg, Willa tells me you're interested in a little free advertising for the Honey Agency."

"I think so. Lord knows I need to get the word out and try to drum up some business."

"You know, of course, *Austin Monthly* has a large circulation and it's mostly upper-class readers. I'm sure an advertisement will bring you clients. So, we'll get to your interview later this afternoon. First, though, we need to take a couple of pictures. My assistant, Mary, will talk with you about the advertisement."

"You want to take care of it all today?"

"Of course, it has to be today. Things move very quickly around here. We've already set aside space in this week's issue for our 'Children of the Rich' article."

"Since when did *Austin Monthly* put out weekly editions?"

"Greg darling, *Monthly* went weekly two years ago. It can be confusing, but the times, they are a changing."

"Okay," I replied lamely. I found the urgency ridiculous—but hey, what did I know about publishing?

Jenna leaned back and called to her assistant through an open doorway.

Mary bounded into the room as Willa said good-bye, crossing her heart in a mock promise to pick me up in an hour. Jenna's assistant handed me the relevant release documents and a pen. I signed without reading, too lazy to slog through the technical crap. I figured this was business between friends. No need to get bogged down in the legal mumbo jumbo.

Mary snatched up the forms before the ink dried and said, "Ready for a few quick pictures?"

"I guess." I didn't disguise my reluctance, but she ignored my lack of enthusiasm. Jenna waved us out the door. As I followed Mary along the hallway, I scanned the walls for a mirror. No luck, so I crossed my fingers and hoped I was having a good hair day.

Forty minutes later, I was seated in a plush leather settee across a glass-topped desk from Jenna. My sight was starting to return after the flash of the camera and there was a trace of makeup dusting the ridge of my nose. We joked around as I waited for the interviewer to arrive.

"Is your mother angry you're gay?"

"Can OJ carve a turkey?"

She giggled. "What do you want to tell me about her?"

"Mother?"

"Sure, you know how I love juicy gossip."

"Well…like any healthy seventy-year-old widow, she diddles the pool boy occasionally," I said, smiling.

Jenna smiled back. "Does she date?"

"I guess so but I don't think she's happy about it. At her age, it can be a little trying. She tells me the only thing separating the men from the dead is Viagra."

Jenna laughed. "Is she seeing anyone special?"

"You mean other than her gigolo?"

We both laughed. Who knew this would be so much fun?

"So your mother visits a gigolo?"

"Probably several, you know how it is with the idle rich. They like to sample the smorgasbord."

Jenna laughed again. I was a riot. "How do you feel about her paramours?"

"None of them are really my type."

More laughter. "Have you ever used one? I mean a rent boy, perhaps?"

"Me, never. I can't afford it."

"But you would if you had the money?"

"I'd do a lot of things if I had the money."

"Such as?"

"Such as move away from my mother, or better yet, pay for a psychiatrist to finally declare her insane and cart her off to the State Hospital where she belongs. But, sadly, I don't even have enough money to pay for this advertisement."

She giggled again, and I began to fidget.

"Is your mother in therapy?"

I ignored the question. "When do you expect the journalist?"

"What journalist?"

I looked at her still smiling. "The one conducting the interview. Just wondering when we're going to start? Time is money for a businessman, you know. I've got a few things to do this afternoon."

"Here I am."

"You mean you're doing the interview?"

"Yes."

"So when do we start?"

"We have started."

I swallowed hard. "But you haven't asked any interview questions."

"Of course I have."

I swallowed again. "You can't be serious?"

"As a heart attack."

"We were kidding around."

"Maybe *you* were kidding."

"But those things I said, I wasn't serious."

"Duly noted."

"And you can't print them."

"Sit back and watch me. You signed the release, remember?"

I glared at her, she glared back at me; she was better at glaring.

"Jenna, this just isn't fair. If I knew you were going to print any of those things I wouldn't have said them. Look, Mother does not have a gigolo or a pool boy. Well, she has a pool boy, but he's eighty-five with a beer belly and hair growing out of his ears. Definitely not her type."

"Do you have his name?"

I looked at her in disbelief. "You can't print this stuff, it's just not true."

"Of course it's true, everything is true. This is just the kind of insider information our readers have come to expect from the *Monthly* weekly."

I shook my head in disgust. I expected shoddy journalistic standards, but I didn't expect this. I said, "If you publish anything derogatory about my mother, she'll sue you."

"Let her try." Jenna pressed a button on her desk and said, "Did you get all that, Betty?"

A voice answered, "Every word, including the threat."

"Thanks." Jenna released the button. "So, I have the tape of our conversation and a signed release statement saying you agree to a recorded interview answering questions about your family. It also gives us the right to publish any of your words in an *Austin Monthly* piece. Legally, our bases are covered."

I slumped back into my seat, sighing. The more I replayed the scene, the more I wished I'd never agreed to the interview in the first place. Silently, I cursed Willa.

As if summoned by my thoughts, Willa slammed through the office door, screaming. Her face was blotchy and her shoes were scuffed, but the most amazing thing was her hair was on fire. Well, it would be more accurate to say it was smoking. I could see blackened singed spots and gaps where ashy bits of hair residue clung to her scalp like dust on a bowling ball.

"What the hell happened to you?"

"I will kill her. I will sew her ass shut and force-feed her laxatives. I will dip her in tar, roll her in feathers, and use her to clean chimneys."

I noticed Jenna reach into her purse and pull out her iPhone surreptitiously.

Willa said, "I will make her suffer and hurt and bleed and scream for mercy. She will lose her teeth and her hair and her fertility. She will sprout warts and pimples and tumors the size of a Mack truck."

Jenna tilted the phone toward Willa and I stepped in front of her to block an attempt to capture the moment in pictures.

I stood and wrapped my arm around Willa. She said, "I will hurt her, Greg…it just got personal."

It just *got personal?*

I shot a withering look at Jenna and bundled Willa's still-smoking form through the door. We reached the stairwell with Jenna in hot pursuit. Luckily, the stairs weren't a possibility for her, so we made it out to Willa's car before Jenna caught the elevator.

"Now, tell me what happened," I said.

She started the car, shaking her head. "I only have one thing to say." She turned to look directly at me. "If you're smart, you'll check your hair dryer for an incendiary device."

We pulled away from the curb.

CHAPTER TWELVE

The afternoon blazed with the heat of a blast furnace as I made my way up the hill toward Lost Wind. I was filled with a building sense of doom. Sweat painted dark rings under my arms and the scorching sun seemed to pour from the sky like molten lava.

But that was nothing compared to the heat I expected from Mother.

I needed to warn her about the interview, even though every fiber of my being seemed to be screaming at me to just run and hide. I knew it wouldn't matter to her that my comments were meant in jest or that I'd been lulled into a false sense of security. It wouldn't count that I didn't believe what I'd said. She would remind me I was a Honey, and as a Honey, I had obligations—chief among them the solemn duty not to sully the family name.

I'd failed at that obligation, and so I trudged up the hill hoping to lessen the impact with a heartfelt mea culpa.

I knocked once on the service door before entering. The anteroom was empty, so I trudged through a darkened corridor into the bowels of the mansion, my steps echoing on the granite floors. I climbed the stairway to the public space and found Chin outside the main gallery. He was carrying a clipboard followed by a guy with a six-foot fuchsia bow balanced across his shoulders.

The party decorators had arrived.

I asked Chin where I could find my mother. He directed me down the hallway. I slunk deeper into the huge edifice, nervously checking rooms. I found her directing workmen in the solarium.

"I told you no mirror ball, José, and for God's sake, move those tables, there's going to be dancing."

She spotted me, and I froze. Her icy stare seemed to suck the heat out of the room.

"Mother?"

"What happened this time?"

I'd forgotten she hadn't seen the new additions to my bruise collection.

I shrugged. "It's a guy thing." Lamely, I added, "You should see the other guy."

She smiled. "I'm sure his fists are very sore."

I smiled back.

She said, "Tell me what happened."

"I was knocked down by a bouncer at a strip club."

"My God, Greg, you're a Honey. What will people think?"

"That I'm manly?"

"That ship sailed a long time ago, dear."

My mother has a withering wit, but she is so well heeled that you have to pay attention to catch the sarcasm.

"I need to tell you something." My voice softened as I rocked back and forth in discomfort.

"I'm busy, Greg, can this wait?" She sounded irritated.

"Probably not."

She frowned and turned with her hands on her hips.

In a soft voice, I said, "I may have inadvertently made a few comments, completely in jest, mind you, that might be construed to be slightly derogatory…to a discerning audience. I was speaking to an *Austin Monthly* journalist at the time…and well, totally by accident… there could be an article coming out that might not shed the most attractive light on the family. This, of course, was all a mistake, but I wanted to mention it just in case you felt it necessary to check out the specifics and possibly call in a few favors."

Her face congealed like uncovered pudding left in the fridge. Her lips barely moved when she asked, "When?"

"Huh?"

"When did you speak with this journalist?"

"A couple of hours ago."

"And when is the article coming out?"

"Thursday."

"This Thursday?"

"Yes, day after tomorrow."

She looked at me again with her coldest stare and I felt my testicles retract.

"What exactly did you say?"

"I was joking."

"What did you say?"

"I didn't mean it."

"Tell me what you said." Her voice was calm and steady but had a rough edge—like the sound of the *Titanic* sliding along the iceberg.

"Um, well, that you enjoyed the presence of young men."

She raised one eyebrow.

"Well, more like you enjoy 'working' men."

The brow dropped.

"I may have used the term 'gigolo.'" I started to sweat. "And that you might be having an affair with your pool boy."

"Henri? An affair with Henri?"

I imagined the sound of rivets popping.

"Well—I didn't name him exactly."

"I see." Icy water began to flood the lower decks. "Is that all?"

"Um—there's a little more."

"What?"

"Not much."

"How much?"

I swallowed hard. "I may have maybe said that you're just the teeniest bit…insane." In my mind the ship tilted, bow upward. Lamely, I added, "Or words to that effect." I could feel my heart pounding. "It was meant as a joke…really."

"To which *Austin Monthly* journalist did you tell these horrible, slanderous things?"

"Jenna Bulldog."

The ship fractured and the bow slammed on the water as the stern headed to the bottom. Icy cold water engulfed me.

"I see." She turned back to her decorators.

I skulked out feeling like a crewmember who'd elbowed an old lady out of the way before heaving himself onto a rowboat.

❖

"So she said 'no one can tell I'm wearing makeup,' and I said 'maybe it would fool the blind,' and she said 'I try to keep it subtle,' and I said 'you should try harder,' and she said 'the trick is to use natural shades that blend,' and I said 'that color would only blend if you were a pumpkin,' and she said 'don't you like butter cream foundation,' and I said 'I prefer pier-and-beam foundations,' and she said..."

We were munching on convenience store burritos in Willa's car and watching Russ Buttons's gingerbread Victorian house, waiting to follow Billy Crenshaw on his nightly excursion. Willa took another bite of her burrito, washing it down with a slug of cola. She was wearing a stocking cap over the patchy remnants of her hair. Willa, being Willa, refused to let a little thing like cranial immolation keep her from an exciting outing with a private investigator.

"She said 'Eau de Plom is such an enticing aroma,' and I said 'I bet it draws flies,' and she said 'it only takes a hint,' and I said 'I wouldn't even give it a clue,' and she said 'it smells like fresh-cut flowers,' and I said 'I think it smells more like the body in the casket.'"

The lights went out in the main room, and Russ began to climb the staircase. Still standing in the kitchen, Billy looked nervous. I stuffed the rest of my burrito into my mouth.

"And she said 'don't you like it,' and I said 'it's very earthy,' and she said 'I like things natural,' and I said 'like cow dung or doggie poo, what's more natural than that,' and she said 'it's subtle, don't you think?' and I said 'like a gynecologist in a gas mask,' and she said..."

The side door opened, and Billy crept along the hedgerow. When the cab light came on in the green Mercedes, I stilled Willa's incessant chatter with a gesture.

"There he is."

"Oh."

"Now, remember, follow from a distance. We don't want him to know we're tailing him."

Willa wrapped the tag ends of her burrito and dropped the foil-covered morsel into her tote bag. The Mercedes backed out slowly, and she started the Honda. I was grateful for the air-conditioning as we idled for a few seconds, waiting as Billy's car rolled down the shadowy street. When he paused at the third stop sign, Willa popped her car into gear.

"I figured we should be armed tonight, especially after what happened last night."

I rolled my eyes.

"I brought this little ole thing since you were afraid of the .38." She stuck her hand inside her bag as we slowed for a stop sign. The Mercedes turned right, and I watched closely, following the path of its taillights through the trees.

"He's heading south toward campus. Pick up the pace, we don't want to lose contact." The tension in the air was making me uncomfortable, and I tried to hide the anxiety in my voice because I didn't want to set Willa off.

She was markedly unconcerned, pulling a shiny silver handgun out of her bag. She waved it around as we turned the corner.

"What do you think about this little fella? Sweet, huh. It's a J frame 642 snub-nose. The kind of gun you drop in your pocket for a quick run to the grocery store."

"Jesus, Willa!"

"It's light and barely packs enough of a punch to take down a debutante. Of course, that means you should aim for the head."

I pushed back against the car door and scrunched down, trying to reduce the chances of catching a stray bullet should Willa pull the trigger inadvertently.

"It's cute as a button and a real pleasure to shoot. I have one around the house all the time. You never know when you're gonna need to bag a possum. Just enough kick to let you know it went off."

"Put the gun away." I said this as slowly and calmly as I could manage with my testicles withdrawn into my abdominal cavity.

"Just hold it for a second, go on." She shoved it my direction, and I pivoted out of the way.

"Willa, I don't…Will you put that away?"

"If you'd just hold it, I'm sure you'd change your mind. It's such a sweet little pistol."

"I don't care how sweet it is, I said no guns!"

"But this is hardly a gun at all…well, not in Texas. Think of it more as a prop, a noise maker, something to chase off intruders."

"No guns, Willa."

"But—"

"No guns!"

"Okay, okay…chill, Honey. Jesus, no need to go all hormonal on me. It's just a puny little pistol, not like a bazooka or a Gatling gun." She turned onto Duval before adding, "*They're* in the trunk."

I rolled my eyes.

We followed Billy's Mercedes through the darkening streets. The road was a black ribbon trailing down the hill before angling across a bridge. Willa held the Honda back, staying close enough to keep him in sight. He veered left onto San Jacinto and entered the UT campus. We inched our way through the campus, crawling along at a snail's pace. We passed the stadium, and I watched the Mercedes weaving along the tree-lined street a few hundred feet in front of us. He followed the curve to Martin Luther King Boulevard and picked up speed going through the light. We trailed along, passing state buildings and parking garages before he turned west onto Enfield.

I said, "Looks like he's going back to Les Furieux Chat."

"Something weird is going on. I don't get it. Why would Russ Buttons's boyfriend spend time in a strip club? Guys don't frequent those places for the watery drinks and stale chips…am I missing something here? Gay guys aren't supposed to enjoy that sort of entertainment, right?"

"Personally, I find it hard to stifle the gag reflex while watching women strip."

"Exactly, so what the hell is Billy doing?"

"That, Willa dear, is what we've come to find out."

She turned the Honda onto Enfield, and we drove past the Capitol.

A few blocks later, the Mercedes pulled to a stop and parked directly in front of Les Furieux Chat. Billy trotted across the street and disappeared through the double glass doorway. Willa turned into the Starbucks lot at the corner.

"Now what?"

"Now we figure out how to get in there." I nodded toward the building.

"That's not going to be easy, especially now that they know us. No way are we getting past that bouncer again."

We sat in the car and surveyed the building. I could see a graveled access to a service driveway that cut south behind the building. "Let's try the back. Maybe there's a way in from the alley."

We scampered across the street. I led Willa around the side of the building. From the sidewalk, I could see the club's back entrance, a gunmetal gray door with *No Parking* painted in faded red letters across its surface. The door was positioned between a rusted chain-link fence and a Dumpster. With Willa keeping lookout from the alleyway, I picked my way carefully through the remnants of smashed bottles and strewn garbage. I took a deep breath and reached for the doorknob.

It was locked.

"Damn."

"Now what?" Willa hissed.

"Give me a minute."

My mind was whirling. *How are we going to get inside?* I scanned the wall, but it was made of concrete and cinderblocks, with no windows. The door was solid steel without external hinges. The lock was a brass double cylinder deadbolt. Short of liquefying my body and pouring myself through the keyhole, I didn't see a way inside. With building frustration, I crunched back across the lot, but before I got to Willa, we heard the sound of keys scraping in a lock.

I darted back to the building and crouched behind the door. It swung wide and I caught it before I was smashed against the wall, letting it drift slowly closed. The thumping sound of bass filled the night air. I peered through the gap and could make out someone's rear end wiggling through the portico. A Hispanic man in a greasy apron pivoted on the doorstep. Two bulky black plastic bags hung from his hands. He caught the swinging door with the side of his body, propping it open with a hip, and heaved the bags over the edge of the Dumpster one at a time. Then he turned and scurried back inside, oblivious to our presence. The door swung slowly shut behind him. I reached out and grabbed the handle before it latched, and grinned back at Willa.

"We're in," I whispered. The thumping music made my words inaudible. I held the door partially shut for a few seconds, giving the man time to get out of the way. Willa jogged across the lot and perched beside me.

I opened the door cautiously. Willa stepped through, and I followed with my head held high like I owned the place. My plan was to bluster if we came across anyone.

We made our way down a well-worn hallway to a passage leading across to the brightly lit kitchen. I could hear voices speaking Spanish and the clattering sounds of dishes. Off to the right, through an open door, we glimpsed a shadowy space. I could make out stacks of boxes and shelves of bottles. A large refrigerator door was centered in the far wall. Across an open area, light shined through the gap beneath yet another door. I led the way into the darkened room with Willa hot on my heels.

"Where do you think that leads?" She nodded toward the door.

"Not sure, maybe the room where we saw Billy last time—what do you think?"

She pulled back, eyeing the entrance, and I could tell she was trying to map out the layout of the building. "Could be. What now?"

"I guess we see what's in there…carefully."

I stepped forward, putting my hand on the knob. It turned slowly, and even though I felt it click, the booming music coming from the front of the building overrode the sound. I eased the door open and Willa squeezed beside me.

We peered through the crack into a bathroom.

"Damn."

"This is great, 'cause I really gotta pee," Willa said, elbowing me aside. She closed the door while I turned to examine the storage room.

It was mostly shelves of liquor bottles and supplies. I could see an open box containing plastic-wrapped stacks of cocktail napkins, a shelf of gallon-sized cans of Planters peanuts, and an open carton of plastic swizzle sticks used to stab lime slices and chunks of pineapple in tropical drinks. In the corner near the back, I found another door. It opened onto another dark corridor. I followed it, sneaking past a pair of swinging doors leading in the direction of the kitchen. At the end of the corridor was yet another door. I slowly edged it partway open and peered into a darkened office space. Across a metal desktop, a smoke-tinted glass doorway was hung with mini-blinds. The blinds were open, and I could see into the bar. Lights from the stage illuminated the floorshow, where two statuesque dancers humped in time to the music.

I thought about entering the office but held back when I caught sight of the same bald man from the night before approaching through the bar. He pulled a set of keys from his pocket as he approached, and

I backed into the hallway as stealthily as I could, leaving the door slightly ajar. I heard the office door swing open and watched through the crack as he flipped the light on. Milton Buttons walked in behind him. Milton was dressed in a white nurse's uniform and entered the room swinging his hips in a parody of womanhood.

The bald man sat at the desk. He began rummaging through a file cabinet.

"It's in here somewhere. I'll kill the bastard if he's trying to pull something on me."

"He's not, Rocco, would you relax? You'll get your money. The guy's flipping out, he's so afraid. You just need to give him a little time."

"That's not the way I work. You know that. I take care of assholes who don't pay their bills."

Willa appeared at the end of the hallway. I held my finger to my lips. She tiptoed to my side.

"Look," Milton said. "It's your call. I'm just saying sometimes it's smarter to go along to get along. If you drop the guy now, we may never have a chance for this big a score again. If we follow through with the plan, you'll get what you want. In the end, it's a smarter play."

"Yeah, and how do we know this is gonna work? What if he doesn't get us in…then what?"

"Would you take a look at him, for Christ's sake? He's about to toss his cookies, he's so scared, and yet he's still out there. Why would he do that?"

"What the fuck do I care?"

"I'll tell you why. Only one reason, he's trying to protect his boyfriend."

"So he's scared. Doesn't mean I trust him. If this doesn't come off big, somebody is going to pay."

"You'll see. It's gonna be big, way bigger than the punk-ass 10K he owes you. He'll get us in, and we know we've already got our ace in the hole on the inside. For sure half the money in Austin will be there. Those old broads will be wearing the crown jewels. From what I hear the place is full of art, they say the silverware alone is worth more than Switzerland."

"That's not what I'm interested in."

"I know, but I'm just saying. They're gonna be rich, and that means they're gonna be traveling in style."

Rocco squinted at Milton skeptically. "Getting in is one thing. Getting out is another."

"We'll get out, the boys will make sure of that."

"Yeah, but you listen to me, Peaches—if we don't get in, if he tries to fuck with us…"

"He won't. Relax, will ya? Come Monday, you'll be lying on a Cabo beach sipping beers and getting your wang waxed by a Mexican broad."

Willa elbowed me in the side. When I looked down at her she nodded back up the corridor. A couple of the dancers stepped into the hallway and began to stretch. One flung a foot up to the doorknob and was leaning forward like a ballerina at the barre. She wore a cowboy hat, holster, leather vest, and leather chaps, but no shirt or bra. The other was rolling her shoulders and shaking out her legs. She had enormous, surgically enhanced breasts and was dressed in a feather headdress. She was wearing a long, straight black wig.

We turned away from the door just as the cowgirl yelled, "Hey, what the fuck are you lookin' at? Customers ain't allowed back here!"

I nudged the door shut with my foot. Willa looked at the women, her eyes full of fear. In a passable Mexican accent she said, "Eeem looking for *mi hermano* José. He wash deeshes *y* mamá, she say eeemagracion, they coming."

The cowgirl glared, but Cher smiled and said, "There's a bunch of Mexican guys in the kitchen, honey. It's that way."

"Muchas gracias," Willa mumbled. We hurried down the hallway and turned through the storeroom doorway. We scrambled out the back door.

Back in the alleyway, still breathing hard, I said, "What the hell was that in the office?"

"No idea."

"It sounded like they're planning some kind of a hold-up or drug deal."

"You think Billy's part of it?"

"Maybe. What do you think we should do?" I asked.

"Hey, this is your party, what do you want to do?"

I squinted at her in the dark. "I don't know—I'm not even sure I heard right. Do you really think Milton is mixed up in something illegal? And what about the guy they were talking about, could that be Billy?"

"No idea."

We heard the sound of a car engine starting and crept back around the edge of the building in time to see Billy's Mercedes back into the street. He angled onto Guadalupe, and I caught a quick glimpse of his face. He looked worried. Obviously Milton was mixed up in something illegal. Probably Billy too—but that was just a guess. My mind flashed to the image of Milton in a nurse's uniform, and I remembered the nurse Billy was sitting with last night. Okay, so Billy might have been meeting with Milton at the strip club. I couldn't quite shake the feeling a pattern was coalescing and I just couldn't see it...yet.

As we walked back to the Honda, Willa started talking. "Didn't you think it was weird to hear Russ Buttons's brother try to sound tough?"

"I guess so."

"Reminds me of the time Wally Proust tried to convince me he was a gangster. You remember Wally, don't you? Pasty and pudgy as the Pillsbury Doughboy, but with a wicked smile and great hands, sexy as hell if you could get past the urge to brush him with butter and toss him in an oven. He wanted me to believe he was dangerous, so he tried to talk all street like he was gonna roll up on someone and cap their ass. It was pretty silly because Wally worked in the lingerie department at Dillard's and the closest he'd ever come to a street fight was the pre-Christmas white sale."

❖

"She said 'I don't know why he rejected my article,' and I said 'you call that an article? I've read better compositions written in crayon,' and she said 'but literature is my strong point,' and I said 'you need to exercise more,' and she said 'whatever do you mean,' and I said 'well, your spelling is atrocious, your grammar is incomprehensible, your word choice is sketchy, and your logic is so shaky it has palsy.'"

Fear sparked Willa's incessant prattle to new heights as we drove through the sparse nighttime traffic. I could feel a headache building.

I brooded over what we'd just witnessed. I was feeling anxious and a little queasy as Willa sped over the rolling hills.

"So she said 'but I love to write,' and I said 'but does anyone want to read what you write,' and she said 'what are you trying to say,' and I said 'that you're a lousy writer,' and she said 'you think I should change my profession,' and I said 'me and everyone who's ever read your stuff,' and she said 'dang, Willa, that's harsh,' and I said 'a good friend will tell you the truth,' and she said 'well, you know my talents, what profession do you suggest,' and I said 'can you dig a ditch,' and she said—"

"Willa, stop! Please stop."

She looked over at me.

"I've got a headache and I need to concentrate."

"Concentrate on what?"

"What we just saw. What it means. What we're going to do."

She glanced back at the road. "Do? What do you mean? I'm taking you home and then I'm heading out for a late date with Wilson Blake. You remember Wilson, don't you? He's the one that snorts when he laughs and occasionally passes gas on the sly, but he's got lots of money and a nice smile. I'm not sure if there's a future in it, but he's good for a quick roll in the hay if you don't mind a clumsy lover and can stay upwind."

"Not that, I mean what are we going to do about what we just heard? What about Milton Buttons and their plan?" I gestured behind us in the general direction of the strip club.

"Jesus, Honey, that's simple. Nothing. We do nothing. It's not like we saw a crime. We have bupkis to report. And even if we did, we still couldn't go to the police. We snuck in there, remember? That's trespassing. What do we really know anyway? They just talked in vague terms about some stuff that may have sounded a little sketchy. For all we know, they were teasing each other or rehearsing a scene from a play or trying to impress someone with big talk. Right?"

"I guess so."

"It's nothing. Really. Just let it go."

"You're probably right."

"Of course I'm right. Besides, Wilson is picking me up in twenty minutes and we need to hurry if we're going to have time for a little ham-fisted romance in the backseat of his car."

I sat back sighing and Willa added, "This time I'm gonna leave the window down."

Willa dropped me at the curb and I climbed the steps to my gate with uncertainty still rumbling in the pit of my stomach.

Or maybe it was just a dodgy convenience store burrito.

CHAPTER THIRTEEN

I arrived at my office the next day full of vim and vigor. Well—full of vigor. I'm pretty sure Matt rinsed most of my vim down the drain in his morning shower. The cat greeted me at the door to my office, standing to stretch before glancing in my direction and hacking up a two-inch hairball at my feet. I watched as he calmly strolled through the threshold, his tail twitching as proudly as if he'd just delivered a bouquet of roses.

I picked up the gruesome pile with my hand stuck inside a plastic sandwich baggie and spent the next ten minutes on my knees scrubbing the hallway carpet. After washing up, I paused to scrutinize the unsavory image staring back at me in the bathroom mirror. The ring of bruises around my right eye was just turning green at the edges. I held out hope that it would fade by the weekend, but the shiner surrounding my left eye was still a puffy mass of blue. I scowled at myself for good measure and sat down at my computer to check my e-mail.

There were twenty-two unread messages in my in-box. The first one informed me I was the lucky recipient of an offer to help a Nigerian prince recover 4.3 billion dollars from his investment accounts in American banks. As a token of his appreciation I would receive 10 million dollars. All I had to do was click the link, enter my credit card information, and send $123.44 to pay a small "banking transfer" fee.

I declined the offer.

The next three messages were companies selling gray-market Viagra and herb-based male-enhancement products. I came across a penis enlargement advertisement I read word for word, considering my options carefully before finally deciding my penis, while nothing to write home about, was adequately sized for my current needs.

The office phone rang as I read a proposition to meet "hot chicks" ready to "service" my every need. Boy, were *they* barking up the wrong tree.

"Honey Investigative Agency, when you need a dick, and you're not too picky."

"Very funny." It was Russ Buttons.

"What's up, Mr. Buttons?"

"What do you mean 'what's up?' I'll tell you what's up. I'm about to go crazy worrying about Billy, that's what's up. We didn't have sex again yesterday. That's three days in a row. Where did he go last night? Did he meet that woman again? Is he sleeping with her?" His voice was high and reedy.

"First, you need to settle down. Following someone without being discovered is a subtle art, and it can take a while to get the whole picture." In reality, I was clueless about to the subtle art of successful stalking, but didn't think admitting that would instill confidence. I added, "Look, all I can tell you right now is Billy went back to the strip club."

"What about the nurse?"

"I didn't see her." I flashed back to Milton in his nurse outfit and realized I wasn't, strictly speaking, telling a lie. Milton, despite wearing dresses and makeup, was most decidedly not a "her."

"What does that mean? Was she there or not?"

His tone was bitchy and it didn't sit well with me. With as much control as I could muster, I said, "It means I didn't see her."

"Jesus, Greg, this is driving me crazy."

"No need to drive, it's a short walk from where you started."

He ignored the dig. "Billy's just not his usual self. He's sad all the time and it's breaking my heart. Something is very wrong." Whimpering sounds came through the receiver. I thought about Billy as I listened to Russ blow his nose. Milton and Rocco at the strip club had talked about someone who owed Rocco money. It seemed logical they were referring to Billy. I decided to ask a question.

"Tell me something, is Billy in financial trouble?"

There were sounds of sniffling and honking. Finally he said, "No, we're fine."

I waited because it felt like there was more to the story. After a moment of awkward silence he spoke again.

"I mean, the salon's making money and his flower shop is okay…I think…Why do you ask?"

"It's just a possibility. Sometimes money troubles can make people act in strange ways." I wasn't ready to tell Russ what I suspected.

"Lord, Honey, this is not a money thing. This is a love thing. My Bill is a sexual beast with raging hormones, and if his manly parts aren't serviced regularly, bad things happen. We haven't had sex in three days. If Billy's not stepping out on me yet, he will be soon. I need help. I need to know."

"Of course you do, but you've got to give me some help here, Russ. I'm flying in the dark. It feels like there's something more going on. If you have any additional information, I need to know it. If not, finding the truth will take some time. So you need to relax. All we know for sure is that Billy has a strange habit of attending a strip club."

"You think he's romantically involved with that woman, don't you."

"No. I just can't picture it. But you know him better than me. What do you think?"

He paused again in thought. "No, no, you're probably right. To put it gently, if Billy were a baseball player he would be wearing a mask and crouching behind the plate."

The sports analogy was so out of character that I almost missed his meaning. "You're telling me he's a bottom?"

"Does the pope shit in a palace? Are you planning to follow him again?"

"I guess so. Maybe tonight I'll figure something out."

He paused breathing heavily into the receiver and I waited for him to continue. Finally he said, "Your mother called and invited me to the party she's throwing this weekend."

Why would Mother want Russ Buttons at her soirée? It's true he did the hair of half the moneyed women in Austin, but that alone didn't explain the invitation.

I said, "Hope you have fun, because you won't be seeing me there."

"Why not?"

"Fear of guilt by association, I guess."

"I was wondering about Billy."

"What about him?"

"What do you think, would it be okay if we came together?"

"Sure, why not."

He was making sounds like he was about to hang up, but said, "Oh, and Honey…"

"Yeah?"

"Figure out what Billy's up to before I lose my mind."

"I will," I said, but I was pretty sure that chicken was already plucked.

❖

Later that afternoon, I started thinking about Milton Buttons. I printed out a blown-up copy of the picture I'd snapped at his apartment. The jumbo-sized falsies were clearly visible lying at his feet. In the picture, he looked groggy, with what was left of his hair flattened on one side like a deflated tire. He was definitely wearing a lacy robe and what looked like a woman's silky teddy underneath. I wasn't sure what it all meant, but I had a ton of questions for Milton.

He might also be able to enlighten me about Billy's trips to the strip club.

I was considering a quick trip back to Milton's apartment when the phone rang again.

"Honey's Investigative Agency, when just about any old dick will do."

"Greg, darling, how's that eye?" It was Gary Weiss.

"Not so lonely anymore."

"Huh?"

"It has a partner, long boring story. What's up, Gary?"

"I'm calling to let you know Bradford Collins finally filed his fraudulent worker's compensation claim and, thanks to you, the police just issued an arrest warrant for our little insurance cheat."

"So Bradford Collins is going to jail?"

"When they find him."

"What's that mean?"

"It means he's on the run."

"Bad move."

"Yes, and there's more. Texas Insurance Purveyors wants to use him in a mail-out. You know what I mean? Sort of a 'you try this and you go to jail' warning. Our clients are going to pass it on to their employees. The hope is it will deter would-be scammers."

"Sounds like a good idea."

"But…"

"But what?"

"But they need him in jail first. That's where you come in."

"Don't tell me…you want me to hunt down Bradford again."

"You got it. It could mean follow-up business, if you're up for it."

"Follow-up business is good—count me in."

"I can drop off a check at your office. When can you get started?"

"Hold on a minute—first tell me what I'm supposed to do when I find him."

"Oh, yeah…well, that's the easy part. APD assigned someone." I could hear him shuffling papers. "Let's see, Officer Ronnie Blake. He's your contact. When you find Bradford just let Officer Blake know. You got a pen? I'll give you his number."

I cringed at the name. I knew Ron Blake better than I was willing to admit. He was probably the most sexually frustrated gay guy at the Austin Police Department. The last I'd heard, he'd married a Texas cheerleader and had a couple of children. His sexual dissatisfaction and position at the APD made him dangerous to any openly out gay guy crossing his path. But I'd always tried to give Ronnie the benefit of the doubt, knowing he would never be happy until he figured out that a repressive childhood could be overcome.

I'd had the misfortune of having sex with Ronnie when we were freshmen at the University of Texas. The tryst started off hot and heavy in a parked car, but soon turned rough and awkward, and finally a little like a salmon sliming its roe. Afterward, he acted like I had leprosy and bolted from the car—which was a little tricky, seeing as how it was his car. I walked home. It took two weeks for the friction burns to heal.

For a long time afterward, whenever our paths would cross he treated me like a stranger—which was fine by me. But recently, things had been a little less abrupt, and chance encounters would bring on lingering stares.

Closeted or not, Officer Blake wanted another go-round.

I said, "Go ahead."

Gary gave me Ronnie's cell phone number and informed me Blake was expecting my call.

"Okay, I guess I can start as soon as you drop off the check. Any idea where I should look?"

"There's always Peggy Maloney's silicone-enhanced neighbor."

That made me shudder.

❖

Before I began looking for Bradford Collins, I decided to drop in for a little discussion with Milton Buttons. It took three bus transfers and a hot, sticky hike up the hill to get to Milton's condo. I arrived smelling as rangy as Oklahoma, but Milton's place was not the kind of spot where one worried about such things. I climbed the steps and pounded on his door.

Silence.

I pounded again.

The sound of a car starting up in the lot behind me drew my attention. When I turned to look, Cicely Wessley drove across the lot in a red BMW. She parked at the base of the stairs and I watched as she rolled down her window. She was wearing a beaded blouse. Her hair fell in casual ringlets around her face. When she stuck her head through the window the breeze caught the ringlets, and they danced around her face like a bunch of yo-yos.

"Greg? What a surprise."

"Uh, yeah." I'm not very articulate when I'm creeped out.

I found Cicely's presence unsettling. I wanted to ask where she'd come from, and wondered if she was stalking me. I realized I was jumping to conclusions. The circuitous route I'd taken from my office made it doubtful Cicely had tagged along.

We stared at each other until I said, "I'm working. What are you doing here?"

"Oh, nothing really. Just a little errand for my father."

"Here?"

She ignored my question. "It's such a surprise to run into you again. I've been thinking about our last encounter and wanted you to know that I really do hope you've decided to come to the party. Your mother seems to think it's going to be quite an occasion."

"I'm sure it will be. Still, I have so much work, you know."

I hadn't planned on dealing with pressure to attend that stupid party, not while sweating buckets on Milton Buttons's porch.

She looked at me, disappointed, and opened her mouth to speak but stopped herself. I wondered if she would try again. Instead, she said, "I guess I've waited around here long enough. I'll let you get on with your work. But if I don't see you at the party, I hope to see you again before I leave Austin."

She waved a gloved hand my direction and rolled up the BMW's window. I watched as she pulled out of the lot, and turned back to Milton's door. I rang the bell again. Still nothing. I silently cursed myself for not calling before leaving the office. I sat down on the steps to wait.

Forty uncomfortably hot minutes later, Billy Crenshaw's green Mercedes turned off South Lamar and climbed the hill to the parking lot. I hid behind the Dumpster and watched the car. It pulled into a slot in front of Milton's place, and Billy stepped out of the driver's side door. My jaw dropped as Brandon Collins crawled out of the backseat.

I couldn't believe my luck. I had just picked up a job to find Collins, and here he was. I speed-dialed Ronnie Blake on my iPhone.

"Officer Blake."

"Ronnie, it's Greg Honey."

Total silence. I pictured confusion playing across his face.

"Gary Weiss hired me to look for Bradford Collins. I'm supposed to call you when I find him, and he's here."

"What the hell?" He sounded pissed off.

"Bradford Collins? You have a warrant for his arrest. He's charged with filing a false insurance claim. I'm looking at him right now."

"Greg Honey? Why are you involved in this?"

"I told you. Gary hired me to track down Collins."

"Hired you?"

"Yeah, I'm a private investigator."

"Well, I'll be goddamned. I didn't think I'd ever hear from Greg Honey again. You still hanging out in the UT bathrooms?"

I barreled ahead, steering the conversation to the subject at hand. "Very funny, Ron. This is not the time. You need to listen. Like I said, Collins is here right now—you want the address?"

"Where have you been all this time?"

He was treating this like it was a social call.

"Look, we can catch up later. I think you better hurry if you want to grab this guy. They've got a car and I don't know how long they'll stick around."

I gave him the address and asked him to hurry. He told me he was on his way.

When I turned back to stare at the porch, Milton and friends were going through the door. I moved around the Dumpster so I could follow their shadowy movement through the front window. I was looking for a better spot to hide when I glimpsed sunshine reflecting off something shiny in the back of Billy's car. As stealthily as I could manage, I edged my way through the lot, keeping low and trying to listen for the sound of a slamming door, or footsteps. I crouched down beside the Mercedes and raised my head up slowly, peering into the backseat. Microphones and a small set of speakers were piled on the seat, next to a couple of pistols.

I ducked at the creaking of the condo door. Crawling away quickly, I heard Milton's voice.

"Be careful with that, will ya?"

Scampering behind a row of parked cars, I squatted low, edging my way across the lot toward a small copse of trees. Hidden in the foliage, I turned back, warily raising my head above the brush. Milton was walking down the steps carrying a massive sequined dress draped across his outstretched arms. Behind him, Bradford held two Styrofoam heads wearing wigs, and Billy struggled under the weight of an enormous makeup bag, its strap looped over a shoulder. Milton waited while Billy unlocked the trunk and stowed the makeup bag, carefully laying the dress on top.

Milton said, "Look, this is it, Billy. As far as he's concerned, you've done your bit, we got the job. You're done. Just keep your mouth shut and everything will turn out right."

"So it's over? I don't have to pay him back?"

Bradford said, "One thing about Rocco, he keeps his word. He *always* keeps his word. But that don't mean he's a nice guy. I wouldn't want to be you if he finds out that you've been telling anyone anything."

Milton said, "Forget about that crap, Bradford. Billy's not a rat. Right, Billy? You have people in your life you don't want to get hurt."

Fear flashed in Billy's eyes as he said, "No one will hear about this from me. My lips are sealed."

"One way or the other," Bradford said as he squeezed into the backseat with the wigs. Both doors slammed shut, and the Mercedes pulled out of the lot.

I watched them turn north on Lamar and disappear into traffic. I climbed out of the bushes. Billy had been uncomfortable, and Milton and Bradford were warning him about consequences if he spoke to anyone about something. Whatever they were into, I was pretty sure it wasn't legal. I was still mulling over possibilities when Ronnie Blake's police car drove up the hill.

"You missed them—they just left."

He looked at me through the car's window and said, "You want to tell me about this?"

So I told him what I saw, describing the car and its occupants.

"What brought you all the way up here to this dump? It's not like your office is in the neighborhood."

"It's a long story. Basically, one of the guys, the guy that lives over there," I gestured toward the condo, "Milton Buttons, he's the brother of a client. I was asked to check up on him."

Discussing a client's case, even with a police officer, made me uncomfortable, so I glossed over the details. As I spoke, Ronnie's eyes trailed down my body and paused briefly at my crotch.

"Been a long time." He smiled.

I didn't know what to say, so I just stood there with a dumb look on my face trying to pretend I'd missed the turn of direction in the conversation. A week ago, I might have found this situation mildly erotic. But a lot had changed for me in a week. Now the idea of sex with a closeted cop seemed pathetic. Even if Matt and I hadn't found each other, and Ronnie and I had somehow managed to squeeze off a few rounds in the back of a cop car, so what? He'd still be a screwed-up homophobe trying to live his life both in and out of the closet. The only difference was, that way I'd be covered in spunk with my self-respect dangling in the wind.

I said, "Yeah, well, I guess we're done here."

Ronnie reached down to adjust himself and I looked away quickly, still feigning ignorance. He said, "You want to get in? We can talk in the car."

"Sorry, I've got to get back to work. Don't want to miss my bus."

"I could give you a ride."

When I looked back at him he had his zipper down and was trying to maneuver his penis free.

Christ!

"Ronnie, I'm in a relationship."

He looked at me. "And I've got a wife. Get in," he nodded toward the backseat, "I'll let you play with my gun."

"No thanks," I said, backing away from the car. "I'll call you if I run into Bradford," I yelled back at him as I pushed through the hedges.

I took a fleeting glance back as I started to follow a footpath down the hill. Ronnie had the passenger door open and his manliness stood proud as a flagpole in his lap.

❖

"So he said 'it's just that I don't think I like sex anymore,' and I said 'if you're saying sex is a pain in the ass, maybe you should roll over,' and he said 'it's not that, it's just that I no longer have any interest,' and I said 'have you considered a change?' and he said 'of what,' and I said 'species.'"

Willa was yammering at me on the phone. I had the receiver wedged against my ear with my shoulder. On the screen in front of me was a threatening e-mail. It was simple and to the point.

It said: *You will burn in hell.*

"So he said 'maybe I'm just tired,' and I said 'well, I certainly find you exhausting,' and he said 'I don't mean to burden you with my issues,' and I said 'then why the hell are you,' and he said 'it's just that I don't have anyone else to talk to,' and I said 'where do I sign up for that list,' and he said…"

I sighed, trying to ignore the prattle. Why was someone so angry at me? I'd obviously made an enemy. Someone was upset enough to send me vague threats and curses. It was getting on my nerves. I was a good guy—mostly—and certainly hadn't done anything intentionally to warrant this. I racked my brain, but the only person I could think of that I'd even offended was Mother.

Vague threats and curses were not her modus operandi.

So far, I'd ignored the threats expecting the nastiness would eventually end. I still held out hope the person behind these threats would grow up and see the error of his (or her) ways. But I was starting to suspect that that wasn't going to happen…at least, not soon.

Maybe I needed to push a few buttons of my own.

I hit Reply and typed in the following message:

I don't know who you are or what I may have done to upset you, but if you want to sit down and talk I'm available. I'm sure whatever this is about must be a misunderstanding. So if you want to meet, name a time and a place and I'll be there.

I clicked Send. Then I broke in to tell Willa what I'd done.

"Hey, Wil. I was checking my e-mail. Guess who I heard from."

"I don't know…Satan?"

Satan?

I pulled the receiver away from my ear and stared in disbelief. With a voice as dry as the Sahara Desert, I said, "No, Satan hasn't written recently…at least, I hope not."

I read the message to her.

"What the hell? That's the sicko who sent you the doll, right?"

"I certainly hope so. I believe more than one stalker is overkill. Don't you agree?"

"Probably. What the hell did you do to get this freak all stirred up?"

"Nothing, honest, at least nothing intentional. I have no idea who it is or what they want."

"That's easy—they want to scare the shit out of you. So what are you going to do?"

"I already did it—I replied with an offer to sit down and talk."

There was silence on the line. When she spoke again, her voice had softened. "You think that's a good idea? This guy is obviously not playing with a full deck. It could be dangerous."

"It's probably just someone who needs a little guidance."

"More likely it's someone who needs a little incarceration. Look, Honey, I know you have a tendency to give people the benefit of the doubt. You're a 'glass is half-full' guy, always seeing the good in situations. You're Pollyanna playing the glad game. It's part of what you are. Hell, I love that about you. But this is different. Whoever this guy is, he has serious issues. He's not Mr. Wilson upset Dennis ran through his roses, he's Joseph Mengele out to procure some twins for a few experiments. You don't send someone a voodoo doll with pins stuck through its crotch because you want to sit down and talk. He's trying to scare you."

"Why?"

"I don't know, could be trying to send you a message."

"What message?"

"I don't know…maybe it's not a message, maybe he's the next Jeffrey Dahmer, with an invitation to check out the barrel in his basement. The thing is, we don't know what he has in store for you, but it's probably not an invitation to tea."

Willa had a point. Perhaps it was dangerous to try to reason with this guy. On the other hand, what else was I to do? I was getting tired of people breaking into my house, leaving threats on my phone and nasty notes in my mailbox. I said, "I'm doing this, Willa. Whoever it is will either back off or kill me. Either way, the messages will stop. This person doesn't know me, at least not the real me. When they do, they'll see I don't deserve this kind of treatment. I'm not afraid."

It was all bluster. In truth, I was terrified and the situation was setting off images from childhood of scary things in my closet. But maybe I was worrying for nothing. Maybe he wouldn't respond, maybe my offer would soften his view and bring him around.

Yeah, and maybe the Vatican would open an abortion clinic.

CHAPTER FOURTEEN

On Thursday morning the weekly edition of *Austin Monthly* hit the stands and my phone began to ring. First to call was Russ Buttons.

"My God, Honey, did you really say all those nasty things about your mother?"

"It was a mistake."

"You compared her to OJ, for Christ's sake."

"That was taken out of context."

"And you told the world she was sleeping with her pool boy. All of Pemberton's chuckling over that one."

"Very funny."

"I particularly liked the part where you said you were afraid she was trying to have you killed because you have sex with boys. That had a nice spin to it, sort of Cosa Nostra meets WeHo."

"I didn't say that."

"And then there was the part about committing Livia to a mental institution. Pure gold."

I rolled my eyes, thinking, *At least the article publicly outed me.* That meant no more pressure from Mother to find a fertile woman with breeding and childbearing hips to marry.

Russ asked, "Does she really have a gigolo?"

"Did you need something in particular, Mr. Buttons, or did you just call to harass me?"

"Mostly the latter, but I did want to tell you that Billy and I had sex last night. Finally."

"Uh…congratulations?" I wasn't sure what he expected me to say.

"Thanks, the point is, whatever was troubling him appears to be over. We talked, well sort of, and he promised he was done sneaking out alone at night. I really think he's pulled himself together. When you asked about our finances, you were right on the money. No pun intended. His flower shop was in more trouble than I realized. But that's over now. Did you know your mother asked him to do the place settings for her party? A big job for sure, and it will lead to more work for him. It already has. When he heard Billy was doing Livia's flowers, the manager of Chez Sneeze called. Now they're talking about Billy's shop delivering flowers to the restaurant on a weekly basis."

The mention of Mother's party caused an image of her face to flash in my mind and I knew that she would soon be reading the article. Perhaps she was perusing Jenna's purple prose even as Russ blathered on. I made a mental note to get a copy and prepare myself for the inevitable onslaught from Lost Wind.

I said, "I'm glad to hear things have worked out for you, Russ. Did Billy mention what he was doing at the strip club?"

"Of course not."

"Did you ask?"

"Honey, Honey, Honey…he doesn't know I know about that, remember? Why would I bring it up now? Here's a little relationship advice you can take to the bank…hold on to dark little secrets, they come in handy when you're divvying up assets in front of a judge."

I wondered briefly about the wisdom of planning for a divorce while in a relationship, and Russ filled the void with a question. "How's your mother taking all this crap?"

I felt my stomach muscles contract. "I haven't spoken with her yet."

"Of course you haven't, and boy, is that gonna be a fun conversation. Wish I could be a fly on the wall. Anyway, Billy is back."

"And?"

"And all is well with my household."

"And?"

"And I really don't think following him is necessary."

"So you're asking me to give up on the investigation?"

"Exactly. You can send me your last bill and we'll call it a success."

I told him I would, and hung up. The phone rang before my hand was off the receiver. It was Willa.

"Jesus, Honey, I hope Livia's got room for a large pet 'cause she's gonna have a cow when she reads Jenna's article. Who would have guessed our sweet roly-poly high school friend would grow up to be a nasty, mean, backstabbing bitch. You have to admire Jenna's spunk, though. All of West Austin is reading her exposé right about now. Can't you just picture the blue-haired Pemberton ladies laughing and snorting and squealing like pigs hoping to wallow in this juicy glop of trash? *Austin Monthly* will sell a ton of copies. I assume you didn't mean to say all those things, right? I know Livia's a pain in the ass, but she's still better than my mom. She comes off sounding a little like Catherine the Great, without the horse in a sling, of course."

"Christ!"

"Did you really say she was porking her pool boy?"

"It wasn't my fault. I was joking."

"About Livia's love life?"

"It was taken out of context. I was set up, and you're to blame."

"Me?"

"Yes, *you*. You're the one that suggested I place the ad. You pressured me into doing the interview. The whole thing was your idea. You set up the meeting with Jenna. You brought me there and left me all alone in front of that sneaky woman. You're the reason for this mess."

"True, I set it up and left you there, but how was I to know what Jenna had planned? And for the record, I didn't think I had to tell you not to dump all over your mother in front of a reporter."

I sighed heavily.

"Look, it's probably not as bad as you think. Livia has dealt with this sort of thing before, remember when your father died?"

Dad's heart attack was precipitated by overexertion during a sexual encounter with a prostitute at a sleazy South Austin hotel. The details were fuzzy, but Willa had heard rumors involving feathers—or chickens—the details were never made clear. Mother weathered the storm with stoic resolve, throwing lots of money at various causes to build back goodwill and strengthen the Honey name. To all of our surprise, it had worked, sort of. Austin is the kind of place that allows for a few black sheep in the flock.

I said, "That's true, but this is different."

"Not really, it's just a little more public…Livia can deal with it. Have you seen the ad?"

"No, and I haven't read the article either."

"Oh, you need to read the article."

"I will."

"The ad's a little staid: *Honey's Detective Agency, professional services handled with discretion for discriminating clientele.* Doesn't have a lot of zip."

"I was aiming for the Junior League and West Austin customers. You know how those ladies can be, one shouldn't rattle their knickers."

"Well the ad didn't do that, but you can't say the same about the article. At least your picture was okay, if you ignore the swoopy bits of your hairdo, I mean."

"I need to get a copy, maybe you could bring me yours?"

"Sure, I'll drop by. Have you heard back from your stalker?"

"Nope, which is fine by me. My life is full of things to deal with today."

"I hear you there."

"Russ Buttons called, evidently they've talked and Billy is going to give up on his nightly forays. Russ is calling off the investigation."

"So no more nighttime jaunts to the strip club?"

"Guess not."

"I'm gonna miss that."

"Uh-huh."

"Did Russ tell you what Billy was doing there?"

"Nope, he doesn't have a clue."

"What do you think?"

"Well, he borrowed some money and couldn't pay it back. That much we know from what I overheard."

"At the strip club?"

"And at Milton's condo, I dropped by there yesterday. I overheard them talking about Rocco easing up on Billy's debt. I still haven't figured out the rest."

"Them, who's them?"

"Milton, Bradford, and Billy."

"What are they all doing hanging out together?"

"Not sure yet."

"Man, I want to know what's going on."

I agreed, but was reluctant to say so. I needed to think through my next move, and at this point, I wasn't sure I wanted Willa along for the ride. I changed the subject. "How's your head?"

"I've had better hair days. I'm gonna shave it when the blisters go down and the burns heal a little."

I cringed at the thought of shaving tender scalp and said, "Don't you think it's time to let go of this little vendetta with Lola?"

"Not quite."

"Why not?"

"It's my turn."

"It will always be someone's turn."

"But she set my head on fire."

"And you put Nair in her shampoo."

"Yeah, after she drugged me and took my underwear."

"Which was after you slept with her husband."

"Who was my boyfriend until she took him."

"Willa…this will go on forever."

"Not forever—only until one of us dies. I'm planning on it being her."

I sighed. There's no reasoning with the truly delusional.

I needed to get back to work, so I gently nudged Willa off the line. Before hanging up, she told me she was on her way over to drop off her *Austin Monthly*.

The office phone rang again as soon as I hung up. I let it roll to my answering machine, figuring I'd screen out the people wanting to talk about the article. I could call back potential clients and important callers later.

I looked around the office, and it felt suddenly claustrophobic. I needed to get out of there. On a whim, I decided to try to find Bradford Collins again. I only had one lead, so I'd have to convince Willa to take me back to Milton Buttons's apartment. As I considered what I would say to Milton, my iPhone buzzed, telling me e-mail had been sent to my private account. It was the reply I'd been dreading. My stalker wanted to meet at Chez Sneeze at six thirty.

Che' Sneeze was a restaurant in the hills of West Austin. A little on the pretentious side, with a baby grand piano played by the type of cheesy musician my mother's peer group preferred—think Wayne Newton crossed with Adam Sandler. Waiters dressed in black aprons served saucy food and Southern delicacies on brightly colored Fiestaware. Fried pickles were on the menu, and so was blackened redfish. The dessert case was impressive and the wine selection allowed patrons to splurge on pricy imports meant to impress their guests more with price than taste. My guess was they'd named the place during cedar season.

Six thirty would still be happy hour, and the restaurant would be full of people—always a good thing when you're planning to sit down with a potential psycho. I typed in a message agreeing to be there and clicked Send.

Willa walked in as I was working out how to ask her to drop me after our little jaunt to Milton's man cave.

"Here's the magazine." She tossed it on my desk. "You talk with Livia yet?"

"Nope, that joy is going to have to wait. First I need a ride."

"Where we going?"

"I thought you might want to come with me to see Milton Buttons again."

"What for?"

"Not entirely sure, but I want to ask him about Bradford."

❖

We pulled into Milton Buttons's parking lot. Willa parked the Honda next to a white Rambler. We hiked up the hill toward the condo. The place was pretty much deserted. The only other car in the lot was a school-bus-yellow Mazda Miata.

The air felt humid and sticky with leaden clouds skittering across the sky from the east. Rain was coming.

I was sweating like a pig as we neared the steps to Milton's porch. Willa asked, "So what's the plan?"

"We knock on the door."

"And then what?"

"Then I ask him if he knows where I can find Bradford Collins."

She grabbed my arm, pulling me to a stop, and glared at me. "Jesus, Honey, you don't really think that's going to work, do you?"

"Maybe, maybe not...but what else can we do?"

She leaned backward and peered around the building. "We could take a little peek in the window first. That wouldn't hurt, would it?"

I thought back to the last time Milton chased the two of us away by blasting buckshot in our direction and shook my head. *Of course* it could hurt—it could kill too.

"Not smart, Willa," I hissed, but she was already creeping along between the buildings. I dropped my head and followed, fairly certain I was making a mistake. Following Willa's lead was never a good idea.

A three-foot gap separated Milton's condo from the windowless wall of the next unit's garage. The hard-packed ground was strewn with empty beer cans and debris. I saw a couple of used condoms and a set of false teeth. The teeth smiled at me, half-buried in the muddy spot where water dripped beneath a window-mounted air conditioner.

Willa had her face pressed against the window's glass.

"No one in this room," she said, then quickly hurdled a garbage can on her way to the next window.

"Here either. Hold on, who's that?"

I scanned the area nervously. In the distance the white Rambler drove out of the parking lot. Otherwise, we were alone.

I was reluctant, having studied Texas law for my licensing exam. State penal code 42.1 made it illegal to intentionally or knowingly "enter on the property of another and for a lewd or unlawful purpose look into a dwelling on the property through any window or other opening in the dwelling." The same statute also made it illegal for a person to "expose his anus or genitals in a public place." Given the pronoun, evidently females were free to expose anything they chose in the great state of Texas. I took solace from the fact that my pants were on, shrugged in resignation, and stepped forward, shielding the window with a hand to look inside.

It was a bathroom. A ratty toothbrush sat sentinel in a coffee cup on a grimy porcelain sink. Mouthwash and deodorant competed with tweezers, nail files, and tubes of lipstick for space on the shelves above the toilet. I could see a bathtub that looked like it was growing mushrooms and a dust bunny the size of a squirrel in a corner.

Evidently, keeping a clean house was not one of Milton's priorities.

"Do you see him?"

"I don't see anyone."

"But he's there."

I looked closer. The walls were a sickly pink and streaked with black splotches that were probably toxic mold. The toilet bowl was dingy gray but thankfully empty, at least from my line of sight. A multicolored mat on the floor was frizzed with dust and sprinkled with dark, crinkly hair. Mold grew in the un-caulked gaps between the floor tile and the wall trim. Rust stains descended below the showerhead into the tub. I half expected a family of rats to scurry into view. This was not a very healthy environment, for sure, but there was still no one in sight.

"Where am I supposed to be looking?"

"Through the door."

A small patch of hallway was visible. More dust bunnies wafted in the breeze, and a filthy rag rug had been dropped atop the grimy tile floor. I could see grease stains where hands had smudged a light switch. Milton was definitely not a picky housekeeper. I said, "So?"

"Can you see the front room?"

I edged to the side to improve the angle, and the space came into view. Bradford Collins was sprawled across a Herculon easy chair. He was wearing a plaid shirt and ratty jeans with a hole in his crotch strategically placed so his business would hang free when he stood. He was strumming a guitar and I could just hear the soulful sound of gentle music. I stepped away from the window.

"Do you see him?" Willa hissed.

"Yes." I pulled out my iPhone.

"Is that your guy?"

"Yeah." I dialed Ronnie Blake's cell phone. He answered on the first ring.

"Officer Blake."

"Ronnie, Greg Honey. I found Bradford Collins again." I peeked through the window as we talked, trying to keep my voice low. Bradford had shoved forward in the chair and was packing the guitar into its case.

"What the fuck, you don't waste any time, do you?"

"No, and neither should you. I have no idea how long he's going to stick around, so hurry."

I told Ronnie we were at that same condo project as before and hung up. That's when Milton walked into view. He came from a part of the room I couldn't see and was dressed in a sparkly ball gown and cha-cha heels. His enormous falsies were tucked in place, but his unshaven face was free of makeup and his bald head was wigless. Willa was standing beside me, both of our heads just above the window ledge. We watched Bradford and Milton until Milton turned our direction, then ducked in unison.

"You think he saw us?" she whispered.

"Maybe."

We heard the sound of scuffling, and I was pretty sure they were about to leave in a hurry.

"Damn it, Willa, they're going to get away again."

"Maybe not. Give me your phone."

"What?"

"Give me your iPhone, quick. I've got an idea."

I looked at her, confused.

"Give it to me." She pointed to my pocket.

I pulled it out.

Willa snatched it and sprinted across the parking lot. I followed slowly, crouching along the sidewall, trying to stay out of view. I heard the front door slam as I neared the edge of the building and held back, watching Willa dive through the bushes on the far side of the lot. Milton waddled across the pavement faster than I thought possible for a big man in cha-cha heels, with Bradford lugging his guitar case in hot pursuit. When they reached the yellow Miata, Milton sat in the passenger seat. Bradford gave him the guitar and dashed around to the driver's side. The engine sprang to life, and the topless convertible zoomed across the parking lot. I stepped out of the gap between the buildings to try to see the license plate, but it was too late. I watched as they turned out the exit and followed the road down to South Lamar.

Willa's head popped up through the bushes and she pushed through the limbs to the lot. I walked across the space, shaking my head in frustration. She was covered in dust and dead leaves. A limb had snagged her stocking cap, jerking it askew. She bent over to dust herself off as I neared.

I said, "Damn, I didn't get the license, did you?"

"Nope, but we don't need it."

"Of course we do. How else are we going to catch up with them?"

"I tossed your cell phone in the side pocket of the car."

"Are you insane?" I looked at her with confusion. "Why the hell did you do that?"

"So we can track them."

It took a few seconds for my mind to engage, but my smile widened as I clued into her plan. Willa was pretty amazing. She could be a pain in the ass—noisy, nosy, crude, abrupt and impetuous—but she was also smart as a whip and a fast thinker. I'd almost forgotten that she'd set up the Mobile Spy app on my iPad. Now we could follow the phone's location across a map of the city, and it would let us know where the Miata was in real time.

"I owe you one, Willa."

"You owe me a million, Honey—but who's counting?"

"Let's roll," I said, and we jogged to her car.

❖

My iPad was stowed at home, so we drove north on Lamar to Twelfth, looped under the bridge at Fifteenth Street, and climbed the hill next to the park. I used Willa's phone to call Ronnie as we drove past the parking lot, noting the irony that this was the location where the two of us had twiddled each other in a younger—and stupider—time.

I clicked the speakerphone icon so Willa could hear, and his response snapped through the connection loud and clear.

"Officer Blake."

"Ronnie, it's Greg."

"Where the hell are you?"

"Where are you?"

"Sitting in the parking lot on South Lamar, same place where I was supposed to meet you and take Bradford Collins into custody." His voice was rough and angry.

"Change of plans. Bradford left."

"Well, that's just great! Thanks for dragging me all the way out here for nothing."

His frustration was to be expected. but I didn't appreciate it. It wasn't *my* fault he'd missed Bradford twice now.

I said, "Ron, they drove off in a hurry. What was I supposed to do, throw my body in front of the car?"

"Hell, yes, if that's what it takes to keep him around until I get here. I'm starting to wonder if you're wasting my time on purpose. That's interfering with a police investigation, a big mistake, *big* mistake."

His attitude might be frustrating me, but it was really ticking off Willa. Her upper lip curled, and she clenched her fists.

I didn't want to agitate him any more than necessary, so I kept my voice light and easy. "How am I interfering, Ron? I'm trying to help."

"You need to back off, Greg. This is a police matter."

Of course he was right, but he was also wrong—my client had a legitimate concern Bradford might escape justice.

Willa leaned over and yelled at the phone. "Look here, buddy, if you were doing your job in the first place, Bradford would already be in jail and I wouldn't be scratched and itchy. You need to put your wee little dick back in your pants and climb down off that mountain of impotence and insecurity. Just do your job, jackass."

I was stunned into silence. The blood slowly drained from Willa's cheeks.

Ronnie's voice crackled through the speaker. "Who the hell are you? Greg, who the hell was that?"

I shot Willa a warning look and held up a hand.

"She's a friend of mine with a quick temper and an odd sense of humor. Look…" I filled him in on our tracking plan and told him I hoped to know where Bradford was in a few minutes. He was dubious, but agreed to stay available.

❖

When we arrived at Niles Road, Willa parked a few slots down from the carriage house. The street traffic was heavy and the curb lined with cars. Someone must have been throwing a party. An uneasy awareness percolated inside me, but I didn't know what was making me so edgy.

For once, my gated entrance was locked. I used my key and ushered Willa through the passageway. As we made our way up the sidewalk, she began firing off questions fast and furious.

"Is your iPad charged? So say we locate Bradford and Milton, then what? You going to call that jerk of a cop again or are we going to take him down ourselves? If we go get him, can I use a gun? And what about Milton? What's up with that? What do you make of a plus-sized drag queen hanging out with a scam artist? Still can't believe he's Russ's brother. You think he was adopted?"

"Jesus, Wil—you planning to write a book?"

"Just asking."

"You know everything I know. First things first, and the first thing is—find the car."

She was as nervous as I was. I picked a couple of leaves from her stocking cap as we climbed the steps to my back door. I found my iPad lying on top of my bed. I clicked on the tracking app, initiated our search, and took advantage of the momentary delay to pick her brain. "What I'm most confused about is the strip club connection. What do you think is going on over there?"

"You mean other than a bunch of dirty old men hoping to provide gynecological exams?"

I nodded.

"Don't know, but my instinct tells me it's not on the up-and-up. It sure looks like Milton is mixed up in a criminal mess. We already know Bradford operates on the shady side of the law. I just hope Billy's not too involved, criminally, I mean. It would kill Russ if he went to jail."

"Why do you say that?"

"It would take Billy about three minutes to become someone's prison bitch and Russ would die of jealousy."

"I see."

"You really think Billy's doing something illegal?"

"No. I've known him a while and he's just not the type. He has no record—I checked, and outside of repeatedly breaking the old sodomy law, it's doubtful he's ever done anything illegal. It's pretty obvious he owes some money to Rocco. I think that's the level of his association."

"Yeah, and Milton got Rocco to back off on that. Not sure I follow the rest, though."

"Me, either," I admitted. "Still, I have the feeling there's a lot more to this story."

The app pinged and Willa crowded closer. A map appeared on the iPad screen with a little blue dot indicating the phone's position. It floated above Sixth and Lamar. When I zoomed in and switched to the satellite image, the dot was sitting in the parking lot of the Whole Foods flagship store.

"You figure they're shopping for organic produce?"

"I think a guy built like a linebacker, wearing a sparkly dress and cha-cha heels, would be reluctant to shop in a crowded grocery store."

"This is Austin, Honey, that wouldn't raise an eyebrow."

As we watched, the little blue dot began to move across the screen.

"Looks like they're leaving. Maybe they just stopped by to use the bathroom."

Nerves were making Willa positively vibrate beside me. She said, "Now what do we do?"

I shrugged.

Willa said, "Well, the way I see it, we've got two choices, go after them or call that nasty cop."

Her tone let me know that was the last thing she wanted to do. I agreed. I didn't want to risk sending him on yet another wild goose chase. Still, I saw a technical problem with the other option.

"Following's going to be trouble. This iPad's not set up to track from the phone system. If it moves outside the three-hundred-foot limit of my wireless transmitter, it loses the signal."

Willa frowned, "You had to buy the cheap option, didn't you, Honey? You are one tight-fisted bastard."

"Frugal, Willa, I'm frugal."

"No, Greg, you're cheap. You realize if you had sprung for the cellular option we'd be on their tail right now. As it is, the only thing to do is sit tight and see where they go."

I shrugged and we both watched the blue dot head north on Lamar. When it turned west on Twelfth Street, Willa said, "Looks like they're coming this way."

The dot turned north again and headed under the Fifteenth Street Bridge. It followed the road alongside Pease Park and slowed to a stop a couple blocks away. I wasn't sure how accurate the GPS was, but the dot seemed to be resting a few feet off the road in a boggy thicket where a small stand of trees separated the street traffic from a creekside hike-and-bike trail.

I said, "What do you think they're doing?"

"Looks like they pulled off the road."

"Maybe they're waiting or talking or something."

Willa said, "I'm going to go see."

She slammed through my back door before I could stop her. I heard the gate clang shut. I crossed my fingers and prayed she would be careful before turning back to the screen. The blue dot still hovered over the thicket.

After a few minutes, Willa's phone rang. I picked it up. My picture was showing. I answered cautiously, "Willa Jensen's phone."

"It's me."

"Willa?"

"Yeah, I've got your phone."

"What happened?"

"They tossed it in the park."

"Damn."

"Yeah, damn. They must have found it in the side pocket of the Miata. Now what?"

"Beats the hell out of me. Come back and we'll talk."

I heard her sigh in frustration before she hung up.

I met Willa at the gate. She was hot and cranky as she handed me the phone. Once again, we trudged up the walk to the gatehouse. We were both grateful for the cool air inside. I called Ronnie Blake to tell him what happened. He was grumpy and something else—something I couldn't quite put my finger on.

When I hung up, Willa said, "Stupid, stupid, stupid!"

"What?"

"I should have thought about it."

"What?"

"I should have muted the bell on your phone. The call log lists an incoming call six minutes ago. My guess is the ring tipped them off. That's why they dumped it."

I looked at the log. It was Mother's number, probably calling about the article. She didn't leave a message. She didn't have to.

Willa said, "What a waste of time."

"It was a good idea, Wil. Next time we'll know better."

"So you're going to track these guys again?"

"I intend to keep looking until Bradford is behind bars. I'm a professional, you know."

"Right. For some unknown reason, you're getting paid for this."

I wasn't sure how to take that.

❖

It was five thirty by the time I convinced Willa I didn't need her help with my upcoming meeting. Her incessant chatter had been driving me crazy, and the peaceful hush after she left was heavenly. I sat at my kitchen table, soaking in the blessed silence until it was time to get ready. I changed into a clean T-shirt and jeans and took a quick peek in the bathroom mirror. The bruises around my eyes were fading. I sneered and turned sideways, using a handheld mirror to catch the view from different angles.

When I'd finished admiring myself, I tossed my dirty clothes into an overflowing hamper, grabbed my cell phone, and pushed through the gate. I hurried down the street, and arrived just in time to catch the number 6 north.

I got off at Balcones Drive and Mopac, three blocks from Chez Sneeze. I hiked up the hill and waited on the light at the crosswalk as rush-hour traffic pumped noxious fumes into the sticky afternoon haze. I choked my way across the street. By the time I entered the restaurant I was hacking up mucus like a three-pack-a-day smoker and sweat had drawn a dark line down the center of my chest. I could feel my formerly fresh cotton T-shirt sticking to my back.

The restaurant was about halfway filled with office workers looking to unwind at happy hour. I scanned the dining room, taking notice of each man sitting alone. All but two were elderly. One of the others was in a wheelchair, and the last was so drunk he was having difficulty balancing on a bar stool. I took heart. I was hoping to avoid trouble, and this spot seemed like a safe place to share a little quality time with a potential psychopath.

No one seemed particularly interested in my presence, so I stepped up to the hostess stand. A flustered-looking woman called a waitress, who took me to a table by the window. I sat with my back to the wall so I could watch the door, hoping to spot the caller before he spotted me. I wanted a beer; instead I asked for iced tea, fearing alcohol might slow my reaction time.

The glorious air-conditioning began to wick sweat from my T-shirt as I blotted my forehead with a napkin. A celebration of sorts was going on at the next table, where a plump woman wearing a "Hi, I'm Sue!" name tag directed six inebriated ladies wearing party hats as they screeched a pitch-challenged version of the birthday song. At the far end of the table, I could see a prune-like creature under a bouquet of Mylar balloons squinting through thick lenses as she rearranged her dentures in anxious anticipation. In front of her burned a conflagration of candles stuck into the pale blue icing of an angel-food cake. When the song had finally, mercifully, been put to death, the birthday girl inhaled. When she blew, her dentures popped out of her mouth and bounced once on the tabletop before clattering across the floor to my feet.

That's when the door opened and Officer Blake walked in. He pushed his mirrored sunglasses to the top of his forehead and waved the hostess off. When he spotted me at the table, his sneer transformed into a grin he probably thought was sexy but made him look somewhat constipated. I was surprised to see him, but not shocked.

I'd always suspected Ronnie had a few screws loose.

I wrapped the dentures in a napkin and handed them to Sue, who returned them to the old lady. She gummed a toothless thank-you as Ronnie sat down next to me.

I stared at him in disgust.

"I'm sorry. I just wanted you to notice me," he said, a feigned look of contrition on his face.

"Let me get this straight. You threatened me for attention?"

"I made a mistake."

"You called me several times."

"I made several mistakes."

"You sent a threatening letter."

"I was confused."

"You broke into my house."

"That was a bad day."

"And left a voodoo doll."

"It was sort of a joke."

"It wasn't funny."

"Sorry."

"What is your problem?"

"I just wanted to get with you again, you know, like we did before."

"And you thought that was the way to do it?"

"Like I said, I was confused."

"You are troubled, deeply troubled."

"I know." He looked at me with sad eyes. "But I still want to get together."

"Ronnie, things have changed."

"Oh."

I wasn't sure if it was disappointment or anger on his face. I said, "And you're married—remember?"

"I was married then too," he said coldly.

"But I didn't know."

"Nothing has changed."

"Yes, it has. For one thing, I know you're married now."

"Does that really matter?"

"Yes, it matters! It matters to *me*."

"My marriage is over."

"I'm sorry to hear that."

"We're separated."

"I see. But that still doesn't make it right."

"Why not?"

"Because things are different for me now. I'm in a relationship."

"Oh."

He fidgeted in his seat until the waitress came by. He ordered a beer.

I said, "So, here's the thing, Ron, I don't know what you're trying to do—"

He interrupted. "Sex. I'm trying to have sex."

"Fine. Go have sex. There's a couple of bars on Fourth Street."

"With you. I want sex with you."

"Well, that's not going to happen."

"I'd settle for a blow job."

"Jesus, will you listen to yourself?"

"I'm just being honest."

"And here's my honest response: no way, José."

"Why not?"

"Hello? I'm in a relationship."

"I won't tell anyone. How about I give you a blow job?"

He read the disgust in my face and turned away.

And that's when Willa came stomping across the restaurant. She must have been hiding in the back. I watched, mystified, as she stepped to the table while fishing in her purse. I started to speak, but her Taser flashed briefly and she zapped Ronnie before I could find words. He convulsed a few times before his legs stiffened and he slipped from his chair.

I peeked under the table where a Jell-O-like mass in a police uniform twitched sporadically.

I stared at Willa. "What the hell?"

"Is that the guy who sent you a voodoo doll?"

"You didn't think to ask first?"

"Is it?"

"You zap someone and then ask who it is?"

"Look, Honey, is that the guy or not?"

"Well, yeah, but still—"

She interrupted me. "He's a criminal, he made threats to you. I wasn't going to sit back and watch you get hurt."

"I'm not hurt, Willa."

"Not yet. Let's call the cops."

"You didn't notice the uniform?"

"What uniform?"

"He is a cop."

"Oh." She peeked under the table.

"Yeah, oh."

At the next table, Sue leaned over. "Is he epileptic?"

Without missing a beat, Willa grabbed my arm and dragged me out of my seat. "Yeah, he is, and we need to call an ambulance. Maybe you could look after him while we find a phone?"

"Will do, sweetie." She turned back to her table. "Anyone have something we can use to hold his tongue down?"

We bolted out of the restaurant. I took a quick peek back at the table. Sue was kneeling beside a couple of other ladies. They had Officer Blake propped against the wall, and she was stuffing a tampon in his mouth.

"Damn, Willa," I said, struggling to breathe as we jogged across the parking lot.

"Restaurants are my third favorite place to tase someone, right after the mall and church. I don't know about you, but I think that went well. I mean, he went down relatively quietly, we got out of there without wearing handcuffs, and he didn't even wet himself…they usually do…best of all, now he knows you mean business."

She popped the locks on her car doors as we approached, and I jumped in the passenger seat.

"He'll think twice before he sends you another doll. Reminds me of the time I had to shoot Stanley Billings. You remember Stanley, don't you? All hands and hair but sexy as hell in a sticky-fingered, furry sort of way."

She started up the Honda.

"One little bullet, barely grazed him, less than a pint or two of blood. Only lost one testicle, still, he went down like a sack of potatoes, and I tell you, he never laid a hand on my backside again. There's one thing you can take to the bank, Honey. If you want someone to leave you alone, all you have to do is knock 'em unconscious and the job…"

I rolled my eyes as we pulled out of the parking lot.

CHAPTER FIFTEEN

Willa dropped me off on her way home to recharge her stun gun. I trudged through the back door and slumped onto the bar stool next to my wall phone. I was already tired, and all I wanted to do was go to bed. But I had a joyful conversation with Mother to look forward to, and Matt and I had plans for a late dinner after the show. I called him first.

"Hi."

"Hi, yourself."

"What's up?"

"Just checking in."

"How was your day?"

"Busy."

"Tell me about it."

"Received a threat, found Bradford Collins and Milton Buttons, chased Bradford Collins and Milton Buttons in cha-cha heels, lost Bradford, Milton, and my cell phone, found my cell phone, met with a lunatic, watched Willa tase the lunatic, helped her escape, disparaged my mother, and outed myself in print. You know, the usual."

"You were wearing cha-cha heels?"

"Not me, that would be Milton."

"You lead an interesting life, Mr. Honey."

"So they say. And now I have the joy of talking to my mother." I explained about the reaction to the article so far and the flames of maternal displeasure I expected to face.

"It's not going to be that bad. She'll be upset, but what's she going to do? You're her son, she'll forgive you."

That was true. However, wolf spiders and hamsters eat their young. I wasn't absolutely certain they hadn't learned that behavior from Livia.

"Enough about my crappy day. How was yours?"

"Me? I went to work as usual, pretty boring by your standards. I'm guessing after a day like that, a late dinner out is somewhat unappealing. You want me to pick up takeout after the show?"

What a guy.

"May Allah bestow many goats and camels upon your house, and may your wives be virtuous and give you many sons."

"You've been watching Al-Jazeera?"

"Don't worry about dinner, it's too much of a hassle to bring it home. I expect you'll need to drop by your place before you come over, and you'll be tired after the performance."

"True, but we have to eat and I want to see you."

That brought a smile to my face. "I want to see you too. I'm just saying Milto's delivers."

"Even better. You know, if we lived together we wouldn't be having this discussion. Everything would be a lot easier. We could stay in bed longer in the mornings too. I wouldn't have to hurry home to get ready for work."

I pictured a large dirigible bursting into flames. The thought of living with Matt made me break out in flop-sweat so heavy I almost slipped off the bar stool. I searched for a response somewhat less lame than "um" in the vast wasteland of pause that followed.

Matt jumped in. "And now you're shaking with fear."

"It's just…"

"Relax. It's just a thought."

"But I want to—I think, I'm just…"

"Freaking out?"

"A little."

"Well, no need. Really. First, no pressure, if we live together or apart, nothing changes, I'm with you, kid. It would just be easier, that's all. Second, if and when you want to make some plans—you know, move things along a little—I'm flexible. All you have to do is let me know."

We both listened to the hiss of dead air on the phone until I said, "Um, okey dokey then," and hung up.

I felt like an idiot for not jumping at Matt's offer to live together. I wondered why the thought bothered me so much. I was fully committed to the relationship. But things were going well right now—maybe *too* well. I didn't want to rock the boat. In the back of my mind, a little voice kept telling me there were reasons to worry.

Of course, it was just insecurity, but if anyone had a right to be insecure, surely it was me. Hadn't Russ hit the nail on the head when he said Matt was at least four levels above me on the gay-boy food chain? I wasn't worthy. There were a lot of things about me that would surely drive him away—eventually. I was notoriously messy, could be whiny on occasion, and my hair was unmanageable in high humidity. And there were things I'd rather not share with anyone. I've been known to string pork chops from my shoulders and lip-sync to Lady Gaga in front of the bathroom mirror—nobody wants to see that.

But those thoughts made me wonder about Matt. What secret flaws might he have that I didn't know about—and would knowing about them change anything for me? I heard Russ Buttons's words: *Hold on to dark little secrets, they come in handy when you're divvying up assets in front of a judge.*

As if the thought summoned his presence, my cell phone rang. Without thinking, I answered as if I were at the office. "Honey Agency, this dick's gotta be good for something."

"Am I speaking to the world's least fashionable detective?"

"What do you want now, Russ?"

"Just a quick call to tell you I'm sending Lenny Wallowitz your direction."

"The salsa guy?"

"No, the samba guy—salsa's what I put on a taco."

"Right, what does Lenny want?"

"He's hiring a new instructor for his dance studio. You remember what happened to Jaime Ramon?"

The story had been grist for the gossip mill for months. Jaime had been Lenny's most sought-after dance instructor, even as he used his position to worm his way into the hearts and pockets of half of Austin's idle rich (mostly the female half—though I suspected a few old queens might have also succumbed to his oily charms). It came to a head when a tabloid photographer snapped a few shots of Jaime doing the nasty with Shirley McCormick in a Port Aransas hotel room. How the photographer gained access remains a mystery, but the resultant published article wasn't amusing to Shirley's lawyer husband, Benjamin McCormick. He sued Jaime, and included Lenny and his business, noting their complicity in committing adultery. The scandal had tongues wagging from Pemberton to Tarrytown. Lenny spent thousands of dollars in legal fees fighting the suit. The story would probably still be on top of the rumormongers' hit parade if it weren't for my little interview.

"Of course," I said.

"Lenny wants to protect himself from that kind of embarrassment this time around. He was looking for some way to screen his applicants, so I suggested he hire you to run background checks. He jumped at the idea."

"I can do that."

"I gave him your number, and he said he'd call in the morning."

"Thanks for sending business my direction, Russ."

"Sure thing, Honey. We have to look after our own, you know."

"True dat."

I was about to hang up when I remembered Milton. I figured this was as good a time as any to ask Russ about his brother.

"So I have a question for you."

"Shoot."

"I was thinking about your brother's situation, and it still bothers me. Won't you please tell me what that was all about?"

"What do you mean? It was about finding Milton."

"Why did you choose to find him *now*? I mean, after all this time."

There was another uncomfortable pause.

I said, "I won't tell a soul, if that's what you're worried about. But I want an explanation. You owe me that much."

"You promise to take this to your grave?"

"And beyond."

He cleared his throat. "I know it's vulgar, but it has to do with money."

"Spill."

"Well, you know the Baldwin brothers, of course."

"Not personally."

"Let's put it this way, Milton and I are like Stephen and Alec."

"You're marginally handsome actors with overblown images and questionable talent?"

"No, not that. I'm saying he's *Celebrity Big Brother* and I'm *30 Rock*."

"Okay, you lost me there."

"Concentrate, Honey. He's a cigar-chomping Republican, and I'm…well, I'm not."

"Okay, so your politics differ."

"Exactly, our politics differ and…?"

"And what?"

"And in my family, that matters. There are factions. And our grandfather was in Milton's camp."

"You're saying he's a Republican?"

"I'm saying he *was* a Nazi."

"Okay, I'm still not following you. How does your grandfather's politics lead to your desire to find Milton?"

"Let me finish, will you? Bernie Buttons the Third assumed room temperature fourteen years ago."

"You mean he died."

"If not, we made an awful mistake burying him in the Texas State Cemetery. Anyway, in his will he left me some money, but the bulk of the cash was kept in trust for his favorite conservative asshole grandchild, Milton, with one provision. If the estate executor went fifteen years without finding Milton, the money would go to the other surviving family members. And everyone else is dead—so that would be me."

"I think I see where this is going. The executor hasn't found Milton yet."

"I don't think he's looking very hard."

"Who is it? The executor, I mean."

"My grandfather's attorney, Walter Wessley."

"Of the Philadelphia Wessleys?"

"Exactly, do you know them?"

"I'm acquainted with a member of the family."

"Of course. Anyway, the deal is if Walter finds Milton in the next two days, then I'm out a bunch of money. But there's not much chance of that, seeing as how Milton is in Austin and Walter's in Philadelphia… assuming you don't tell."

"You're a client, Russ. I don't make it a habit of pissing off my clients."

"Good. Then as long as Walter stays in Philadelphia, all is good."

But Cicely Wessley is in Austin, I thought.

I briefly considered the chance that Cicely's appearance had something to do with the will, but I couldn't picture it. And even if it did, it wouldn't matter unless Cicely somehow ran across Milton.

Then I remembered seeing her in Milton's parking lot. Cicely struck me as a bit of an airhead. I couldn't picture a law firm sending her out to hunt down a lost beneficiary...Still, she'd said she was there for her father. *Of course* she was there looking for Milton—what were the chances she would show up in Russ's brother's parking lot on her own?

After I hung up from Russ, I dialed Mother's number. Her cell phone rang through to voice mail, so I hung up without leaving a message and dialed Lost Wind. Chin answered on the second ring and informed me Mother asked not to be bothered. He offered to take a message, so I asked him to let her know I called. Eventually, I would need to make contact, but I felt no need to push the issue.

CHAPTER SIXTEEN

I must have drifted off, because the next thing I heard was an annoying caterwaul of marimba music morphing into the ring from my cell phone. It was Matt, calling from the sidewalk outside the gate. I told him I'd be right there and rolled out of bed, padding through the house in my stocking feet.

"You okay?" he asked through the gate.

I slipped my key into the lock and the latch clicked open. "I think so, just tired. Where's your key?"

"Oh, man, I totally forgot you gave me one. Guess I need to get used to that." He smiled and tossed an arm over my shoulders. "When's dinner getting here?"

It took a moment before I understood what he was asking. "Um, I forgot to call. Guess I fell asleep. Sorry." We stepped through the back door of the cottage.

"You sure you're okay? You look beat."

"I am."

"Still want dinner?"

"Not really."

He looked disappointed and gave me a sad smile. "Why don't you go on to bed? I'll find something to eat and call you in the morning."

I grabbed him by the arm as he turned to go. "Don't leave. I don't want you to leave."

"You're exhausted, mister."

"Yeah, but I still don't want you to leave."

"You need your sleep."

"I sleep better with you."

The disappointment vanished and his smile widened. "You sure?"

"Positive."

"Okay then, I'll stay, but you get to bed." He gestured toward my bedroom. "I'll grab something quick and be back in half an hour."

I watched him slide through the gate before heading for the bathroom. I thought about his disappointment and realized my exhaustion might have felt a little like impending rejection to Matt. If the shoe were on the other foot, I'd probably be cutting my losses and looking for the door. The thought scared me. *Why am I doing this to Matt? Am I subconsciously trying to ruin the best relationship I've ever had?*

I resolved to make a decision soon.

I crawled into bed and was asleep in seconds. I didn't hear Matt come in, and only marginally woke when he wriggled into bed beside me. It seemed like only seconds before the sun blasted through the blinds. I woke Friday morning to find Matt had dressed and snuck out, leaving a sweet note inviting me to dinner before the show.

I gargled and brushed my teeth before calling him at his office.

"How's sleeping beauty?"

"Up from the dead, but I missed my prince this morning. And we're on for dinner. I promise not to fall asleep."

"Great! Why don't you bring Willa? Maybe you guys can come to the show."

"Are you sure? She can be a little much."

"I think she's funny, and she's your friend."

"Well, yes, but that doesn't mean you have to put up with her."

"You mean the chatter?"

"Mostly."

"Tell me this, before we got together, didn't you two have dinner together most nights?"

"I guess so. Yeah."

"And you think of her as your best friend, right?"

"Most of the time."

"Well, there you go. I don't want her to feel threatened by our relationship. I want her to feel included."

"But like I said, she's my burden, not yours."

"Don't worry, I can handle it. Besides, I like her."

"Liking her is not the problem. Standing her is the problem."

"What do you mean?"

"You know what I mean."

"Still, she's your best friend and I want her to be my friend too."

I thought about Willa thinking Matt had hurt me. Maybe the two of them getting to know one another better was not a bad idea.

"Okay, I'll extend the invitation, but I hope you understand what you're getting into."

"What?"

"Willa's friendship comes at a price."

"Do you mean the prattle?"

"I mean *the danger*. You might find yourself dodging bullets or catching a punch. On the up side, if there's a gunfight she's usually armed."

He smiled. "I think I can handle it."

After we'd said our good-byes, I considered calling Mother but dropped the idea quickly. The sun was shining and it was a beautiful morning. I didn't want to mess it up. I showered and dressed quickly and caught the bus downtown.

❖

The cat stretched and showed me his butt at my office door. He'd obviously had a rough night, judging by the blood dripping down the side of his head. I opened the door and picked him up gently. He squirmed for a second, not liking the contact. But he settled down, allowing me to examine his wound with only a halfhearted moan of discontent. The blood came from a small gash just behind his right ear. I parted the fur carefully, then took him to the bathroom, where he let me clean the gash with hydrogen peroxide.

I carried him back to the kitchen and filled his water bowl. I added kitty nibbles to his food bowl and set him down. He sniffed the food, looking up at me with disgust before disappearing behind the foliage.

Cats are not good at showing appreciation.

I made myself a cup of tea and called Willa from my office phone, extending Matt's dinner invitation. She said she'd drop by to pick me up at six. I settled down to go through my messages.

My e-mail was mostly spam, but there were twenty-two messages on the answering machine. A warning light told me the tape was full, so I assumed others had called only to be turned away. I grabbed a pen and notepad and pressed Play. The first three were marginal friends calling to "sympathize" over the article. I was just about to listen to the fourth with the phone rang again. I answered, "The Honey Agency, dicks are us."

"Well, hello, stranger. Long time, no see."

"Lenny?"

"On the button, partner. How're things over at the Honey spread?" Lenny Wallowitz grew up in the Bronx, but he liked to pretend that he was from the country.

"The corn is as high as a pony's eye. What can I do you for?" Evidently, acting country was contagious.

"Partner, I need some help screening potential employees."

"Sure, I can do that."

He explained his predicament, and we discussed options and prices. In the end, he asked me to run preliminary background checks for ten dance instructor applicants, asking what I needed to get started.

"Well, my regular up-front cost for a job like this is five hundred dollars for a day's search."

He agreed to drop by with a check and I asked him to bring along the applicants' résumés.

After I hung up, I did my little happy dance before screening the rest of my messages. Six were from potential clients. I made a list and called each one back, securing three jobs and deflecting three others toward other agencies. That's one of the good things about working for yourself; when business is good, you can be choosy.

Flush with optimism and ready to take on the world, I decided to call Mother. I dialed her cell phone first, but got no answer. I left a message asking her to call me back.

Three minutes later, my cell phone rang.

"Hello."

"Greg, it's your mother."

"How are you this morning?" I kept my voice light and airy.

"In no mood for your good humor."

"So, you've read the article," I said, realizing I still had not. Willa's magazine still sat unopened on my desk.

"Of course, and I want you to know how truly disappointed I am."

"What can I say? I've already told you Jenna took my words out of context. I was joking."

She made a noise that sounded like a blowtorch igniting, and I waited for the onslaught of threats and abuse while my mood darkened like a biscuit in the oven.

"There is nothing humorous about my sex life."

Well, there certainly was no arguing with that. I apologized again. "I'm sorry, but it doesn't mean anything. Everyone will be able to see that I was joking."

"What were you thinking?"

"I wasn't thinking, I was joking."

Static crackled through the receiver. and I wondered how many more mea culpas she needed to hear.

"Greg, I know you find it hard to live up to the expectations of this family, but why do you always have to lash out in such a public way? Yes, you're gay. I know that, we all know that...but do you have to call attention to the fact? And why must you always, always try to hurt me?"

I caught an uncharacteristic hint of vulnerability in her voice. She was truly wounded, and that made me question my intentions. I knew I didn't want to hurt her—at least not consciously—but I wanted her to see things from my point of view. I began to wonder if that was fair. What about me? Had I really tried to see things from her point of view? The realization gave me pause. I understood family image mattered to Mother. What I had just done was tantamount to hanging the family's dirty laundry from a flagpole. Maybe I *was* trying to hurt her.

"Mama," I said, pausing. The word seemed to waft through the air like a feather in the breeze, and I knew she caught the significance. It was the first time I'd called her *mama* since I was a little boy. When I spoke again, my voice was softer. "I don't want to hurt you. Really, I don't. I feel lousy about this. I'm so sorry." My throat began to tighten as I listened to the silence on the line.

Finally, she said, "Oh, Greg. Why can't we just get along?"

"I want to, and I'm trying. Really."

"I know you are," she sighed again before adding, "and I'm trying too."

❖

After we hung up, the echo of her words kept playing through my thoughts. I glanced over at the magazine but still had no interest in reading the article. I decided to distract myself with work and spent most of the morning carefully combing through the pile of résumés Lenny Wallowitz had left. I worked through the stack, one at a time, doing Internet searches to verify facts and locate criminal records. I was down to the last three when Willa dropped by.

"You've got to admire Jenna. Her tactics may be suspect, but she writes a mean slam piece. How's the world's most fabulous private detective?"

"Swamped."

"The jobs are rolling in, then? Told ya. A little advertising was all you needed to kick-start this business. So, you have anything new that's interesting? Maybe I could help you chase after a wayward woman this time—for a cuckolded husband. Or how about hunting down a murder suspect? I'd love that; we could go all CSI for a change. I could wear gloves and take samples from the corpse. Oooh, I know, I know, we could spy on someone…I want to spy on someone…maybe a little international espionage. You know, follow a foreigner, wear a wire… maybe I could take pictures or break into an apartment. I've never broken into an apartment—professionally, I mean. If you have a spy job, I could help with that for sure."

"Sorry, fresh out of spy jobs, Willa."

I stared at the magazine still lying on my desk.

"What's up, pumpkin? You look a little down in the mouth."

"Just talked to Mother."

"Don't tell me, the queen of the Honey hive is not happy."

"I don't know, Wil. I think I really hurt her this time. She sounded sad."

"Well, she doesn't come off well in the piece. You told her you didn't mean those things, right?"

"Several times, but I don't think she cares."

"You have to admit, it does come at a bad time for Livia, what with the party tomorrow night and all."

I hadn't thought about that. *Of course* the scandal would burn red hot through the bitchy crowd of women she called friends. And tomorrow night, she'd have to welcome Austin's elite into her home, knowing they were all talking about her behind her back. I grabbed the magazine, and Willa sat on my office couch while I read the article. It was exactly what I expected, but on steroids. Jenna made the comment about Mother's pool boy sound like she was banging him on the front lawn. When I'd finished, I looked at Willa.

She said, "Nasty little piece, huh? So what do you want to do about it?"

"I don't think there is anything to do."

"You're probably right, but one thing is for sure."

"What's that?"

"If you don't show up at the party tomorrow night, people will think you've abandoned your family altogether. And that will only compound Livia's shame."

I knew she was right. Not going to the party was no longer an option. I would have to show up now and stand by Mother. And when people asked, I would tell them the truth, that Jenna had stabbed me in the back and the article was a bunch of lies.

Willa and I met Matt for dinner at Schlotzsky's Deli before the show. Afterward, all three of us walked across the crunchy grass to the Zachary Scott Theater. Matt said his farewells and made his way backstage while Willa and I waited in the lobby for the show to start.

Mickey Craig was working the box office, leaving Willa free to mingle. We found Doodle Brendell sitting in one of the ratty sofas in the theater lobby.

Willa said, "Well, look at what the cat drug in."

Doodle smiled. "I wondered if I'd see you two here. I love the hat, Willa."

Willa was still wearing her stocking cap.

"Thanks, didn't expect to see you here again. Can't get enough of *Rent*?"

"I'm on a reconnaissance mission. I'm supposed to report back to Janet about the new Mimi."

"How's Janet doing? Still taking it hard?" I asked.

"Actually, she's much better. She landed another job. And it's show business, sort of. She's in training to be a clown at the Travis County Livestock Show and Rodeo. It's a pretty good fit for her too. There's no singing or dancing, but she gets to wear stage makeup in front of lots of people."

Willa said, "There you go. Janet's good at wearing makeup."

"So far the main problem is squeezing into the barrel. She has to oil her hips."

I shot a quick grin at Willa, who said, "I can see Janet as a rodeo clown. She kind of reminds me of a country girl. Did she grow up on a ranch?"

"She grew up in Detroit."

"Well, there you go, that's kind of like the country. Rodeo clown is a good job for her. I assume it pays the bills, and I bet they have good medical coverage. She has nothing to worry about, as long as she can keep away from the hoofs and horns."

"She's surprisingly nimble for a big woman, and her size actually helps. I think she intimidates some of the bulls."

Willa smiled. "They are about the same size."

I excused myself to make a quick pit stop. On my way back to the lobby, I spotted Lola Riatta in the parking lot with Bradford Collins. They were smiling and holding hands as they strolled together across the pavement toward the door. I couldn't believe my luck. I'd run into Bradford three times in two days now. This time I wanted to make sure Ronnie got here in time to arrest him. I hurried to the lobby.

"So I said 'sometimes when you want a banana you have to be willing to climb a tree,' and she said 'it's been so long since I had a banana I'm willing to scale a sequoia,' so I said 'a girl's gotta do what a girl's gotta do,' and she said 'which way to the forest,' and I said…"

I waved Willa off with a hand and turned to Doodle. "I apologize for butting in, but I need to grab Willa for a minute. Please excuse us."

I grabbed Willa by the elbow and dragged her quickly down the back hallway and around the corner before she managed to free herself from my grasp. Irritated, she said, "What the hell was that all about?"

"Bradford's here," I hissed.

"What?"

"Bradford is here."

"Where?" She stepped around the corner to peer back into the lobby. I grabbed her arm, jerking her back behind the corner and out of the line of sight.

"They're just now coming in the front, but don't let them see you."

"He's not alone?" This time she peeked around the corner, careful to stay mostly hidden.

I pointed toward the entrance. "Over there."

"Who's he with?"

"Right. Um, he's with—now, don't freak out about this, but he's with Lola."

She looked at me with undisguised rage and said, "Don't tell me that bitch is coming to my theater?"

"Well, technically it belongs to the city."

"I can't believe that hag has the nerve to show up here, of all places. She'd better stay away from me, that's all I have to say. If she gets within spitting distance, so help me God I'll cut her, I'll punch her, I'll slap her so hard the wall will be wearing her makeup."

"Please don't make a scene."

"I won't make a scene, I never make a scene."

Strictly speaking that was a lie; still, I decided not to argue. Instead, I said, "I'm going to call Ronnie. Hopefully he can get here in time to grab Bradford before he spots us."

She peeked around the corner again and said, "Look at that bitch, strutting around like she owns the place. Who the hell does she think she is?"

I knew Willa was working herself up for a confrontation. I only hoped Ronnie would get to Bradford before the fireworks started. After that, as far as I was concerned, Willa was free to whale away on Lola to her heart's content.

I said, "I think we should stay hidden. If Bradford sees either of us, he'll run again."

"Ronnie who?"

"What?"

"You said you were going to call Ronnie. Who is Ronnie?"

"Ronnie Blake."

"The guy I tased last night?"

"Yep."

"Don't you think he'll be a little upset over that?"

"I'm hoping he's over it. Anyway, I don't think he even saw you and probably doesn't know what hit him. I'll just tell him he passed out and I went for help."

"And never came back?"

"Good point, I'll have to think up a more viable excuse."

"Good luck finding a good reason for leaving someone passed out under a table."

"I didn't say it was going to be easy."

"How about this, you thought he was tying his shoe and got an urgent phone call. So you had to leave quickly."

"Something like that."

I stepped through the theater door in search of a quiet place to make the call. It was empty, except for two volunteer ushers busy stacking playbills. I speed-dialed Ronnie. It wasn't hard to hear the anger in his voice when he answered.

"What the hell happened at Chez Sneeze?"

"That's what I want to know. You ducked under the table, I figured you were embarrassed or something." I decided playing dumb was my best option.

"You left me on the floor."

"You looked comfortable."

"I can see the red bumps."

"The what?"

"The contact points from a stun gun. I know you zapped me, I just don't remember how, exactly."

I played ignorant. "You're insane, I don't know what you're talking about."

"One minute I'm sitting at the table looking at you and the next thing I know I'm lying on the floor with a mouth full of cotton and you're nowhere to be found."

"Wow, well, that's weird. Like I said, you slipped under the table, it was a little odd but I took it to mean you were done talking, so I left you in peace. I have no idea what happened after that. Look, Ron, we don't have time to talk about this now. I'm at Zach Scott Theater and Bradford Collins just walked into the lobby."

A tremendous crash echoed up the hallway.

"What the hell was that?" Ronnie asked.

"Hold on." I pressed the phone against my chest and stepped back through the doorway. Willa had disappeared. Cautiously, I peered around the corner. A group of patrons crowded together, blocking my view to the lobby, but I sensed the bloodlust of a prizefight.

"Oh, crap, I gotta go." I sprinted down the corridor as catcalls sparked the air. As I neared the lobby, I caught a glimpse of Bradford's yellow Miata pulling out of the parking lot through the glass doors.

I pushed into the rowdy crowd of onlookers to find Willa straddling Lola on the grimy carpet. People were whistling and someone yelled, "Punch her!"

Lola's arms were pinned to her sides. She looked up at Willa with venom. Willa began banging Lola's head into the floor, and the crowd clapped to the rhythm of the pounding. I nudged ahead and reached out, trying to pry Willa's fingers from Lola's ears. She kicked me away, screaming, "You baboon-humping, camel-toed jackass! If you ever show your lizard-face, chicken-bumping pig butt in here again I will pound that hippo smile right off those wormy lips!"

I grabbed her by the waist and hoisted her off Lola, holding her at bay with one hand while Lola scrambled to her feet, flailing at Willa, trying to slap her with an open palm. I grabbed her hand too.

She yelled, "Let me at her! I'll kill that pox-infested pus-filled boil! I'll slap that oily smirk right off her butt-ugly face!"

"Will you stop? Both of you, right now!"

I held them apart, turning my head to glare at each in turn. I shoved Willa ahead and dragged Lola behind as I guided them through the crowd like a kindergarten teacher dealing with a playground fight. I ushered them to the storage room behind the concession stand, nudged the door open with a hip, and shoved them inside, shutting the door behind us.

They circled each other like fighting cats, hissing and spitting.

I stepped between them and said, "Jesus! What the hell was that?"

"She attacked me," Lola said, pointing a glossy red fingernail at Willa.

I looked at Willa, but she ignored me. She stepped toward Lola and said, "Listen, bitch, this is my place. You come into my space again, they'll carry you out in a pine box."

"Excuse me—your space? I don't think you own this theater."

Willa lunged at Lola, and I caught her by the shoulder. With a voice as authoritative as I could muster, I said, "Stop it! You're both acting like children."

They glared at each other in silence.

I said, "Look at the two of you."

They both looked at the floor, avoiding eye contact.

"Go on, look," I demanded.

Slowly, they turned toward each other. Willa's stocking cap had slipped off in the melee, exposing a blistered patchy bald head matching Lola's shaved cranium. They both had scrapes from the tussle in the lobby, and blood dripped from Lola's elbow and Willa's knee. Willa's blouse was missing three buttons, and Lola's skirt had been wrenched to the side, displaying much more of her nether regions than I wanted to see.

I said, "I don't get it. Really. Will someone please explain to me what Ralph Mason had that makes the two of you fight over him like a pair of jackals?"

They each looked down at the floor.

I broke the silence, insistent. "Go on, explain this to me. What was the deal with Ralph? Was he that good a lover? He must have been a hell of a guy for you two to carry on like this. What was his secret?"

No one spoke. I waited. Finally Willa said, "Hell, I don't know. He was pretty lousy, really."

Lola added, "With a puny little pickle dick."

"And childbearing hips."

"Hung like a weasel, smelled a little like one too."

"Worst lay I ever had," Willa said, smiling.

"Like sleeping with a sack of potatoes," Lola added, grinning.

Willa said, "All ear hair and toe jam."

"Cried like a baby if you said anything bad about his mama."

"Probably breast-fed into his twenties."

"What the hell was I doing marrying that bastard?"

Willa's smile widened. "Worst decision ever."

Lola chuckled. "He had this annoying way of snorting. You remember that? Sounded like a pig looking for a truffle."

"And when he slept, he snored."

"Like a pachyderm passing gas."

"Speaking of passing gas..."

I left the two of them amiably discussing Ralph's flatulence in the storage room and went back to the lobby just as Ronnie Blake stepped through the doorway. The lights were flashing and patrons were making their way to their seats, so I grabbed Ronnie by the elbow and dragged him to the back wall.

"He's gone."

"Again?"

"Yes, I'm sorry, but he's quick. He must have spotted Willa and made a run for it."

"God damn it, Matt. That's it, I've had it. You call me out repeatedly to pick up a nonexistent Bradford Collins, you refuse to trick with me, and you zap me with a Taser. I'm getting the impression you don't like me."

"Hey, you sent me threatening messages and a voodoo doll."

"Next time it will be a letter bomb."

"Look, Ronnie, I'm sorry you missed Bradford again. What can I say? He was here and now he's gone. You need to hurry when I call you. The guy is slippery as a pig in grease."

"I have a better plan. Stop calling me."

He stormed out.

CHAPTER SEVENTEEN

So I said 'where's my order,' and she said 'there may be a delay,' and I said 'I've been sitting here for twenty minutes,' and she said 'there's a problem in the kitchen,' and I said 'I'm in a hurry,' and she said 'the waitress is on fire,' and I said 'but I didn't order anything *flambé*,' and she said 'can you hand me that fire extinguisher,' and I said 'I'll take that to go,' and she said..."

The five of us were perched along the wall, waiting for a table at Kerbey Lane Café. We had come for pie after the show, and Willa, as usual, was talking. Matt, looking freshly scrubbed and absolutely beautiful, watched intently, trying to keep up with the gist of the story. Doodle was watching Willa too.

I looked over at Lola. Without doubt, she'd gotten the worst of the scuffle in the lobby. She sat at the far end of the bench with what looked like a Cheeto dangling from her patchy hair and new red scabs on both of her knees.

It was odd seeing Willa and Lola together without fur flying. The two had apparently bonded over poor Ralph Mason's failings as a lover, but I was skeptical. Willa had even asked the house manager to move Lola's seat next to ours so she wouldn't be alone in the theater. Obviously Lola's date with Bradford Collins was a non-starter since he'd abandoned her when Willa started pounding her head into the lobby carpet. So far, the calm had held. Still, in my view, prospects for lasting peace were meager, but even as a temporary reprieve it lacked fervor. I found myself praying that the next bout of violence wouldn't come in the restaurant.

The crowd waiting for tables was full of faces I recognized from the theater. Furtive glances flashed in our direction, and I was sure Lola and Willa were the topic of several whispered conversations. The smell of maple syrup and soft tacos wafting over from a couple of nearby tables made for an unappealing combination that turned my stomach.

Maybe I'd just drink tea.

"Oh, my goodness, it's Greg."

I looked up to see Gary Weiss. He was wearing a flowing mid-length skirt in a flowery pattern and a simple white blouse. His hair was pulled back into a ponytail, and there was excitement in his eyes.

"It's perfect running into you like this! I have a request."

"Hey, Gary, what's up?"

"Late dinner with the girls." He nodded to a group of rough-looking drag queens waiting at the door.

"Looks like a fun group."

"Yeah, they're fun, but you have to watch your lip gloss." We both looked at the queens and Gary shrugged, adding, "I need your help. What are you doing tomorrow afternoon around two?"

"Not much."

"Great. Wally's mother died." Wally was Gary's partner.

"I'm sorry to hear that."

"Yeah, yeah, yeah…thanks, and all that—but the truth is it didn't ruin my day. She was a nasty old biddy who stole my makeup, cursed like a sailor, and smelled like rotten peaches. Now at least we can bury the body. The thing is Wally had to drive to Houston to deal with the funeral."

"Tough time for him, then?"

"As far as I'm concerned they should have just dropped her at the curb on bulk trash pickup day."

I looked at him with raised eyebrows. "You really didn't like her."

"She was the spawn of Lucifer."

"So you're not going to the funeral."

"Wally's on his own there. I'm booked to do Cher at the *Queen's Revue* tomorrow. Ads have already been run. So I'm committed. It's going to be at the Fussy Pussy."

"The what?"

"Fussy Pussy, it's a traveling performance venue, they have

afternoon tea dances and drag shows. This month it's at a little club over by the Capitol."

"Okay," I said, still not understanding how I figured into his plans.

"So, I was counting on Wally as my Sonny."

"And now you're asking me to play Sonny."

"Bingo."

"I'm not much of a singer—you remember last time."

"I remember. You were a little weak-voiced, behind the beat, and off-key. An absolutely perfect Sonny."

"Don't you think you deserve someone better?"

"But there is no one. Come on, Honey, please."

He looked at me, tears already forming in his eyes. I don't know how drag queens do it, but I had never met one that couldn't cry on cue.

I said, "How long will it take?"

"Couple of hours, tops." Magically the tears disappeared.

I figured Cicely's party wouldn't start until eight, so that gave me plenty of time.

I shrugged. "I guess I can do it. I've got plans in the evening, though."

"No problem, tea dance has to be over by four thirty or they don't have time to get the place ready for the evening crowd." He grinned. "How about I pick you up around one thirty."

"I'll be ready."

"Thanks, Greg, darling, you're a life saver. Wear neutral colors, I'll bring the knee pads." And with that, he skipped through the door.

Matt looked over at me with a smirk. "Who was that?"

"Gary Weiss, he's a client and a friend."

"He?"

"He, she, pronouns are a challenge when it comes to Gary."

"She, Greg. Definitely she."

"Yeah, guess you're right. She asked me to help her out with a drag show tomorrow afternoon. You interested?"

"What time?"

"Two."

"Got a Saturday matinee, remember?"

"That's right, I've got to get used to your schedule."

He smiled, and a thought hit me. It would be great if Matt could join Willa and me at Mother's party. I knew he had the late performance, but it wouldn't hurt to ask.

"And what about tomorrow evening?"

He smiled. "What about it?"

"I know you have the show, but…" I let the unspoken request hang in the air, unsure how to phrase it.

Matt's grin widened. "You want some company at your mother's party—right?"

"Right."

"Guess I need to let Dave know and call the understudy."

"You, Mr. Kendall, are the loveliest thing on the surface of the earth."

❖

I spent Saturday morning at home working my way through the stack of dance instructor résumés, running background checks to verify training and job history. I also cross-referenced online court records, looking for criminal and civil charges. The entire stack scored a few hits, mostly divorce proceedings or drug-related run-ins with the law, but I was totally taken aback when one applicant, Melvin Bostic, turned out to have spent twenty-three years in Huntsville Prison on a second degree murder charge. I was pretty sure that disqualified him as a potential dance partner, so I printed out the information along with Melvin's picture, and set it aside to show Lenny Wallowitz.

My cell phone rang as I was cleaning up after lunch.

"Hello."

"Greg, you ready for this?" It was Gary.

"Guess so. I'm wearing khakis and a short-sleeved white button-up shirt. Is that going to work?"

"Perfect. I've got a sparkly pullover vest. If that's not Sonny, what is? I'm parked at the curb."

"Be right there."

Gary was dressed in pink sweatpants and a white T-shirt with *Hide the Candy* printed across the chest. His hair was pulled back into a knot behind his head. His eyebrows had been plucked clean and drawn back in at an acute angle with an eyebrow pencil. Two-inch false eyelashes encrusted in purple glitter were glued on, and red smudges enhanced his cheekbones like war paint. He was using a hair pick to fluff the fuchsia afro-style wig adorning a Styrofoam head held between his legs. A mass of sequins sparkled from the backseat.

"We're in a hurry, Honey," he said as I opened the door.

I sat down, and he handed me the head. The Mercedes tires chirped before I could fasten my seat belt. I braced against the door handle as he pulled a sharp U-turn. We drove down Lamar to Twelfth, cutting east in the direction of the Capitol. I was shocked when he pulled into the parking lot across the street from Les Furieux Chat.

I peered through the Mercedes window at the building. "The drag show is in there?"

"Yeah, come on." He stepped out of the car and opened the back door, grabbing a jumbo-sized makeup kit and a mass of sparkly material from the backseat. I followed him, carrying a gray box under one arm and the Styrofoam head out in front of me like the host at communion. My heart beat irregularly, matching the staccato sound of his high heels as they clicked across the pavement.

We pushed into the building, and a cold finger of fear ran down my spine. The front desk was unmanned. I noted the pictures of strippers hanging on the wall had been replaced with headshots of drag queens. Gary led the way through the curtained passage. I tucked in close behind, trying not to draw attention. The neon overhead lights filled the space with a cold glare, and the room looked even grungier than I remembered.

Groups of drag queens and their helpers had set up staging areas along the back wall. Curling irons and mascara wands waved in the air. Lacquered fingernails grasped industrial-sized tweezers as several performers stared into mirrors plucking wayward eyebrows and nose hair. Others were being helped into costumes. Padding enhanced hips and bosoms; corsets squeezed tummies; tape created cleavage and held down unruly appendages. Four-inch press-on nails adorned hands, lipstick painted half an inch beyond the lips adorned faces, and sparkly eye shadow in shocking shades glittered on eyelids.

I trailed behind Gary as he sailed right into the middle of the group, air-kissing a host of astonishingly bedazzled beauties. When they spotted me, the mood in the room shifted. I began to feel threatened, like a male spider navigating the web of a black widow.

A large African American queen wearing six-inch platform sandals stepped into my path. Hoops the size of piston rings adorned her earlobes, and a bright yellow baby doll dress barely covered the questionable parts of her anatomy. She licked her lips and said, spitting the words out in slow rhythmic tempo, "Who is this pretty little thing?"

Her eyes moved up and down my body like a rancher checking out a calf at an auction. Extending a hand, she added, "Hi, sweetie, I'm Tess Tosterone. You can come over and sit with me, and I'll teach you a thing or two about how to diddle a banjo."

Tess grabbed my arm and began dragging me toward the back when another queen elbowed her out of the way.

This one had to be at least seven feet tall in her six-inch heels. She had hands that could easily palm a beach ball and shoulders Olympic swimmers would envy. She wore a billowing dress made from acres of emerald taffeta and had on more eye makeup than you could buy at a Mary Kay convention. Tossing one muscular arm over my shoulder, she moved in close to whisper in my ear, "Don't do it, pumpkin. That one doesn't know a thing about a banjo. Why don't you come sit with Chlamydia, and I'll show you where I hide my candy."

I gave Gary a concerned look, and he set his dress carefully on the table before coming to my rescue.

"Ms. Infection, you're a hot pink mess." Gary pried Chlamydia's arm off my shoulder and turned me toward the group, clearing his throat to get their attention.

"Ladies, this little piece of heaven is Greg Honey. Greg, meet Tequila Mockingbird, Wanda Lollipop, Alexus Sedan, Kaye Mart, Ivana Twat, Krystal Klear, and Ham Sandwich. You already met Tess and Chlamydia. Now, I want all of you ladies to keep your hands off Greg. He's got an honest-to-God boyfriend and doesn't need any of you bitches rubbing up on him."

The group turned away slowly, grumbling to themselves as they went back to primping.

I heard Ham say, "That poor boy doesn't know what he's missing. Chlamydia can suck a bowling ball through a hundred feet of garden hose."

Wanda added, "Mmm-hmm, and don't I know it…a little piece of heaven, especially when she pulls out her dentures."

Milton Buttons pushed through the door behind the stage. He

carried a clipboard and looked almost classy in a platinum blond wig styled into a neat little bob and a floor-length shimmering gown. The enormous falsies were tucked in place, and his face was almost understated compared to the garish colors of most of the other queens. I ducked behind Chlamydia and edged along the wall toward the bathroom, careful to stay out of sight as Milton stepped up to the microphone.

"Listen up, ladies, the lineup's posted on the DJ booth. Make sure Jeff has your music and knows your number. I'm up first and I'm doing two songs."

There was general grousing in the room, and someone said, "Bitch is always taking over. I'd like to slap the happy right off her face."

Milton said, "Stop your bitching, Alexus, I'm the emcee, and that means I run the show. If you don't like it, take a Midol and shut the fuck up. Now, ladies, when I finish, and the thunderous applause dies down—"

Alexus broke in with a stage whisper, "That shouldn't take long."

"I'll make a little speech and bring on Wanda. From then on, every performer introduces the next, so work out your intro with the bitch ahead of you and don't bother me. We're in a hurry today, so punch it up and keep it moving. Our feathers and fluff have to be out of here by four. Let's make it snappy, ladies. There's already a line forming outside, and the door opens in thirteen minutes."

There was flurry of activity as a group of drag queens made their way to the DJ booth. Others grabbed their gear and headed to the doorway. Evidently, the back hallway was being used as a staging area. As I watched, Milton pulled a chair onstage and began shuffling through sheets of music.

Gary's head popped through the doorway. I caught his attention with a wave.

"We're up third. I'm going to go put on Cher now." He gestured back through the passage. "Whenever you're ready to get on your knees, come find me. I figure we've got about fifteen minutes from when they open the doors. You remember the words to the song, right?"

"I got you, babe."

He grinned. "Don't be late."

I handed him the box and wig and glanced back at the stage. Milton was whispering to himself, so I snuck over to the DJ's booth and hid behind a half wall, hoping to hear what he was saying. The band was setting up onstage. The drummer looked familiar. I recognized him as the bartender from my first trip to Les Furieux Chat. Something about the piano player made me uncomfortable. Bradford Collins brought out his guitar.

"You part of this?"

The voice floated down at me from the booth. I looked up to see a skinny young girl with an asymmetrical haircut wearing headphones peering over the partition. She tugged at the headphones, sliding them down so they hung around her neck.

"Helping out a friend," I said. "What's the story with the band?"

She looked up, squinting at the stage. "That's the Gene Spleen Combo, it's the emcee's group. The only ones that don't lip-sync."

"Oh?"

"Yeah. I guess they're pretty good, if you like that kind of music. Me, I'm into techno beat."

"So you've seen them perform before?"

"Every Saturday afternoon for a month. Sometimes she comes out in a nurse's outfit. Then the group's billed as Nurse Betty and the Bedpans."

I looked back at the stage. "Same band?"

"Yep, just different costumes. They even do the same songs."

So Bradford was a bedpan. I thought about Milton in a nurse's outfit and realized he must be the one I'd seen with Billy the first night. I wanted to ask the DJ if she knew anything about the owner of the club, but couldn't figure out how without raising suspicions.

"Does Gene always emcee these events?"

"For the last month or so, anyway. I hear Rocco recruited her from Oklahoma."

"Rocco?"

"He owns this dump and runs these shows on the side. Kind of oily for my taste, but he's a hell of a businessman. Rumor has it he's a bit of a gangster too, but that's just lady talk." She drew quotation marks in the air around the word "lady."

"You say she came from Oklahoma?"

"That's what I heard. Talk has it she's big in the queen world."

"The queen world?"

"Yeah, it's like they live on a different planet. They all know each

other and there's this circuit of performers and hundreds of contests...
Miss Gay Yada Yada. Seems like every one of them has a sash and
crown from somewhere."

"You always DJ for them?"

"Whenever I can. The pay's good and I love the music. Old disco
mostly."

We heard sounds coming from the stage, Milton's band was
warming up.

"I guess you better get back there." She nodded toward the door.

"In a minute—which one of these guys is Rocco?"

"Oh, he never comes to these things. He shows up in the evenings
when it reopens as a strip club."

"Not into daytime socializing?"

"Not really, he just rolls that way."

"What way?"

"Rocco likes big-breasted ladies dancing in g-strings."

She smiled and pulled her headphones back to her ears, saying,
"Break a leg."

I made my way backstage, careful to avoid detection. Milton was
talking with Bradford as I passed, and I turned away, shielding my face.
I didn't want them to spot me before I could call Ronnie.

As I passed the stage, I could just make out a few words of their
conversation. Milton was assuring Bradford they wouldn't be stuck
doing these shows much longer.

I hurried on through the door and down the hallway. The performers
had broken into small groups and were helping each other into wigs,
more makeup, and clothing. I found a deserted area and pulled out my
cell phone. I called Ronnie Blake.

"What the hell are you calling me for?"

"Look, I found him again. I'm at a strip club named Les Furieux
Chat off Enfield. There's an afternoon performance, and Bradford
Collins is playing in a band. He's out there tuning up right now. All you
need to do is get here in the next twenty minutes and we've got him."

"I told you, I'm done with this. I'm not wasting any more time
chasing after your tips. I don't even believe Bradford Collins is there—
you've been jerking my chain."

"Ronnie, will you listen to me? Bradford's here right now and he
has no idea I'm here."

"Not interested."

"But it's your job."

"I don't need you to tell me what my job is."

"You're mad because I don't want to fool around."

He was silent. Finally, I said, "Look, Ronnie, I can't believe you're going to mess this up just because your feelings are hurt. Bradford is out there...warming up on the stage, right now."

"Still not interested."

I hung up and dialed 911.

"Nine-one-one, what is your emergency?"

"I'm calling about someone who is wanted on an arrest warrant."

"What is the emergency?"

"Well, he's here and the police can—"

"Is anyone harmed or in danger?"

"Well, not technically but if you'd just—"

"Is this an emergency?"

"Not so much, but if the police would just come over—"

"Sir, nine-one-one is an emergency response service only. Please call three-one-one for non-emergency calls."

"That's just great!" I said, but she had already hung up.

I was still staring at my phone when the distant strains of the show's prelude music echoed down the hallway. I edged to the stage door and watched as Milton stepped up to the microphone. To my complete disbelief, he belted out the introductory phrase and his voice was surprisingly wonderful, both resonant and soulful...and uniquely asexual.

Backstage, the activity level kicked up. The space was full of feathers and fur, and a few celebrity look-alikes strolled the hallway. Gary's Cher was dead-on, and Alexus made a surprisingly realistic Bette Midler, but Krystal's Judy Garland could have done with a little less shoulder...and leg hair.

"Aren't you guys up third?"

I looked over to Ham.

"Yeah, I think so."

"You better get ready, honey, these things go pretty fast."

I sighed, shoving my cell phone back in my pocket, and took the elements of my costume out of the gray box. Gary had cut the toes out of a pair of work boots and glued them to the kneepads. I put them on and dropped to my knees in front of the mirror. I looked like a midget barely four feet tall. With the pageboy wig and sparkly vest, I'd make a passably cartoonish Sonny. I was practicing walking on my knees when the music ended. There was a smattering of applause before Milton launched into his second number, and Wanda began to warm up, stretching her hamstrings.

Gary stepped up beside me, and we looked in the mirror. On my knees, he towered at least a foot and half above my head. We ran through our number whispering the words so we didn't disturb the show.

When Milton's second number ended, he introduced Wanda.

"It's time to bring out a girl that needs no introduction, well, no introduction to the nurses down at the STD clinic. She's a regular at these affairs, even though everyone hopes that streak will end soon. Straight from the county jail and still smelling like a French whore, give it up for Austin's very own Wanda Lollipop. God save the queen."

Shirley Bassey's version of "The Banana Boat Song" started, and Wanda pushed through the doorway in an outfit that looked a little like an ice cream float.

Milton slipped backstage with the boys from his band right behind him. They grouped together at the far end of the hallway, where the players began packing up their equipment. Bradford huddled with Milton next to the storage room. I pretended to check myself in the mirror, edging closer to the door so I could listen to their conversation.

Bradford spoke first. "What if he shows up tonight?"

"Won't matter. Look, we've got this covered, will you relax? We'll be on our way to the islands at midnight."

"But what about Rocco?"

"What about him? I told you—this is totally separate from his business. His score is going to be big enough that he's not going to care. Hell, he probably won't even notice we're gone."

"But he'll figure it out."

"Yeah, but by then, we'll be on our way. What's he going to do, call the police? I don't think so, he'll be busy shipping stuff south."

"I don't know, this is the biggest job I've ever worked. If we screw it up, we go to prison."

"What do you have to lose? You're already going to prison."

"You don't know that. They haven't convicted me yet."

"But they're going to. Insurance companies have a lot of lawyers just dying to make sure people like you spend time in Huntsville."

"I still don't know."

"What the hell, you can't do anything about it now. It's too late to back out. So just keep your mouth shut and think about the islands."

I heard ruffling sounds, so I moved back toward the others. Three minutes later, I crawled out onstage behind Gary.

We moved quickly through our number, receiving a standing ovation before, true to form, Gary mooned the audience.

By the time I hobbled offstage, Bradford was gone.

I wondered what it was going to take to bring him in.

Maybe I should unleash Willa with her stun gun.

CHAPTER EIGHTEEN

I still don't know why you wouldn't let me carry the little snub-nose. I promise I'll keep it in my purse…mostly."

"No guns, Willa."

"But it's such a sweet little Cobra .38 special. And it's just perfect with these shoes."

"I said, no guns."

"Why not? This is Austin, Honey, a girl's gotta defend herself from oilmen and lawyers and the Texas legislature."

Matt nodded agreement and grinned. I rolled my eyes.

Willa said, "What about all those snakes?"

"What snakes?"

"There are fifteen different poisonous species in Texas, and my guess is every one of them will be attending the party."

"I promise there won't be any snakes at the party."

Matt said, "I wouldn't count on that. You said your mother invited the governor."

A quick smile flashed between them, and I stared at Willa's eyes in the rearview mirror. There was a weird bonding thing going on in the front seat of Willa's Honda—and I wasn't sure I liked it.

She said, "I feel practically naked without protection. Besides, your mother's peer group is made up of right-wing NRA fanatics. Everyone will be packing heat tonight."

"You've got your pepper spray and I'm pretty sure your stun gun's stuffed inside your clutch. That's enough protection for anyone."

Willa frowned. "But they aren't lethal, and you never know when you'll want to bring them down for good. Besides, the pepper spray canister is red."

I looked at Matt, who shrugged.

Willa continued, "Red clashes with my shoes."

"No guns, Willa." There was no compromise in my voice. Lethal weaponry should not be used as a fashion accessory.

She sighed in frustration. "But it's such a cute little snub-nose."

Willa turned her blue Honda Civic into the Lost Winds gate and rolled down the driver-side window. Up the hill, we could see cars inching along the driveway. At the parking station, a host of red-coated valets handed out claim checks and held doors for people dressed in evening wear. The well-heeled crowd formed a line that climbed the steps, wove through a set of Ionic columns, and angled across the tiled porch to a pair of ornate French doors propped open by a pair of uniformed footmen.

Willa pulled the Civic to a stop at the security station. I leaned forward and shouted from the backseat, "Hi, Wilber, are we the last to arrive?"

Wilber nodded and dragged a coal-black finger down a clipboard. "Looks like they're mostly here, Mr. Greg. So far, I've checked in fifty-two invited guests, and the band just started playing. Going to be quite a party. The press is here en masse and the governor's assistant called, their group is running late, but I suspect they want to make an entrance."

"No doubt."

"You all have fun now, Mr. Greg," he said, waving us through. Willa pulled away from the security station slowly.

We got out of the car at the parking kiosk and Willa handed her key to an attendant wearing a name tag and skipped on ahead. Matt held the door for me, and I bumped into the attendant as I exited. When he looked up to apologize, there was something familiar about his eyes, and I scanned the name tag quickly. It said *Melvin B*.

A cold finger of dread crept up my spine. I was trying to recall where I'd seen that name when Matt grabbed my hand and tugged me toward the walk. We scaled the steps quickly and he looked at me with those impossibly green eyes and smiled.

He said, "This is going to be fun."

"That's a judgment call." I took a couple of quick breaths before speaking again. "Matt, there's something I have to say. I have no idea what we'll face in there, but I want to apologize in advance for what's about to happen."

His grin widened. "Relax, mister. It'll be a hoot, no matter what comes."

I was concerned about Matt's interaction with my family. He'd met Mother, of course, but this would be his first taste of the full Honey experience. The opulence, the snobbery, the snide comments, and peer pressure. And then there was Grandmother; she could always be counted on for one or two uncomfortable and embarrassing incidents. I sighed as we ambled over the threshold.

We caught up with Willa just beyond the doorway. Crowd noises emanated from down a carpeted hallway, and I gestured toward the hubbub. Willa linked arms with Matt and me. The three of us followed the noise to the anteroom outside the solarium.

"Will ya look at that, whoever thought you could sculpt a twenty-foot penis from a block of ice."

"It's not a penis, Wil. Our family emblem is the pickle."

"Well, this is the first time I've ever seen a pickle with a scrotum."

Matt and I looked down. The sculptor had added the whimsical extra in such a way that it was only visible to those standing directly above it.

I smiled. "I like it."

"Me too," Matt agreed.

"Boys, boys, boys…remember, this is a high-class party. No humping the ephemeral artwork."

The lilt of music wafted out from the solarium, but we were still too far away to catch the tune. As we plodded across the plush carpet, I glanced into the set of gilt-framed mirrors that lined the walls. I was looking sharp in my new tuxedo. No matter what I felt about molestation during alteration, Mother's tailor was very, very good. The jacket hung so well no one could see the outline of the iPhone tucked inside an inner pocket. The drape of my pants was elegant, comfortable, and gave me such a big box I could have been sued for false advertising.

Matt looked stunning as always in a black fleece Brooks Brothers tux. He was debonair and elegant enough to star in the next James Bond movie.

Willa, despite missing her snub-nose accessory, was stylish in a wispy chiffon gown. The blisters had receded from her scalp, and she had shaved her head. The effect was surprisingly beautiful—sort of Sinead O'Connor meets Halle Berry.

We sailed into the ballroom. The first thing I saw was Cicely in a floor-length Jovani jeweled gown in midnight blue, featuring sheer net overlays of beaded tulle. The jewels lining the bodice caught the light from Mother's Waterford chandelier and shimmered like the Andromeda galaxy. Extensions had been added to Cicely's hair, which was arranged in a braided, coiled concoction piled on top of her head and reached near-nosebleed heights. No doubt she was paying homage to Texas, the big-hair state.

"Get a load of that," I said, nodding in her direction.

Willa said, "Damn, that's big hair. Maybe Livia will ask Cicely to stick around after the party. It's time to dust the light fixtures."

Rustling sounds came from the alcove behind us. The three of us turned in unison to see the luxurious coiffure of the best hair in Texas politics float above a sea of conservatives. Bankers, oilmen, and legislators bowed their heads in reverence as the governor waded into the room. He wore a western-cut tuxedo and black polished cowboy boots. In one hand he carried a felt cowboy hat that he used to wave to the crowd.

The governor far outshone his wife, who looked dowdy and somewhat gray in a dress that could have been made from a feed bag. They were surrounded by fawning admirers and watched over by a security detail wearing wrinkled suits. The governor waved his hat again, and a handgun slipped from his cummerbund. It clattered on the floor. Without missing a beat, one of the security detail bent down to pick it up.

Frowning, Willa said, "What'd I tell you? Even the governor is packing heat."

My grandmother steered her scooter across the tiled floor. She drew the attention of the security detail, and a young man built like a linebacker with a military haircut and a shark tooth earphone moved to block her way.

Willa pointed. "Is that your grandmother?"

"Yep."

Matt said, "I want to meet her."

"Now's as good a time as any. Come on."

We moved across the floor and climbed the steps to the foyer. Grandmother was wearing a sparkly dress and a matching cap. A dainty parasol, circa 1903, was laid across her lap.

"I'm sorry, ma'am, but this is as close as you're going to get," the security man said.

"But I want to talk to the governor."

"You'll have to do it from where you are."

"But he can hardly hear me."

"I can't allow the cart to get any closer."

"Hey, Governor!" Grandmother yelled. The three of us settled in along the railing to watch the show.

"Hey, over here!" She waved her parasol, and the security guard knocked it out of her hand. Undeterred, Grandmother yelled, "Hey, you!" She pointed and waved toward the governor, who was trying to ignore her, but Grandmother was not one to be ignored. "Come over here, young man, right this minute. I have something to ask you."

A flash from a camera lit the space and the governor turned to Grandmother slowly. Ever the consummate politician, he flashed a hundred-watt smile and said, "Hello, ma'am." A small man wearing round glasses and a $200 suit casually slipped beside him and whispered into his ear.

He said, "You must be Livia's mother-in-law, Lucille."

"Why, yes, I am, and I knew your granddaddy from over at Paint Creek."

His smile widened. Sensing a media opportunity, he stepped closer.

"Yes, ma'am, I hear the Honey ranch was out that way."

"It was. I also knew Waller Overton, your old scoutmaster, and he was telling me that you had a little bed-wetting trouble back in high school. Said they used to call you Rubber Sheets. Well, Lord knows I know all about incontinence, I squirt a little every time I sneeze. But that's not what I wanted to ask you about."

The group around the governor shuffled restlessly, and I saw a couple of heads ducking to hide smiles. The governor froze, eyes wide open like a deer caught in headlights. A dozen or more reporters pointed tape recorder microphones at Grandmother.

The area was flooded with light as a television camera began to roll. Grandmother held up a hand to shade her eyes from the glare, and continued, "I was watching the TV with my friend Iola, and we saw you in that Republican presidential thingie where you couldn't name the three federal agencies you wanted to close down, and Iola said you were making the state of Texas look pretty damn stupid."

He tried to turn away, but Grandmother's voice grew louder, and the camera panned the audience, finally settling on her face.

"Well, Iola's a Democrat, so I try not to pay too much attention to her, but still, it was sure hard to argue with her point. I was going to cut you some slack, you see, you're from Paint Creek and everyone knows people from Paint Creek can't alphabetize M&Ms. But Iola reminded me about the time you appointed that Enron guy to that state commission and the next day Ken Lay gave you a check for $25,000. And then you told the press it was totally coincidental. Really? Nice coincidence, would you say?"

He smiled his aw-shucks smile. "Every once in a while I get lucky."

"I guess you're right. It was a nice break for you for sure…still, I can't help thinking it made Texas look pretty damn stupid again. And then there was the time your spokesman said that in Texas we base our policies on sound science and went on to deny the existence of global warming…and the time you told that TV commentator abstinence works when he'd just pointed out that Texas has had an abstinence program for years, right along with the third-highest teen-pregnancy rate in the country. And then last night I was talking with Iola again and she reminded me about that video clip we saw where you told that little boy Texas schools teach creationism…Creationism? Really?"

His smile faded slowly.

"So I'm sure even someone from Paint Creek can see the connection here—if you give them enough time, that is. So my question to you, Governor, is this: Are you *trying* to make the state of Texas look stupid?"

Finally, he said, "We're here for the party, Mrs. Honey. I don't have time for questions."

A host of reporters scribbled notes and bulbs flashed as photographers shot pictures of Grandmother. She just shook her head and said sarcastically, "Well, if that don't beat all. The great state of Texas thanks you, Rubber Sheets."

She put her scooter in reverse and began the slow process of turning around in a small space.

Matt leaned over and whispered in my ear, "I thought you said she was senile?"

"It comes and it goes."

As the scooter rocked gently forward, Matt picked up the parasol and handed it to her. She smiled at him, and he said, "I love you already."

"I love you too, sweetie, whoever you are."

Matt and I watched as she backed her scooter up again, pulled a K-turn, and puttered toward the hallway.

CHAPTER NINETEEN

"What do you think of that hair? Looks like she slept inside a stove pipe." Willa gestured across the ballroom to where Cicely stood chatting with Russ Buttons. I had to admit, her immaculately coiffed hairdo was a marvel of stylistic engineering. Who knew that extensions, braiding, and hair spray could rise to such unprecedented heights?

Russ wore tight, shiny, red knee-length breeches and a shirt so flouncy it rippled in the breeze from the dance floor. His legs were covered in white tights. On his feet were what could only be called elf shoes—ankle booties with toes so pointy and curled up I found myself looking for little bells. On his head was a do-rag pulled tight to cover his newly permed curly locks. All he needed was a hook and a ticking crocodile, and he could captain a pirate ship.

He spotted our group, still perched along the railing, and waved us over. He looked angry, which worried me.

"This is unacceptable, Honey. I can't believe it—your mother of all people should have known better."

"Hi, Cicely," I said, ignoring him. We exchanged nods, and I gave her plenty of distance lest she whack me in the face with her hairdo. Someone called her name and she walked away, trailing her satin train like a dog scooting its backside across the carpet.

I turned to Russ. "Very swashbuckling."

Despite his anger, the edges of his mouth lifted. "You think so? I was thinking it's a little much for this crowd, but when one is a fashionista, one must uphold a certain level of style."

Willa said, "What, couldn't you find a parrot?"

"Very funny."

He turned to me with a sour expression. "This will destroy the Honey name."

"What's got your pantaloons in a wad?"

He glared at me. "I've never been so embarrassed in all my life."

Willa said, "That's unlikely."

I said, "What's wrong?"

"That." He pointed toward the bandstand.

A small band was playing softly. I could make out a drummer, sax player, bass, and lead guitar scattered around Mother's baby grand piano. Sitting at the piano belting out a soulful rendition of "My Funny Valentine" was a large woman with big hair and a small nurse's cap. She wore a white nurse's costume, filling out the top with breasts so big she had to nestle her chin between them to read the sheet music. I said, "So?"

"So? So look closely."

I studied the group. Something about the drummer looked vaguely familiar. I wasn't sure where I'd seen him before, but I was sure I had. The horn player was unknown to me and I couldn't see the guitar player; he was hidden behind the piano. The singer was big and flashy. Her talent was obvious—the girl could carry a tune. As she sang, she glanced across the audience and I caught a side view of her face.

Uh-oh.

"This is a travesty, an absolute travesty!" Russ stomped off in a flurry of rippling fabric.

Matt leaned over to whisper in my ear, "You should know that I'm having trouble keeping my hands off you."

He touched my side. Testosterone flooded my system, and I considered looking for a place slightly classier than the hallway bathroom in which to molest him; but there was a problem at Lost Wind and I was a Honey.

This was no time for a romp in the broom closet.

I said, gesturing toward the band, "What do you think of that?"

"The band?"

I nodded.

"It's the Nurse Betty Combo…they're pretty good."

"You know them?"

"Of course I know them. I caught them last Sunday afternoon at Walter's downtown studio. The whole cast went to see them after the

Sunday afternoon performance. Gene's cool, she even let me sit in for a set."

"But that's a three-hundred-pound drag queen tinkling the ivories."

"I know. Isn't it a hoot?"

"It's a hoot all right. It's also Milton Buttons."

"What?"

"Russ Buttons's brother—you remember, the one I tracked down?"

He smiled. "So Gene is Milton?"

"Looks like it."

"I didn't know your mother was hip enough to hire a band fronted by a drag queen."

"She isn't. Either she doesn't know or…" I let my voice trail off.

"Or what?"

"Or something is going on."

Willa moved closer. "What're you guys talking about?"

I nodded toward the band.

"Yeah, I like them. The music's nice…Holy crap! Do you see that?"

"Yeah."

"Is that Milton?"

"Yeah."

"Livia's going to give birth to a cow when she figures it out. Can I tell her? Please let me be the one. I really want to tell her."

We stared at the band, and an uncomfortable image ran through my mind. I remembered where I'd seen the drummer. I said, "And that's the guy that punched me at Les Furieux Chat. "

"Sure the hell is," Willa said.

The three of us watched in stunned silence for a few seconds. Willa broke the quiet. "And the bass guitar player, isn't that…?"

"Hell, what is going on here?"

Matt asked, "Who is it?"

"Bradford Collins," Willa said. "He's the guy we've been tracking for Gary Weiss."

"The guy that you found jumping out a window in Waco?"

"Yeah."

That's when I remembered where I had seen the valet. I'd printed out his picture a few hours earlier. It was Melvin Bostic, the guy charged with second degree murder who had applied for Lenny Wallowitz's dance instructor position.

Willa said, "Maybe that explains the little jam session we interrupted at Milton's place."

I nodded. "Probably."

Matt said, "So they're in a band with some of the guys from the strip club? What do you think it all means?"

"I think it means we're in trouble. You remember what we overheard at the club, Willa?"

"You're talking about when that guy said something to Milton about getting his money back?"

"That guy's name is Rocco. He owns the club. They mentioned a big score, remember?"

"Sort of."

"Well, I saw Milton and Bradford at the drag show today. They were talking about it again." They both looked at the band as I continued, "I don't remember exactly what they said, but it sounded like they were planning on something big and Rocco was running something else, something also illegal, at the same time."

"But they're all here. I mean Milton and Bradford and Rocco."

"Rocco's here?" I asked.

She nodded, pointing across the dance floor. I could see his bald head gleaming in the light reflected from the stage. He stood next to a group of well-heeled ladies holding a platter of canapés.

"This can't be good."

Willa's eyes got big, and all three of us scanned the room. Diamonds bedazzled women's necks, fat wallets bulged from tuxedo pockets, and Rolex watches peeked out from sleeves. She said, "Oh, shit."

"Yeah, oh, shit."

The song ended, and a smattering of applause emanated from the crowd as dancers started to leave the dance floor.

Willa asked, "What should we do now?"

Mother was making a beeline across the dance floor. She had a huge smile on her face as she edged through the throng heading toward the governor. The crowd of overly pomaded men and seriously bejeweled women chortled with glee and began to clap as the governor stepped up to the railing.

Willa asked, "Do you think we should tell your mother?"

"Probably."

We began to weave our way through the crowd, and Matt said, "Do you think she knows about your grandmother's little tirade?"

"If not, she'll find out later. It'll probably play for a week on the news shows."

The governor waved once more, and his own bling caught the light from the chandelier. A three-carat pinkie ring sparkled and fluttered in the air like a firefly. Mother bolted up the steps and attempted to maul him with a huge bear hug. It was his moment of glory, and she meant to share it.

They were immediately surrounded. Old men wearing belt buckles the size of dinner plates jostled for space with silicone-enhanced women lacquered in enough makeup to paint a portrait.

We were caught on the periphery of the crowd as the governor began slapping backs and shaking hands. As I listened, I could tell his words had taken on a much more pronounced West Texas drawl.

Willa said, "This is starting to feel a little like a Nazi rally. Next I expect they'll sing 'The Eyes of Texas' and make plans to purify the race."

"I know what you mean," Matt said, "There are so many Tea Party supporters here it's making me itch."

"Come on," I said, taking Willa by one hand and Matt by the other. We pushed into the mass, elbowing our way forward. Mother led the governor's party to their table and flitted about making introductions with the plastic smile still illuminating her face. We caught up with her as she turned to leave.

She stepped backward, taking a deep breath, and glared at Matt's hand in mine. She looked into my eyes with the warmth of a pit viper and said, "Greg, I'm so glad you could make it."

"Hello, Mother, you remember Matt."

"Of course. I'm surprised to see you again so soon, Mr. Kendall. I didn't realize we would have the pleasure of your company this evening."

Without a hint of sarcasm, Matt said, "Thank you for inviting me, Mrs. Honey."

"That appears to have been my son's doing."

I grabbed her by the elbow. "I need to ask you something."

She looked down at my hand with unsuppressed irritation.

"Where did you get the band?"

"What?"

"The band." I nodded toward the stage area. "Where did you find them?"

"Why?"

"I need to know."

"My florist arranged the entertainment."

"Your florist?"

"Yes."

"You don't have a florist." As I said it, another piece of the puzzle fell into place.

"I do now. He helped with the caterers too. He's been such a lovely surprise, assisting with all the preparations, I th—"

I cut her off. "Who is your florist?"

She looked at me, bewildered. "Billy Crenshaw. He has this charming little shop over on Lamar Boulevard."

Queasiness bubbled in my stomach. Billy's late-night forays to Rocco's strip club, the conversation Willa and I had overheard between Milton and Rocco, even what Milton and Bradford had been discussing four hours earlier. Things were starting to make sense. Billy had borrowed money from Rocco, probably to keep his shop from going under. When he couldn't pay the money back, Milton must have approached him with an offer to set things right with Rocco if Billy could get them into Mother's party.

And now all these people were at Lost Wind serving canapés and soft ballads. Soon they would execute the rest of their plan, whatever that was. What could they be here to steal? What would bring them a lot of money? The most valuable thing at Lost Wind was the artwork. French impressionists hung from the walls, and Rodin statuary decorated the gallery. The solarium was festooned with Miró, and a couple of pricey Chagalls adorned the private quarters.

Still, I doubted anyone could manage pulling down the paintings or hoisting off the statues unobserved. The flatware was priceless, but again, how do you steal plates and silverware without being noticed? There were certainly a lot of wealthy people in attendance. Holding them up at gunpoint seemed unlikely. For one thing, the governor had his security detail, and there were tons of cell phones around. Anything so obvious would instantly trigger dozens of calls to 911.

I could feel Willa vibrating with excitement beside me.

"Damn, this is so cool. A real live crime in the making right in front of us, and to think I almost missed this party because of bloating and cramps."

Mother's voice brought my focus back. "Why are you interested in the party preparations?"

I looked at her, squinting. Her auburn hair was pulled back from her pale face and wound into a knot at the base of her neck. The faintest hint of makeup colored her cheeks and tastefully darkened her eyes. Her gown was the standard Mother-wear, soft and wispy chiffon below a form-fitting bodice that emphasized her trim figure above. The only additional adornment she wore was the Tiger's Eye necklace, glittering like the sun from her cleavage. As usual, she had trotted out the museum piece to flaunt the family wealth. I squinted at the jewel, trying to determine if it was the legitimate article or the paste reproduction provided by the insurance company.

Mother noticed me staring and laid a hand on the jewel. "Greg?"

"Is that the real one?"

"What?"

"Are you wearing the real Tiger's Eye or the fake one?"

She frowned and looked around warily. A couple sitting at a table to her right toyed with their dinner. I could tell Mother was afraid they were listening to us. She grabbed me by the elbow and steered me through the crowd. I looked back to see Matt mouth, "what now?" I nodded toward Milton, hoping they would keep an eye on him while I talked with Mother. I caught a quick glimpse of Willa on her tiptoes whispering in Matt's ear before Mother tugged me down the steps.

She nodded and smiled to guests as we wove across the dance floor and sailed through to the hallway. She escorted me into her office and closed the door.

"What is this about?" she demanded.

Instead of answering her question, I asked again, "Is that the real Tiger's Eye?"

She stared at me, distrust furrowing her brow. "Why?"

"Just tell me."

As I watched, the suspicion turned to uncertainty in her eyes. She said, "The governor, the Mexican ambassador, and the owner of half the oil in Canada are in that room. Did you actually think I'd try to pass off fake jewelry?"

"So it's real?"

"Of course it's real, Greg. Now, what is this about?"

I was pretty certain I knew what Milton and Bradford had come for, but what about Rocco and his thugs? What were they doing here? There had to be something in this for Rocco, or else why was he willing to trade access to the party for what Billy owed him?

I stared through the window. Dusk was rapidly approaching, and I could see rows of Mercedes and Bentleys parked in a roped-off area the valets had set up across the lawn. The place was sheltered from the road by a stand of cypress trees. I searched for groups of drivers milling about, but the late-afternoon heat must have driven them inside to the air-conditioning.

"Greg?" I felt Mother tugging on my arm.

I looked at her and said, "Tell me where you got the valet team."

"Okay, I've had just about enough of your questions."

"Just tell me—did Billy also suggest your valets?"

"Of course not. They came from Fuego Del Sol, as usual."

Fuego Del Sol was an expensive Argentinean restaurant. Mother knew the owner and had used their valets for numerous formal affairs at Lost Wind. Still, I was sure Melvin Bostic had parked Willa's car, and since he had served time on a second degree murder charge, the odds he wasn't one of Rocco's thugs seemed remote.

Mother sighed in exasperation. "Look, if you're not going to tell me what this is about, I'm going back to the party. I've got guests to attend to."

She turned to leave, and I grabbed her arm. "Please do me one favor before you go."

She looked down at my hand. Her voice icy, she said, "What?"

"Swap out your necklace."

"What?"

"Before you go back to the party, just replace the one you're wearing with the other one. The fake one the insurance company gave you."

Her head angled sideways.

I said, "They've already seen the real one, what can it hurt?"

"I'm not going to do that. I'm Livia Honey, I don't wear paste jewelry." And she sailed through the office doorway.

I turned back to the window. The sun had just set and the last hint of color in the sky was leeching away. Everything looked calm and peaceful, but there was something else out there, I knew it. I just couldn't figure out what Rocco was up to.

I sighed in frustration.

When I got back to the ballroom, I found Willa huddled with Matt. They'd spent the time while I was with Mother cataloging suspicious-looking people.

Willa said, "There are four or five waiters, and at least one more in the kitchen. Outside of Milton and Bradford and the others in the band, I didn't recognize anyone…but a few looked as dodgy as three-day-old fish."

Matt said, "That's ten, give or take a couple. We've been watching Milton and Bradford, but so far they're just doing the music thing."

I looked over at the bandstand. Milton was standing behind the microphone belting out a fair rendition of an Adele song, and Bradford strummed along on his guitar.

"So what now?" Willa asked.

"I think Milton and Bradford are here for the Tiger's Eye. I still haven't figured out Rocco's angle, though."

"The what?" Matt asked.

"The Tiger's Eye, the fourteen-carat yellow diamond that Mother is wearing."

Willa said, "That rock is real? Damn, Honey, it looks like a cantaloupe."

"I know, tacky, isn't it?"

Willa said, "I used to wear big jewelry."

"When?" I asked.

"Don't you remember that time in high school after we pantsed the debate team? I wore those heavy silver bracelets."

"Willa, those were handcuffs, you were under arrest."

"Yeah, I guess you're right." She looked down at her feet. "On the bright side, I was never formally charged."

I looked over at Matt, whose eyes were scanning the audience.

They stopped when he found Mother. She was at the governor's table, talking to the lieutenant governor. He was obviously sloshed, weaving back and forth as he reached out to steady himself against the back of a chair.

Matt said, "So what do we do now?"

"Not sure. I want to call Ronnie Blake to tell them to come pick up Bradford again, but I've just about worn out my welcome there. I doubt he would take me seriously."

I was also worried that the police wouldn't take me seriously if I told them about Rocco—at least until I figured out his angle in all of this.

I looked around the room. "Where is Rocco?"

Willa said, "Over there…no, wait. He *was* over there."

We looked around the room again. Rocco and the rest of the caterers had disappeared. People were sitting in front of empty plates, and more than a few were holding empty glasses.

Willa said, "This can't be good."

Slowly, an image began to form in my mind. I wasn't sure if I was right, but I knew how to find out. I turned to Matt. "Come with me?"

He nodded, and I grabbed him by the hand. "Keep an eye on Mother," I yelled to Willa as we bolted up the steps and into the hallway. Chin stood guard at the front entrance. He looked up as we appeared from the ballroom, and the thought he was the inside man Rocco had mentioned crossed my mind.

"Is there something I can do for you, Mr. Greg?"

"No, no, we were just going to Mother's office." The lie was instinctive. I wasn't sure about any of this, but I sure didn't want to tip my hand yet. It was important to not let them know we suspected anything. If we had an advantage, it was that they still didn't know they were being watched. Matt followed as I hurried into Mother's office, closing the door behind us. The first thing I noticed was the blinds had been closed. I remembered leaving the office after Mother. I was sure they were open then. No one else should have been in here, so why were they closed now? I crept over to the window, hooked a finger around the edge.

Matt watched in silence.

In the distance, I could just make out the image of a tow truck heading down the driveway dragging a black sedan. I shrugged, figuring one of the drivers must have had engine trouble, but as I went to drop the blinds, another tow truck pulled into the driveway.

"Uh-oh."

Matt raised his eyebrows.

CHAPTER TWENTY

W hat do you see?"

"Okay, I get it," I said.

"Get what?"

"Rocco's men are stealing the cars."

"What?"

"They're out there right now with tow trucks. They're stealing all of Mother's guests' cars. That's what they're here for."

I turned off the light and opened the blinds. More than half of the cars were already gone from the parking area. As we watched, a truck hitched its rigging to a midnight-blue Mercedes coupe. Willa's battered blue Honda sat alone in the open area, presumably not worth stealing.

Matt eased his cell out of his pocket. He said, "I'm calling the police."

"By the time they get here, that lot's going to be empty and they'll be long gone."

"So what do we do?"

"You make the call, I'm going down there to see if I can hitch a ride on a tow truck." I hurried toward the door.

I could hear him explaining the situation to the 911 operator as I jogged down the hallway. I didn't want to leave only Willa watching over Milton and Bradford as they stalked Mother's necklace, but what else could I do? Somehow we had to stop Rocco.

Chin was still manning the door as I approached the exit. He stood across the space with his feet spread.

"Excuse me, I just need to check something." I tried to push past him. He grabbed my arm and shouldered me back. I looked down at his hand on my arm.

He asked, "What seems to be the problem?"

"I need to get by."

Chin smiled his pleasant smile and said, "You don't want to go out in this heat dressed like that, Mr. Greg. Whatever you need, I'll be happy to get it for you."

Down the corridor I caught a glimpse of Matt sneaking across the hallway. I wished I had had time to tell him of my fears about Chin, but somehow he seemed to sense what was going on. He stepped back out of view.

"Oh, it's not that hot now that the sun's almost down. I'll be fine, I wouldn't want to bother you when you're so busy."

"It's no bother at all." His eyes were serious.

"I'll just be a minute." I tried again to squeeze through the door, but Chin pushed back.

I glared at his hand on my arm.

"Please, Mr. Greg. Whatever you need, let me get it for you. That's what I'm here for."

Matt climbed through a hallway portal and dropped softly onto the lawn. I watched through a window over Chin's shoulder as he snuck along the hedgerows and dipped behind the border fence out of sight. My spine tingled, and fear pulsed through my body. I was pretty sure Matt had seen I couldn't get past Chin and decided to go in my place. Now there was no turning back, and all I could do was get back to the ballroom and help Willa protect Mother.

"I guess it's not that important," I said. "You're probably right. Too much trouble in this heat." I kept my words light and easy.

Chin said, "Are you sure? I could make the run for you no problem."

"Thanks," I said. "But it wasn't important, I just wanted to make sure Willa's windows were rolled up. You never know with Texas weather."

"I imagine the valet took care of that, but I'll make sure."

"Thanks, Chin," I said with as much nonchalance as I could muster and turned to leave.

My mind was racing. I was angry with myself for not seeing it all earlier. I was also worried for Matt, but there was no time to stop. I hurried down the hallway back to the solarium. Willa and Cicely were huddled together just inside the door.

Cicely said, "Russ Buttons did my hair, do you like it?"

"It certainly is interesting. How is it held up that way? I mean, is there a stick in there?"

"No, it's all done with extensions and hair spray."

"Must be strong hair spray."

"I wanted big hair—after all, this is Texas."

Willa said, "Well, it certainly is big."

"It took four hours in the salon chair to get this effect. I love your look too."

"Thanks, I did it myself. It took three minutes with a disposable razor."

Willa turned to me as I arrived. "Greg! What happened?"

I ignored the question, asking, "Where's Milton?"

"Milton who?" Cicely asked.

Willa said, "He's over there…no, wait, he was over there a minute ago."

"Where's Mother?"

"She's over…oh."

I was starting to panic. Milton and the entire band were AWOL, and Mother was nowhere to be seen.

Cicely asked, "Milton? Who's Milton?"

I snapped, "Jesus, Willa, one thing…you only had one thing to do…keep Milton away from Mother." I was so exasperated my voice sounded high and reedy.

"They're around somewhere—they were just here, I promise. They can't have gone far."

People were standing around talking, fidgeting as they searched for servers and waited for the music to start up again. I bolted across the dance floor, scanning faces as I went. No sign of either Mother or the three-hundred-pound drag queen. I rushed back to the hallway, turning away from Chin at the front door toward the private quarters. I poked my head into Mother's office again, but it was still empty. Willa and Cicely followed in my wake. I checked each door as we scurried down the corridor.

Separate bathrooms had been set up for men and women at the party.

"Check the women's loo," I yelled to Willa as I pushed through the men's room door. A bald gentleman stood washing his hands at the sink. He stared at me in the mirror and said, "I'm almost finished here."

I apologized quickly and exited.

"Empty," Willa said, leaving the women's room.

We hurried on to the end of the corridor. A set of double doors separated the public space from the private rooms. They were closed and locked. I pulled up, wondering where next to search, when I heard voices coming from the stairwell down to the servants' area. I took the steps two at a time, pulling up short at the bottom. They were in a small alcove off the kitchen. A set of windows filled the far wall. They looked out on the shadowy grounds, and I could see dark figures reflected from the shadowy space. Milton was waving a knife in front of Mother. He said, "I'll take that now, Mrs. Honey."

"You'll do nothing of the sort," Mother snapped indignantly.

I searched the reflection for Bradford or any of the other band members, but Milton was alone.

He stepped closer to Mother and said, "I assure you, I will not hesitate to use this." The blade glinted in the hallway light.

She leaned forward with her hands on her hips and feet spread in a posture of defiance. If she refused to give Milton what he wanted, I had no doubt he would take it.

I eased into the alcove slowly and inched toward Milton, but lost my footing and banged into the wall. They both looked at me before Milton turned his attention back to Mother.

I said, "Give it to him. Whatever he wants, just give it to him."

"I will not."

"It's not worth your life, give him the Tiger's Eye." My voice was soft, but serious. I wanted to find a way to send her a signal, to let her know everything would be okay, but she didn't move.

"Your son is a smart man, Mrs. Honey. You should listen to him."

I looked into Mother's eyes, trying to bend her iron will. It took a moment, but she finally tugged the necklace off her neck and held it out to Milton. He snatched it from her hand.

Willa and Cicely stumbled from the steps behind me. They

gathered themselves along the wall, and Milton looked at all of us before reaching for Mother. I lunged forward, batting his hand away. He grabbed my wrist, wrenching it around behind my back, and pulled me close to his body. With my back pressing against the hard rubber of his breast prosthesis, and my arm cocked awkwardly behind me, he applied some pressure.

It brought tears to my eyes.

Milton jerked me closer, squeezing my neck with one meaty appendage. With the other, he pressed the knife's edge against my cheek. Distant sirens wailed. Through the window I could see a set of police cars moving up the hill.

Mother's eyes glinted again with steely determination. Ever the one in control, she stepped forward, glaring at Milton.

"You will not escape. Surely you can see that your efforts cannot succeed now that the police are here. All you can do is cut your losses. Let him go."

Milton's voice hissed into my ear. "If I go down, you go down."

Steps echoed from the stairwell. Russ Buttons and Billy Crenshaw, hand in hand, skipped into the room. The amorous couple was kissing and cooing. I hoped they would open their eyes before Mother got a demonstration of the mechanics of gay sex. They finally looked up after bumping into Cicely.

"Watch the hair, will ya?"

"What the hell?" Russ squinted into the shadows and added, "Oh my God, Milton, you sorry sack of shit. You're a disgrace to the Buttons name. Let him go right this instant."

"Get out of here, Russ," Milton hissed. I could feel myself being yanked backward toward the door. To my right, Willa groped frantically through her purse and I thought, *Okay, maybe I should have let her keep the gun.*

Cicely said, "Wait, did I hear you right? Your name is Milton Buttons?"

Her brow furrowed in confusion and Willa moved behind Cicely, edging her way closer. Even in the shadows, I could make out Billy's red cheeks.

Milton said. "What's it to you?"

She said, "You're the grandson of Dick Buttons?"

"Yeah, so?"

I could see Russ's eyes widen. They looked like evil glowing orbs in the shadows.

Cicely said, "Oh my God! I've been looking all over for you. My daddy is a lawyer in Philly and—"

But Russ didn't let her finish; he pushed away from Billy and bolted forward yelling, "Wait!"

Everyone stared at him, and he fidgeted in discomfort. I could see his mind working, trying to find the words. After a pause he turned to Mother. "I think it would be better if we let him go, Mrs. Honey. He's dangerous, this is dangerous. If he leaves now, no one important gets hurt."

No one important gets hurt? What the hell about me? I wanted to shout it from the rafters, but that wasn't possible. I was struggling to breathe with Milton's arm squeezed tight around my neck.

Russ shrugged my direction and added, "Milton will set him free…eventually. And—"

Thump!

The sound echoed in the air, mixing with the smell of burned flesh.

Milton's grip released and he crumpled to the ground like a flaming dirigible. The knife clattered on the tiled floor and we all looked at Willa, standing with her still-smoking Taser above the fallen figure.

She said, "I love this thing. Best four hundred dollars I ever spent."

❖

The police arrived within minutes. We all watched as they cuffed Milton's inert body. When he came to they hauled him out of the alcove. Through the window I could see Bradford and the rest of Milton's band being loaded into a police paddy wagon. Rocco and his men had disappeared.

As the police began directing us back up the stairway, I frantically searched for information about Matt, but all that anyone could tell me was the authorities had located the partygoers' cars already loaded onto trucks in a lot south of the river.

The police took statements from everyone at the party, including the governor, his press detail, and the limo drivers who'd been found tied up inside the Lost Wind cabana. Mother, Willa, and I were taken downtown for more detailed interrogations. Grandmother tagged along, mostly for the excitement. On the way over in the back of the police car, I tried to call Matt on his cell phone, but it rolled through to voice mail.

Halfway through my interrogation, I heard sounds of men in the hallway outside. Rocco and his men were in custody, but there was still no word on Matt. By the time the police had finished with me, I was nearly frantic. I bolted out of the interrogation room intending to call Matt again, but when I looked up I saw him chatting with Lucille at the end of the hallway. Relief rolled over me, and I almost yelled his name. I stood and watched, mesmerized, for a few seconds. What could they have in common? I was surprised they looked so happy together. I decided to sneak over and hear what they were saying to each other. I rounded the corner and sat down across the hallway, careful not to draw their attention.

"Mrs. Honey, you're a hoot."

"Oh, thanks, darling, I think you're a hoot too. And I have to tell you, I'm so glad to hear you've been doing the nasty with our Greg. He's sort of geeky and a bit of a stick in the mud. I was afraid he might die a virgin."

"You can rest easy on that score. I'm so glad you approve of our relationship. His mother isn't supportive."

"Oh, I wouldn't worry about Livia, Sugar. That woman is wound so tight she can't pass gas."

Matt laughed. That's when Willa sat down beside me. I held my finger to my lips and gestured toward Matt and Grandmother.

"It's true. My daughter-in-law thinks she knows what's best for everyone, but the truth is she doesn't even know what's best for herself."

The words caught me off guard. Lucille had Mother pegged and was in rare form. This was the woman I remembered from my youth, but who would have guessed she could rally and be this sharp again?

The night was full of surprises.

Matt said, "It's really cool that you don't mind the gay part."

"Mind it? Hell, I wish I could be it. It may not look it, but I'm pretty sure there's a gay man rearranging furniture inside this wrinkled old frame."

Matt laughed again.

She added, "It sucks being this old. Everyone I used to hang out with is either dead or can't find their dentures. And I'm here to tell you there's nothing sexy about a man with no teeth."

Willa snickered beside me.

Grandmother looked down in her lap, and with a little shake of her head, added, "I miss the good times. I miss the fun. I miss the men."

Matt's voice was soft and I leaned forward to hear. "I guess you've seen a lot of changes."

"When you've lived as long as I have, the world moves forward and change is all you know. You may not know this, young man, but I grew up in a poor family. There were days when we nearly starved. Of course, times were tough for everyone back then. We made do, and a little went a long way. Why, I remember my daddy giving me a dollar and sending me down to the store...I'd come back with a dozen eggs, a pound of bacon, six loaves of bread, a sack of pecans, and a gallon of milk."

"Wow! You sure can't do that anymore."

"I'll say...now they have surveillance cameras."

Willa snickered again.

I felt a warm fuzzy feeling watching Grandmother bonding with Matt. But it wasn't going to last, because we heard Mother marching up the hallway. Ten thousand dollars' worth of flowing chiffon billowed in her wake, and the Tiger's Eye necklace shimmered at her throat. She looked absolutely regal.

The sound of her footsteps drew their attention. Matt and Grandmother turned to look down the hallway. Matt smiled as he noticed Willa and me, and he leaned forward to give Grandmother a kiss on the cheek. Willa and I stood as he joined us, and all three of our heads turned to watch Mother's approach.

A surly expression darkened her face. As she sailed past, she said, "Come along, Lucille, we're going home. I have a busy day planned tomorrow. I have to find a new butler."

Grandmother waved to us and steered her scooter down the hallway after Mother. They pulled up at the door, and Mother turned to look in our direction. She said, "I am aware of how much I owe the three of you. I will not forget."

She stepped through the door and held it for the scooter.

Willa said, "Well, I'll be, that's the first time ever I've seen Livia Honey admit to owing anyone anything. What do you think it means?"

"I think it means she's forgiven me for the *Austin Monthly* article."

CHAPTER TWENTY-ONE

Matt and I fiddled and fondled each other through most of the night and well into the next morning. We finally rose from bed about eleven thirty and lunched with half of West Austin at Texas French Bread Bakery. We were perched together at a tiny table next to the window.

"So, tell me the story again, all of it." I took a bite of my turkey sandwich.

"Well, it was simple really. I figured you couldn't get past Chin, and someone needed to find where they were taking the cars."

"And how'd you do that?"

"I just jumped in the backseat of one of the limos."

"But surely it was locked—how did you get inside?"

"I have talents you may not want to know about." Matt said this with an air of mystery.

"Undoubtedly."

"It was quite a ride as they towed the car."

"I bet."

"I just followed our progress with the GPS on my phone and called the police when we stopped."

"Very clever, Mr. Kendall."

"Thank you, Mr. Honey."

"I think everything went well, wouldn't you say?"

"Yes, but there's still one thing I don't think I understand."

"What's that?" I took another bite of my sandwich.

"What was that thing with Cicely and Russ Buttons at the police station?"

I took a swig of iced tea before I spoke. "Well, Cicely's father was the Buttons family attorney and the executor for their grandfather's will. Evidently the law firm had tracked Milton down just like I did. They sent Cicely to Austin to talk to Milton so he could claim his inheritance. She was celebrating because she had managed to get his notarized signature on that document for her father."

"So that was the paper you were all looking at?"

"Yeah."

"I guess that means Milton gets his inheritance. Well, maybe it will help pay for a good defense team."

"One would think."

"And what about Russ? Why was he acting so strange?"

"First, he was angry because if Milton wasn't found, the will was written so the money would go to the surviving family members. And the only other Buttons is Russ."

"So he stood to inherit the money?"

"You got it. That's what made him so angry."

"Well, that makes sense, but then why was he smiling after you spoke with him?"

"Simple, I just pointed out that the document was notarized after midnight."

"And that is significant because?"

"Because the will stipulated fifteen years."

"What?"

"Cicely's father had to find Milton within fifteen years or the money was Russ's."

"And?"

"And that period ran out yesterday. Well, technically at midnight."

"Ah, and that makes you the clever one, Mr. Honey."

"Thank you, Mr. Kendall."

After lunch, Matt dropped me back at the carriage house and left for the theater for his Sunday afternoon performance. From my front window, I could see that Mother's gardeners were already working to get rid of the ruts the tow trucks had left when they pulled the cars across the lawn.

Matt and I had decided to give the living together thing a try, so I rose after a few minutes to start clearing space in the closets for his clothes. I was in the closet when a thump from the back wall drew my attention. I stepped out to look through my bedroom window just in time to see Larry Lawson sneak past. I shrugged. After the night I'd had, I wasn't all that interested in any more drama. Thirty seconds later, the wall thumped again. This time it was Larry's wife Viola creeping stealthily along the walkway. That drew my attention, and I hurried to my back door. I opened it slowly and leaned out. She was hiding at the corner of the gatehouse watching Larry scoot through the bushes.

I bolted through the cottage to the front door and sprinted up the hill. I arrived at the big house just in time to see Larry disappear through the kitchen door. I followed. The kitchen was empty, and I was about to search the pantry when I heard sounds coming from the back hallway. It was the way to Gladys's living quarters. I snuck along the passage, listening. Giggling sounds were coming from Gladys's room.

I burst through the door to find Larry's pasty white body wrapped in Gladys's chocolate arms. They both stared at me with shock and surprise. Gladys's sturdy torso wobbled a bit as her eyes widened.

I said, "Oh, my!"

"Mr. Greg? What are you doing here?"

"What is he doing here?"

"Nothing yet, but that's going to change."

Larry looked like he'd eaten a bad apple. He said, "I'm such a sinner."

A wicked smile broke across Gladys's face and she said, "Not yet, honey, that part comes later. Now, what is it you need, Mr. Greg, 'cause if you're just here to visit you're gonna have to come back. Right now, we need a little privacy."

She moved to usher me out into the hallway, but I resisted. I found it hard to believe that Gladys, with her fundamentalist Baptist upbringing and strong Southern values, would knowingly commit adultery.

I said, "Sure, I'll go, but Larry should know that Viola is following him. I just saw her behind the gatehouse."

Larry looked like he had eaten a bad potato.

Gladys asked, "Who is Viola?"

She looked at me and I looked at Larry. He sat down on the side of the bed with his head in his hands.

I said, "So, you haven't told her?"

Gladys said, "Told me what?"

I said, "Are you going to tell her, or am I?"

Larry stared at his feet for a few seconds.

Finally, I said, "Viola is Larry's wife."

Gladys's smile dissipated and her eyes turned from me toward Larry. "Mr. Greg, you had better be mistaken, because I know no one wants to be telling me that this man has been trying to make me into a harlot and a sinner." She gestured toward Larry, who'd assumed the fetal position on the bed.

"Well, I'll let the two of you sort this out." I backed quickly out of the room.

On my way out the kitchen door I met Viola on the walkway. I held the door open for her, saying, "What's left of him is in the back."

About the Author

Russ Gregory was raised in New Mexico and attended the University of Texas in Austin where he received an engineering undergraduate degree and an MBA. He writes in multiple genres including mystery, thriller, and comedy. His first book, *Blue*, garnered critical acclaim for its compelling plot and character development. Gregory lives and writes in Austin, Texas.

Books Available From Bold Strokes Books

Lake Thirteen by Greg Herren. A visit to an old cemetery seems like fun to a group of five teenagers, who soon learn that sometimes it's best to leave old ghosts alone. (978-1-60282-894-0)

Deadly Cult by Joel Gomez-Dossi. One nation under MY God, or you die. (978-1-60282-895-7)

The Case of the Rising Star: A Derrick Steele Mystery by Zavo. Derrick Steele's next case involves blackmail, revenge, and a new romance as Derrick races to save a young movie star from a dangerous killer. Meanwhile, will a new threat from within destroy him, along with the entire Steele family? (978-1-60282-888-9)

Big Bad Wolf by Logan Zachary. After a wolf attack, Paavo Wolfe begins to suspect one of the victims is turning into a werewolf. Things become hairy as his ex-partner helps him find the killer. Can Paavo solve the mystery before he runs into the Big Bad Wolf? (978-1-60282-890-2)

The Plain of Bitter Honey by Alan Chin. Trapped within the bleak prospect of a society in chaos, twin brothers Aaron and Hayden Swann discover inner strength in the face of tragedy and search for atonement after betraying the one you most love. (978-1-60282-883-4)

In His Secret Life by Mel Bossa. The only man Allan wants is the one he can't have. (978-1-60282-875-9)

The Moon's Deep Circle by David Holly. Tip Trencher wants to find out what happened to his long-lost brothers, but what he finds is a sizzling circle of gay sex and pagan ritual. (978-1-60282-870-4)

Straight Boy Roommate by Kevin Troughton. Tom isn't expecting much from his first term at University, but a chance encounter with straight boy Dan catapults him into an extraordinary, wild weekend of sex and self-discovery, which turns his life upside down, and leads him into his first love affair. (978-1-60282-782-0)

Raising Hell: Demonic Gay Erotica, edited by Todd Gregory. Hot stories of gay erotica featuring demons. (978-1-60282-768-4)

Pursued by Joel Gomez-Dossi. Openly gay college student Jamie Bradford becomes romantically involved with two men at the same time, and his hell begins when one of his boyfriends becomes intent on killing him. (978-1-60282-769-1)

Timothy by Greg Herren. Timothy is a romantic suspense thriller from award-winning mystery writer Greg Herren set in the fabulous Hamptons. (978-1-60282-760-8)

In Stone by Jeremy Jordan King. A young New Yorker is rescued from a hate crime by a mysterious someone who turns out to be more of a something. (978-1-60282-761-5)

The Jesus Injection by Eric Andrews-Katz. Murderous statues, demented drag queens, political bombings, ex-gay ministries, espionage, and romance are all in a day's work for a top secret agent. But the gloves are off when Agent Buck 98 comes up against the Jesus Injection. (978-1-60282-762-2)

Combustion by Daniel W. Kelly. Bearish detective Deck Waxer comes to the city of Kremfort Cove to investigate why the hottest men in town are bursting into flames in broad daylight. (978-1-60282-763-9)

Night Shadows: Queer Horror edited by Greg Herren and J.M. Redmann. *Night Shadows* features delightfully wicked stories by some of the biggest names in queer publishing. (978-1-60282-751-6)

Wyatt: Doc Holliday's Account of an Intimate Friendship by Dale Chase. Erotica writer Dale Chase takes the remarkable friendship between Wyatt Earp, upright lawman, and Doc Holliday, Southern gentlemen turned gambler and killer, to an entirely new level: hot! (978-1-60282-755-4)

Secret Societies by William Holden. An outcast hustler, his unlikely "mother," his faithless lovers, and his religious persecutors—all in 1726. (978-1-60282-752-3)

The Jetsetters by David-Matthew Barnes. As rock band the Jetsetters skyrocket from obscurity to superstardom, Justin Holt, a lonely barista, and Diego Delgado, the band's guitarist, fight with everything they have to stay together, despite the chaos and fame. (978-1-60282-745-5)

Strange Bedfellows by Rob Byrnes. Partners in life and crime, Grant Lambert and Chase LaMarca are hired to make a politician's compromising photo disappear, but what should be an easy job quickly spins out of control. (978-1-60282-746-2)

Fontana by Joshua Martino. Fame, obsession, and vengeance collide in a novel that asks: What if America's greatest hero was gay? (978-1-60282-675-5)

The Dirty Diner: Gay Erotica on the Menu, edited by Jerry L. Wheeler. Gay erotica set in restaurants, featuring food, sex, and men—could you really ask for anything more? (978-1-60282-677-9)

Sweat: Gay Jock Erotica by Todd Gregory. Sizzling tales of smoking-hot sex with the athletic studs everyone fantasizes about. (978-1-60282-669-4)

The Marrying Kind by Ken O'Neill. Just when successful wedding planner Adam More decides to protest inequality by quitting the business and boycotting marriage entirely, his only sibling announces her engagement. (978-1-60282-670-0)